AN OUTPOURING OF PRAISE FOR
LOUISIANA POWER & LIGHT

"Readers . . . will be rewarded. Dufresne's outrageous and sad family saga brandishes both grit and charm."
—*Cleveland Plain Dealer*

"Billy Wayne's story assumes the immediacy of revelation. . . . Along with bits of family history and breezy philosophizing, there are passages of unlikely beauty." —*The New Yorker*

"Precisely what one wants . . . Dufresne, capable of raising a chuckle or ten, doesn't play things just for laughs."
—*Boston Sunday Globe*

"It's the voice of someone sitting on a porch at twilight, quietly telling a passerby what's going on behind the closed curtains across the street. Sometimes it wanders around a topic before getting to the point and doesn't always use the best grammar. But that voice has people hanging on every word." —*Augusta Chronicle*

"Dufresne spins a rollicking yarn, often funny and full of drama . . . gritty, nasty, wild and absolutely American."
—*Memphis Commercial Appeal*

"This is the type of book . . . that you can't wait to tell your friends about. So, my friends, read *Louisiana Power & Light*."
—*Tampa Tribune-Times*

"A delightful comic meditation on everything from love and marriage to gun control and Louisiana politics."
—*New Orleans Times-Picayune*

"With *Louisiana Power & Light*, cackle for a while, then hope for a sequel." —*Pittsburgh Post-Gazette*

JOHN DUFRESNE has won the *Yankee* Magazine Award for Fiction, a PEN Syndicated Fiction Award, a *Transatlantic Review/* Henfield Foundation Fiction Award, and is the author of the short-story collection *The Way That Water Enters Stone*. He lives with his wife and son in Dania, Florida. He misses Louisiana.

Also by John Dufresne

The Way That Water Enters Stone

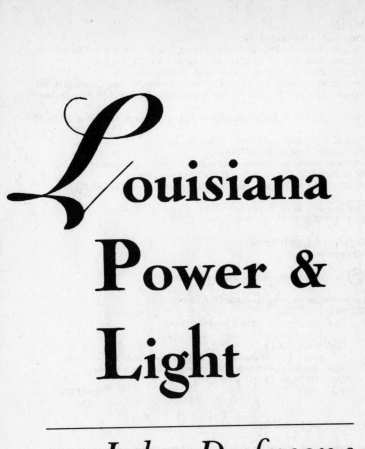

Louisiana Power & Light

John Dufresne

A PLUME BOOK

PLUME
Published by the Penguin Group
Penguin Books USA Inc., 375 Hudson Street, New York, New York 10014, U.S.A.
Penguin Books Ltd, 27 Wrights Lane, London W8 5TZ, England
Penguin Books Australia Ltd, Ringwood, Victoria, Australia
Penguin Books Canada Ltd, 10 Alcorn Avenue, Toronto, Ontario, Canada M4V 3B2
Penguin Books (N.Z.) Ltd, 182–190 Wairau Road, Auckland 10, New Zealand

Penguin Books Ltd, Registered Offices: Harmondsworth, Middlesex, England

Published by Plume, an imprint of Dutton Signet,
a division of Penguin Books USA Inc.
This is an authorized reprint of a hardcover edition published by
W. W. Norton & Company, Inc. For information address:
W. W. Norton & Company, Inc., 500 Fifth Avenue, New York, NY 10110.

First Plume Printing, November, 1995
10 9 8 7 6 5 4

Ⓟ REGISTERED TRADEMARK—MARCA REGISTRADA

LIBRARY OF CONGRESS CATALOGING-IN-PUBLICATION DATA
Dufresne, John.
    Louisiana Power & Light / John Dufresne.
        p.   cm.
    ISBN 0-452-27502-4
    1. Marriage—Louisiana—Fiction.   2. Family—Louisiana—Fiction.
    3. Men—Louisiana—Fiction.   4. Louisiana—Fiction.   I. Title.
    [PS3554.U325L68   1995]
    813'.54—dc20   95-31672
                                                                CIP

Printed in the United States of America

PUBLISHER'S NOTE
This is a work of fiction. Names, characters, places, and incidents either are
the product of the author's imagination or are used fictitiously, and any
resemblance to actual persons, living or dead, events, or locales is entirely
coincidental.

BOOKS ARE AVAILABLE AT QUANTITY DISCOUNTS WHEN USED TO PROMOTE PRODUCTS
OR SERVICES. FOR INFORMATION PLEASE WRITE TO PREMIUM MARKETING DIVISION,
PENGUIN BOOKS USA INC., 375 HUDSON STREET, NEW YORK, NEW YORK 10014.

In Memoriam

This book is for Charlie Willig,
for his friendship and his stories.

Acknowledgments

I want to thank Florida International University and the Florida State Arts Council for grants that facilitated the writing of this book. I also want to thank Dan Whatley for all his help with the manuscript and the research, and Bill Cousins for his music. And thanks to Peter Mladinic, Doris Bartlett, Dick McDonough, and my wife, Cindy Chinelly, for their insight, encouragement, and support. Special thanks to Jill Bialosky, who found the story hidden in the manuscript, and to my colleagues and students in the writing program at FIU for their patience, understanding, and inspiration. And to my friends in Monroe (and those who've left): Dev and Martha, Herb and Marilea, Steve and Mel, David, Jack, Rodney, Fae, Jo, Marjolynne, and Sharon. And thank you, Tristan.

Contents

If therefore the light that is in thee be darkness, how great *is* that darkness!

—Matthew 6:23

The great principle of light touches all objects in the night sky, stars and nebulae, with its own blank tinge, and the palsied universe lies before us like a leper.

—Herman Melville
Moby Dick

God's everywhere and nowhere until He reveals Himself—then He enters time and space, and He's no longer God—He's just power and light.

—Shug Johnson

Louisiana
Power &
Light

Prologue

*Y*ou're there, and here we are in Monroe, Louisiana, City of Steady Habits, Crossroads of Pipelines, Corrugated Paper Capital of the North Delta Parishes, elevation 65 feet, population 56,600. And you, where you are, and we here, are all of us situated about halfway between stars and atoms, gazing first toward the ones, then the others, and every once in a while, closing our eyes and looking within.

Telling stories about the Fontanas is our attempt at creating the truth of the past by considering its facts and exploring its sequence. Narrative has a long tradition here in northeast Louisiana. About the time that Moses was guiding the Israelites out of Egypt, we already had the largest city in North

America just east of Bayou Maçon at what we now call Poverty Point. The two main streets of this city were aligned with the summer and winter solstices, and the citizens carried on a brisk commerce with aboriginals across the continent. They told their story by sculpting the earth into effigies. Told how they arrived, descending from their heaven on the back of a falcon, how they settled here, prospered, and then vanished. All of that just a few miles from where our own tale begins.

A story, we believe, and perhaps we are out of fashion here, should exert a moral force, should charge and illuminate. Like light, it must have direction, intensity, and color. This, then, is not the family's unmodified chronology, if indeed such a contrivance exists. (And if it did, would it matter?) This is Billy Wayne Fontana's story, an emblem of the family's history—the story of stories that have been changed to make new stories, altered to illustrate how the one thing causes the next thing to happen. Our story is what we say and how we say it.

And it's what we remember. This business of memory got some play at a recent Great Books Club meeting in the Boscobel Room of the Ouachita Parish Public Library when Shug Johnson closed his Proust and cleared his throat like he does, said memory was a myth-making machine. What we do, he said, is we keep revising our past to keep it consistent with who we think we are. Then he looked at his neighbors around the table. He asked each what his or her earliest memory was. Cicero Wittlief remembered playing Peter Pan, jumping off his bed and flying all the way to the bedroom door. Tommie Nash said she couldn't remember a thing before she was ten. Said her first memory was when Mrs. Dement, her fifth-grade teacher, humiliated her by picking nits from her plaited hair and showing them to the other children. Ted Muto said, yes, he remembered the day that happened. Bobby Sistrunk said maybe something even worse happened when Tommie was younger and that's why she couldn't remember. Tommie excused herself and walked to the lavatory. Shug looked at Margaret Grimes, right at her, and said, "It's like the tree falling in the forest." And something seemed to pass between Shug and Margaret, something that made the others lower their gazes to the seminar table. "Is there a past," he asked, "if there is no one here to remember it?"

Anyway, our Fontanas, you will see, have suffered unduly and not always with the dignity, the steadfastness, attributed, reasonably or not, to Christians. They have acted irrationally at times, many times, criminally at others, and in so doing have become not so much a controversy as a public spectacle. We are all of us here caught up in their business. The intrigue is not in what they do or in the style of their performance. What we all the time wonder is "Why?" What kind of engine, what manner of fuel, drives that hapless familial machine?

Part of the public speculation has to do with the relative tenacity of genetic and cultural inheritance. And for the moment, the late Dr. Rexito Graves, M.D., has had the last, though perhaps not the definitive, word on the subject. Dr. Graves's unnatural death has become a droll footnote to our Fontana story. On the day that his monograph, "Genetic Drift among the Fontanas of the Chauvin Basin, 1918–1940," was accepted for publication in the *Louisiana Journal of Procreation*, Dr. Graves decided to celebrate. Still, he should have left Simmie's Diddy wah Diddy before Tremaine Davis and His Pleasure Kings came back on stage for their second set. Most likely then, and despite his succession of imprudent decisions, he'd be alive now and could explain to us all about his theory on the "dissolving effect" of sexual reproduction, which refers not to lust or corporal evanescence, you understand, but to the exhaustion of the materials of existence.

But Dr. Graves did not check his watch or consider his scheduled 7:00 A.M. hysteroscopy on Raymond Chisholm's wife at Glenwood Regional. Instead, he switched off his pager, ordered himself another bourbon and water, no ice, his sixth, a scotch and cola for the young lady, her fourth if he was counting right, and listened to Tremaine sing "Terraplane Blues." Dr. Graves studied Donita Ann as she watched the Pleasure Kings dip, spin, and drop to their knees. He noticed a tiny birthmark behind her left ear and wondered how it had eluded his attentions earlier in his office. Now he leaned toward her and circled his tongue over the nevus. Her eyes closed. He suggested that they take a drive out along the levee. Timing is everything, Dr. Graves used to say.

He escorted Donita Ann to the gravel parking lot, smiled at her, and fished in his trousers pocket for his keys. He heard the squeal of tires and looked up in time to see someone else driving away in his German car. Of course, had he been where he was supposed to be, at his office in the Ouachita Women's and Infertility Clinic where he had told his wife he'd be working late again, then he would not have been chasing after what he naturally enough assumed to be a car thief, but was instead a repo man in the employ of Wade-Maddox Import Motors; would not have charged out onto Winnsboro Road without looking; would not have been struck, shattered, and launched by a Louisiana Power & Light bucket truck.

His obituary in the *News-Star-World* did not mention how that very paper had labeled him the "Little King of Sepulchres" in an editorial supporting the right-to-lifers who were then trying to close up the family-planning wing of his clinic. It did report how he grew up across the parish line in Eros, went to LSU Medical School, and how he left a wife, the former Leslie Hatten, a brother, Fleming, of Bovina, Mississippi, and several nieces and nephews.

We mention Dr. Graves for the first and last time because of his brief though significant (well, maybe "significant" is too strong; let's say "notable"), his notable role in the enduring debate surrounding our Fontana family—the aforementioned monograph in which he attempted to dismiss what he belittled as "that popular Calvinist notion of the genetically elect and the genetically damned." He included in his article a chart labeled "Pedigree Collapse" which illustrated how the proportion of the genes one shares with a given ancestor is one-half squared by the number of generations separating one from said ancestor. So what he calculated was that by 1940, any living Fontana retained only one thirty-second of the genes of Peregrine Fontana. (And by extension any descendant of General Elihu Lamkin had only one thirty-second of the general's illustrious Confederate genes. So you could see where such a calculation might lead to resentment among our patrician element.)

While it was just that one thirty-second that worried some of our citizens, other, more unswerving determinists smiled knowingly at each other and mentioned the Luckenbills over to the east side. There have been, oh, eighty, ninety Luckenbills have lived in town over the years and each and every one has had that dimpled chin (the "lucken bill"), and all of them, male and female, educated and un-, could tear down an automobile engine, smell out the problem, then fix the deal and reassemble the motor over a weekend. Then there are the Soileaus. Twenty-seven of the thirty-one progeny of the late Achilles Soileau are color blind. You go figure your one thirty-second into that, Dr. Graves, the Reverend Drew Stringfellow said. He held as to how Jesus don't cipher; He just fit you with any damn gene he feel like. There were many who agreed with Dr. Graves that genes and chromosomes and whatever had little enough to do with any family's fortunes, but who disagreed with his contention that sociological and economic factors did. The Fontanas, they assumed, were simply traipsing in the sins of their fathers. Well, the argument goes on. Dr. Graves does not.

6 · Prologue

You should read this story with your eyes closed. You're out on Herb and Marilea Bryant's front porch, let's say, and it's dusk. You can just about see the blue irises in the drainage ditch by the road. There's a katydid fastened to the wall beneath the yellow porch light. You're sitting back on the glider with a gin and tonic. There's Herb's dog, Vera, asleep on the porch with a tennis ball by her muzzle. Her back leg twitches. When the breeze kicks up, you can smell the honeysuckle that grows along Danny Whatley's rail fence. You put your head back. You hear these strange voices.

I

Fontana in Excelsis

Had a wife. Couldn't keep her.
Live alone. Big empty house.
Queen-size bed. I can't sleep there.
Sleep alone. Big empty house.

—Earlene Fontana and Tremaine Davis
"Big Empty House Blues"

1

The Solitary and the Chosen

*W*hen Billy Wayne Fontana's second wife, Tami Lynne, left him for the first time, he walked into Booker T. Washington Elementary School, interrupted the fourth grade in the midst of a hygiene lesson, it being a Thursday morning and all, apologized to Miss Azzie Lee Oglesbee, the substitute teacher, fetched his older boy, Duane, and vanished for a year and a half from Monroe. Tami Lynne remarked how spiteful it was of Billy Wayne to take just the one child and not the other. "He's always been partial to Duane," she told a reporter from the *Citizen*, "and it just breaks my heart." She patted her tiny, salmon-haired six-year-old on his head. "Poor little Moon Pie," she said.

Channel 10 has this part of the news called Crime Busters

where our sheriff's department acts out some unsolved crime or other and asks you, the viewing audience, to call this one special number should you have a lead of any kind which might result in the apprehension and/or conviction of the alleged perpetrators. So one night they perform the "Billy Wayne Kidnapping," which is what they were calling it then, and Sheriff Buddy Tidwell himself plays Billy Wayne and Buddy's boy Boogie plays Duane. They get one call on the special number and it's from Steve Yarborough over at You-All Rental, the guy with the hairline mustache and sorghum voice you see all the time on the cable TV commercials. Steve Yarborough says that Billy Wayne did come by on the afternoon in question, rented a cap for his pickup and two very expensive down sleeping bags. So Buddy tells him you best call your insurance company in the morning. Might as well tell you now that Steve Yarborough's insurance agent is Billy Wayne's first wife, Earlene. That's the kind of town Monroe is.

To be honest, we were not at all surprised at this episode or at the calamities which ensued. The fact is that the Fontana family has had a celebrated history of catastrophe in our parish. They have what folks used to call a curse, but now we know better. What the Fontanas may have is bad water in the gene pool.

AROUND 1840 THE first known Fontana sloshed his way out of the spongy gumbo of the Delta somewhere between here and Vicksburg. Rose up out of that sticky, primordial ooze, one person said, like sin percolating up through the slime of your subconscious. Madison Tensas, in his antebellum history of northeast Louisiana, mentions this first Fontana, who stunk like marsh gas, had webbed fingers, and caused a panic among the women and children of Talla Bena when he appeared on Main Street in nothing but alligator-hide drawers. This was Peregrine Fontana, who sired twin albino sons before he was drowned by Yankee soldiers in Bayou Maçon.

Mangham and Bosco Fontana, their several wives, dozen children, converts, and hired hands wandered the Delta for forty years claiming to be the Lost Tribe of Israel. They made a living fishing, trapping, and selling acres of swamp land that they did not own to freed slaves and the occasional carpetbagger. About the time that the effects of Reconstruction had mitigated, a time when everyone found, or was led to, his rightful niche in the new society, the Fontanas appeared at the banks of the Ouachita River at a marshy clearing just north of Monroe called Chauvin Bottom, the very spot where the last buffalo in the territory had been shot in 1803, claimed it was their Promised Land, and settled in for good and all. That's when our great-grandfathers first noticed that all of the Fontana children were male and dispatched a worried delegation of ministers and physicians to investigate. Some of the gentlemen who gathered daily at the Biedenharn Pharmacy for phosphates and dominoes considered the Fontana reproductive anomaly to be a most propitious phenomenon and wondered if it might not be a matter of some easily learned technique. Other folks, however, thought the circumstances peculiar at best, while one or two whispered their suspicions of infanticide. But that was not the case. It was a simple, if ineffable, manifestation of the Lord's will, the delegation concluded. Perhaps this is God's only way of keeping the Fontana men from committing the abominable sin of incest, they went on.

In 1909, Bosco's two youngest boys, Jupiter and Saturn, went cahoots, robbed the Merchants and Farmers Bank claiming to be Frank and Jesse James, and then walked across to the Grand Hotel, bought two La Flor Degulfo cigars and ordered two shots of Old Oscar Pepper bourbon. They were the first of twelve Fontanas to be hanged for crimes against property, the last being De Soto Fontana in 1935 for setting a loaded cotton wagon on fire and driving it into the lobby of the Sugar Theater, which had refused him admission to the new Walt Disney cartoon show, on bank night no less, and on the frivolous grounds that he possessed neither money nor shoes.

In addition to being the most executed white family in the history of Louisiana, the Fontanas have also been the sickest. In 1914, influenza swept Chauvin Bottom, a full four years before the pandemic that followed the Great War, and reduced the Fontana population by two-thirds. Some years later, at about the time the Chicago Mill and Lumber Company was killing off the world's last ivory-billed woodpecker along the Tensas River, yellow fever ravaged its way through our peckerwoods here along the Ouachita.

And between these epidemics, there befell the tribe seven documented cases of fatal encephalitis, annual eruptions of black measles and breakbone fever, a legion of consumptives, and a single, extraordinary case of leprosy named Napoleon Fontana. It had been Napoleon's curious dream to husband the nine-banded armadillo, a vision conceived that twilit evening he had witnessed a brace of doddering matrons cloaked in fox-pelt stoles standing on the glittering deck of a passing sternwheeler. He reasoned that any woman who enjoyed the effect of a weasely muzzle draped across her shoulder would certainly take to a leathery, nearly hairless, and admirably capacious handbag. Sew the bony tail into the tiny mouth and you've got a durable handle even.

Ever a secretive man, Napoleon carried his pair of armadillos to a secluded spot along Bayou Bartholemew which he fenced with chicken wire. Napoleon sat and watched and waited for his capital to increase and multiply. Twenty-nine months after he had sauntered out of the Bottom with an investment under each arm, Napoleon limped back home with four of his toes wrapped in a knotted calico neckerchief, each toe hardened like a nugget of coal.

Throughout this time, the Fontanas kept pretty much to themselves except for the yearly cane harvests. The townsfolk, though periodically and understandably apprehensive, were content to stay their distance, and the Fontanas were reasonably amenable to their social quarantine, so that after the flood of '27—this was before the levee, now—the Fontanas even refused the town's official offer of temporary food and shelter. There they were, out in what was now a shallow lake, all hunkered down in their pirogues some of them, others nestled in the limbs of the sweet gums, chewing the resin off strips of bark—all of them just waiting for the sun of God to shine once again. Claimed the flood was the vengeance of the Lord for the sins of Monroe, and they figured, the Fontanas did, to stay clear of such perilous depravity.

Among those thirty-two Fontana survivors of the flood was a youngish woman so debilitated, so haggard and brittle that she was hurried directly to St. Francis Hospital over the muttered objections of her clan. Tests sure enough proved that Aphrodite Fontana was both profoundly syphilitic and seven months pregnant. On that Fourth of July, a day so unbearably hot that water moccasins dropped from the trees into Bayou DeSiard, a day still remembered by our old-timers as the day it rained snakes, on that Independence Day, Positive Wassermann Fontana was born blind, feebleminded, and otherwise congenitally cursed. Aphrodite was not so lucky and did not survive the birth. Nor did doctors expect little "Pee Dubya," as he came to be nicknamed, to live much beyond his first weeks, given the nutritional and environmental hardships he was certain to encounter there with his family back in the Bottom. One of our professors at the state college first speculated that perhaps a kind of reverse Darwinism was at work among the Fontanas and that somehow "survival of the sorriest" was the rule.

At any rate, by 1946, Positive Wassermann was the only living male Fontana, the only carrier of the inherited material therefore, and the town dared to think that at last the durable Fontana chromosome had played itself out. But Positive Wassermann lived twenty-six years and begat a son and called him Billy Wayne. And all the days of Positive Wassermann were twenty-eight years, and he died ingloriously enough in Monroe's Mental Jail. Billy Wayne's mother, a defective child of thirteen, unable to care for her baby or even to comprehend their relationship, was shunted off to a juvenile facility in West Carroll Parish.

The Fontana tribe, reduced to its women, converts, and assorted hangers-on, and deprived of even the dubious leadership of Positive Wassermann, drifted quietly and mysteriously away from Chauvin Bottom and Monroe. One morning that fall, when the fog had lifted, all that remained of the Fontana settlement was the smoldering ashes of the fire in which they had burned everything they could not carry, everything except a leatherette Recline-o-Chair which had served as Positive Wassermann's throne and now sat in a puddle of green water beneath a basket oak. The infant Billy Wayne, the only breathing descendant of Peregrine Fontana and tabernacle of his formidable gene, was abandoned to the care of the good Sisters of St. Francis Hospital, who, with the unspoken complicity of the town, devised and executed a strategy to rid the world for good and all of the Fontana aberration, a solution at once so inspired and so diabolical it could only have originated, our Pentecostals believed, with the Pope of Rome himself. Billy Wayne was to be groomed for the priesthood.

2

Cold Water to a
Thirsty Soul

*L*ittle Billy Wayne grew up in the convent
wing of the hospital, coddled by his twenty-
one wimpled, maiden aunts, and trained in theology by Monsignor Pargoud, the hospital chaplain. Billy Wayne spoke Latin
before Southern, a circumstance so peculiar that he was put
on Art Baker's "You Asked for It" television program and
driven down to Baton Rouge to meet Governor Jimmie Davis,
the singer and actor. For his part, Billy Wayne was an enthusi-
astic student who was often heard memorizing his Baltimore
Catechism in the shade of the convent's grape arbor. He took
to wearing his altar-boy cassock regularly, even in the extreme
heat of summer, and even on outings to Forsythe Park. This
set him distinctly apart from other children.

Mostly Billy Wayne went to the park with Sister Helen who was not so much older than he, not so far removed herself from the spiritual anxieties and emotional agitations of child-hood. Some mornings they'd stroll on the levee to the boat landing or walk down to the slough where the great blue heron nested. Whatever they did, they'd usually wind up sit-ting at a picnic table under a mossy live oak, and they'd talk. Billy Wayne would say something, like none of the kids at school worried about the things he worried about—like how to accept grace modestly or how to examine but not question the gift of faith. None of them, he said, concerned themselves with the concept of eternity. And Sister Helen would say, Oh, but they will, Billy Wayne, and she'd smile. The fortunate ones will, she'd say.

"You really think so, Sister?"

"I hope so."

"It's not just us then?"

"A person's got to have a spiritual life, Billy Wayne. It's the most natural thing."

It is probably unwise, unhealthy even, for a child who has yet to reach the age of reason to entertain notions of martyr-dom and sacrifice. Consider what profound disappointment must await the boy who understands himself to be a tool for the salvation of others. We must be mindful, however, that Billy Wayne grew up pedaling his three-wheeler along the tiled corridors of the chronic wards and so was early on ex-posed to the unlovely countenance of the human condition. Perhaps it is inevitable that an impressionable child who con-stantly wanders through a cloud of loss will confuse the igno-miny of illness with the nobility of suffering.

When he turned eighteen, Billy Wayne was shipped to a Dominican novitiate up north in Kentucky. In seven years he figured to be ordained a priest, to take the solemn vows of poverty, obedience, and chastity. We held our breaths and prayed for Billy Wayne. He had been called to God, so he claimed, to serve the sick. He proposed to spend his life in service to the lepers at the lazaretto in Carville. And he would begin his training that first summer vacation ministering to the sick right here at St. Francis.

While other nineteen-year-old boys played Dixie League baseball or maybe worked trotlines on the bayou, Billy Wayne performed the Corporal Works of Mercy at the hospital, visiting the conscious, feeding the weak, bathing the sores of the terminal. You're going to make a fine priest, a holy priest, aren't you, Billy Wayne? we'd say to him. After Billy Wayne had brought Lanny Johns back to life, Monsignor Pargoud wrote the bishop in Alexandria and told him how Mr. Johns's heart monitor and the other machines had all gone quiet, and how the duty nurse was already on the phone to Poteet Funeral Home, and how Billy Wayne prayed over the corpse and touched its cold brow, and how Lanny blinked his eyes just like Lazarus must have and whispered, "There's a hole in the world where the light comes in." And the bishop answered, yes, Billy Wayne did seem to be on his way to sainthood, but the path, he cautioned, was rugged and tortuous. We felt honored as a community to have nurtured such a special child. (At least those of us not busy insinuating that Billy Wayne was the AntiChrist felt honored.) Two of the older nuns claimed to have witnessed an aura around Billy Wayne; another said that ambrosia lingered in his wake.

Still there are some things that you quite simply cannot escape. One is fate, another heredity, though sometimes we wonder if they aren't one and the same. That summer, while at the very pinnacle of his spiritual powers, Billy Wayne took his first step along that aforementioned rugged path and tripped. That summer our novice, regrettably, inevitably, belatedly, discovered his manhood.

What happened was this. On one of his regular evening

visits to the infirm, Billy Wayne had occasion to comfort and aid one Earlene deBastrop, a poor young thing being treated for female problems. Earlene lived alone with her eighty-year-old grandfather, Papaw, in Bawcomville out by the paper mill.

Billy Wayne tapped on the door, opened it, stuck his head into the room. "May I come in?" he said.

"Sure you can."

Until his eyes adjusted to the crepuscular light, Billy Wayne squinted toward the bed when he spoke.

"You're a tad young for a priest, ain't you, Father?" Earlene said.

"Well, you see, I'm not actually a priest. And call me Billy Wayne."

"If you ain't no priest, why you wearing that sorry black what's-it then?"

"Cassock," he said. "I'm a novitiate."

Earlene smiled, told Billy Wayne to take a load off his mind. Then she said he might could move his chair closer by her bed. She switched off the gooseneck lamp on her bedside table. "I need to speak with someone."

"That's what I'm here for," Billy Wayne said. "Your name is Earlene?"

"That's right."

"Well, Earlene, I'm listening."

"I need forgiveness."

"Yes."

"You can do it, can't you?"

"You mean Confession?"

"Yes."

"No, I can't do that, Earlene."

"Please."

"I told you I'm not a priest."

"I need to tell somebody. That's what Confession's about, isn't it?"

Billy Wayne knew Earlene was right about that, about the desire for human forgiveness. God's, you can always get. The room now seemed close, airless. Billy Wayne's hands shimmered and dissolved. He blinked. Yes, if you stare at something long enough, it disappears.

"Just listen to me," Earlene said, "and when I'm finished, tell me it's all right. Tell me that people will want me still, that I'm not just a cracked pitcher like Papaw says."

Billy Wayne listened as Earlene poured out her heart like water, like cool water to his thirsty soul. Her voice, like a river, washed over him. He had looked at God for so long that God had vanished suddenly, and all Billy Wayne saw before him now was Earlene, and he looked upon her as upon the face of the water and saw himself reflected there. Saw his yearning. Was that it? An emptiness? He had not sipped, yet could taste the sweet draft of intimacy.

"Did you hear what I said. Billy Wayne?"

Billy Wayne nodded, placed his missal on the nightstand. "I'll close the door," he told Earlene. He stood.

"And shut down the air conditioner at the window," she said. "I want to whisper, and I need you to hear."

Earlene, fragrant with lilac water, began. "Bless me, Billy Wayne, for I have sinned."

Billy Wayne shut his eyes, dropped his forehead onto his folded hands, smelled Earlene's womanly substance on the bedsheets, and listened.

"These are my sins," she said. "I did it to this boy, Marzell Swan, and Marzell Swan did it to me. Then Marzell and me went all the way."

Suddenly it was like Billy Wayne was underwater and couldn't breathe, couldn't talk, couldn't fathom this whirlpool in which he was drowning. He could not imagine what "it" could possibly mean that was different from "all the way," and he had only a clinical notion of "all the way," but he understood from the solemn tone of Earlene's voice, from her tears, and from his own lightheadedness that it must be miraculous, all of it.

Earlene continued. "Every blessed night for three months no matter where we was, we was on it. Just like frogs in a slough."

Billy Wayne knew about the frogs, all their furious croaking and the other moist noises. He saw them now, coupled, wet, the jerky little spasms, that frothy business clinging to their slimy thighs.

"I didn't love Marzell. I didn't even want him around. He's just a dumb redneck shitkicker. Excuse my French, Billy Wayne. All's he cared about was driving his truck and working his little wand up inside me somewhere. But every night I ached for him."

Billy Wayne opened his eyes. He heard a call for Dr. King on the hospital intercom. He saw himself as if from the ceiling, a figure in black, sitting on the edge of his chair, bent toward a bed on which a woman in a white slip sat, pillows at her back. Can any man forbid water? he thought. He wanted to say something. He heard the whisper of the vinyl seat cushion as he stood.

Earlene looked up at him. "Billy Wayne?" she said.

"It's all right," he said. He lifted a damp curl from her cheek. "Your sins are forgiven."

And whatever else they whispered in the dim light of that semiprivate room so stirred our Billy Wayne that, well, one thing led to another and so on. In the morning they were gone.

Monsignor Pargoud lapsed into drink directly upon learning of Billy Wayne's nuptials some weeks later, and no one, except perhaps the bishop, blamed him. When the good Sisters were at last unable to conceal his behavior, the monsignor was retired to a retreat house in Mt. Lebanon. His room overlooked the exact spot where Clyde Barrow drove into an ambush in 1934.

3

Any Bus in a
Storm of Love

*A*s disappointed as we all were with Billy
Wayne, we were duly impressed with his
ambition. Billy Wayne worked two jobs to support his young
bride. Two mornings a week, he fried doughnuts at the King
Louis XIV Doughnut Shop on Highway 80, and afternoons
sprayed roaches for Haddad Pest Control. On free mornings,
Billy Wayne looked for something better—a job with security
and benefits. He put his name in all over the place—at Path-
way Paint Supply and Jericho Masonry, at the phone company
and the paper mill, at the gas works and at LP&L. A man
could realize a comfortable future with the Power & Light.

He recalled having first seen that LP&L logo on the building downtown. He was nine then and Monsignor Pargoud

had pointed it out. The logo was this sun with its rays of lightning bolts shining down on some cypress swamp. Monsignor said God was like the utility company, offering grace and comfort to people. Only some folks, like your kin, Billy Wayne, refused the gift and chose instead to live in darkness. Billy Wayne wondered was he talking about sin or electricity. First thing God did was create light, Monsignor said. He closed his eyes. Light and lust are enemies, he said. "Lust" to Billy Wayne meant wanting something, like a bicycle, wanting it bad. He knew that the nuns slept with their lights on and he wondered what they were afraid of wanting.

And for several years, that's how Billy Wayne chose to imagine God, as a benevolent and luminous sun, wanting and needing nothing from him, emanating warmth and burning with love. And whenever he thought of God like this, the child Billy Wayne felt at peace, felt apart from the material world. Yes, it would be a treat to work for the company that had unknowingly supplied him hours of transcendence. But LP&L, like everyone else, wasn't hiring just then.

In less than a year, Billy Wayne managed to take a mortgage out on a shotgun house on the northside and fix it up with wallpaper and linoleum. And when, after two years of marriage, the couple remained childless, we assumed that Earlene's "female problems" had rendered her barren. It seemed evident to us that at last some providential hormone or, perhaps, a simple and fortunate physical occlusion had affected the laudable and issueless future that our nuns had been unable to insure and for which we had so earnestly prayed and devoutly anticipated. And so we wished the pair a long and prosperous life together.

However, prosperity, as you may have imagined, was not in the cards. Billy Wayne was a Fontana, after all. It may be that Earlene never forgave her erstwhile confessor for the penance of their honeymoon, where the only intercourse performed was social, when, instead of conducting his husbandly duties with her, Billy Wayne committed the sin of fellowship with that Pakistani what's-his-name.

GEORGE BINWADDIE OWNED the Palms Motel which is where, by the merest chance, Billy Wayne and Earlene spent their first night as Mister and Missus. The marriage ceremony, such as it was, had taken place in the courthouse which meant that Billy Wayne's "aunts" were unable to attend. Sister Helen met the couple in the lobby and apologized for the nuns' absence. She mumbled something that she was clearly embarrassed to mention about a call from the chancery. Otherwise, she said, they would be here. We all wish you the best, you know that, she said. And then she took Billy Wayne's hand. We'll talk, she said. As for Earlene's Pawpaw, old Clifton, well, he was at a loss, imagining, as he did that this cassocked visitor to his home was a priest. He had read all he wanted to about the new liturgy and these hippie folk-Mass clergy, and so he chose to ignore Billy Wayne's presence, preferring instead to believe that his grandaughter had gone loonified and had taken up with an imaginary playmate. "Goddam world," he was happy to tell anyone who'd listen, "has gone shit-side up ever since we put that fool on the moon."

As word of the unexpected wedding spread through town, there were the sighing and the shrugging of shoulders, the expression of a collective sentiment not unlike "Well, you try and you try, and this is the thanks you get for your troubles." Some of our more petulant citizens were openly critical of Billy Wayne's guardian nuns. Our hardshell Baptists speculated that maybe this was Jesus's way of punishing us for allowing the luxuriant cancer of humanism to flourish unchecked in Ouachita Parish. Dr. Grady Oliver tried to put the response into perspective on his call-in radio therapy show on

KDNA. He explained that what we were witnessing was the classic southern response to all manner of adversity from Reconstruction and Evolutionary Science to the boll weevil and kudzu: 1. frustration; 2. indignation; 3. resignation; and, 4. anticipation.

The couple themselves figured, as we all would, "Any old bus in a storm of love" and boarded the first one that pulled to the curb outside the courthouse, the #1 DeSiard, running four minutes late because of an accident near Second. They rode out to the final stop, then walked on the shoulder of Highway 80 past the cotton field, the A&P, over the viaduct and beyond the police impoundment and the LP&L substation, until they reached the Palms Motel, an unpretentious, yellow-brick affair.

"This okay?" Billy Wayne asked.

Earlene wiped the beaded sweat from her upper lip with her baby finger. She squinted at the unlighted neon palm. "It's okay."

Before our young couple enter their New Jerusalem, we will invoke the storyteller's prerogative and momentarily change our direction, if not our subject, and perhaps in so doing rectify a popular misconception of the South while reporting a minority hypothesis regarding the dismal fate of Clan Fontana. Fact is we don't all wear ball caps and dip snuff down here. Truth is there isn't much difference any longer between South and North and West for that matter. Like everywhere else we've got our stockbrokers, our entrepreneurs, our artistic element. The only difference between Monroe and, say, Big Rapids, Michigan, is that we continue to allow ourselves to be defined by our past, as peculiar and unpleasant as that past may sometimes seem, believing as we do that you cannot continue a journey unless you know from which direction you've come. We are stuck with that for now.

At any rate, our bohemians frequent the Strawberry Fields Cafe for poetry, Mexican beer, and conversation. When Billy Wayne went missing with his boy, and their names were on all of our lips, Devereaux Wickelhaus delivered his epic-poem-in-progress at the Tuesday night open mike, and it was his contention, explored at length in *The Fontanaead* that the matter with Billy Wayne was just bad timing: Didn't he just by chance meet Earlene deBastrop, who had been scheduled, research tells us, for release a day earlier, but wound up staying on another evening because of a clerical foul-up, and didn't they just happen to settle at the Palms that wedding night and there meet Binwaddie, and wasn't it through Binwaddie that Billy Wayne got himself involved in all that Angelo Candela mess, and isn't that what drove him beyond all normal bounds? And so, you see, Billy Wayne's trials have nothing at all to do with genes or curses, even, or stars, or any of that, just a piece of damned catastrophic luck! All of that in heroic couplets. Polite applause. Whispered misgivings.

It does seem curious though that benevolent fortune shines down on generations of Rockefellers and Biedenharns while disaster sticks to the world's Fontanas like pine resin. You think about it, and at some point maybe you say, this much sorrowful luck, this much unfortunate timing or whatever, must total up to something large. Not even chaos or divinity can explain or excuse some things.

Now, you'll recall we left Billy Wayne and Earlene tramping across the tarmac parking lot of the Palms, Billy Wayne wondering what's that smell I smell, and Earlene imagining the cool caress of percale bedsheets. Billy Wayne rapped at the jalousied office door, peeked in through the streaked office window, called hello.

"He's out back," someone said.

Earlene pinched Billy Wayne's forearm and pointed with

her chin at the buckled and torn window screen beside the door to Room #1. Billy Wayne stepped toward the screen. "Excuse me?" he said.

"Follow your nose," the voice said. "You'll find him."

Earlene decided she'd wait in the shade of the office by the oscillating fan while Billy Wayne collected the proprietor. Billy Wayne led her inside, placed their plaid suitcase beside the potted sanseveria on the window ledge. "I'll be right back."

"Billy Wayne?"

"What's that?"

"You might could bring me a Mr. Pibb if you spy a Coke machine."

"All right then."

Seeing her reclined like that, all moistened with sweat, white cotton dress clinging to her thighs, tops of her perfect ears showing through her damp hair, Billy Wayne was moved to manhood. He knelt before her, placed his face in her lap and breathed. She moaned, heaved, pressed Billy Wayne's head to her.

"Not now, Billy Wayne," she said. "Not yet. You go fetch that man out back like the voice said."

4

My Tears Have Been My Meat Night and Day

*B*illy Wayne spied George Binwaddie sitting out behind the motel, cross-legged beside a listing metal tool shed, sort of absentmindedly massaging the great toe on his sandaled left foot, watching curried chicken breasts grill on the hibachi, and crying. Binwaddie wore a tannish, short-sleeved jumpsuit and his features—his eyes, lips, nostrils, everything—were thinly outlined in black as if he'd been sketched first in charcoal and then watercolored. Billy Wayne hesitated in the face of such intimacy, took a step backwards, then remembered this his honeymoon and his readied bride, and said, "Pardon me."

Binwaddie looked at him.

"Excuse me, are you the manager?"

"Yes, yes." Binwaddie sprung to his feet, steadied, then animated himself. He was all energy and motion. "Room?" he said. "Single? Double?" he said. "For how many nights?" he asked. And, "Follow me, follow me," and "Watch your step, please," and so on, as he took Billy Wayne by the hand and led him back past the dumpster to the office where they found Earlene glistening with perspiration and soundly sleeping.

Billy Wayne angled, dipped, and sidled Earlene through the red metal door of #15, tapping her forehead only slightly on the door jamb. He thought he heard scratching in the wall. He cocked his ear. "What's that noise?" he whispered.

Binwaddie shrugged, turned on the window air conditioner. It squealed to life, shook, hummed. "I hear nothing." He brought his index finger to his lips, winked at Billy Wayne, bowed, backed his way out of the darkened room. And closed the door.

Billy Wayne placed Earlene clumsily, head first, then heels, back last, on the bed. He arranged the window blinds so that a bar of light striped the papered wall above the bed. He slid the plaid suitcase beneath the coffee table, drew the straight-backed chair to the bedside, straddled the seat, his elbows on the seat back, and studied this wife of his. She moaned, said something like "married" or "scary" and turned on her side. Billy Wayne wondered what she might be dreaming. He tried to envision her images, but could picture nothing beyond his own kind of empty face, the grizzled bulk of Papaw, and the cotton field that runs alongside the parking lot of the Bawcomville paper mill. He knew nothing else about her fears.

Billy Wayne didn't know Earlene at all but knew her more completely than he had ever known anyone. Still they were man and woman, now and forever, till death and all that, and he saw himself, fortyish, with graying temples and hair in his ears out in a soybean field with his boy and his boy's boy and they all three are waving to someone floating down the Ouachita toward Caldwell Parish, someone who seems to be waving back or maybe calling for help, and in that reverie, Billy Wayne understood what he had accomplished this day. He was no longer the only Fontana.

Earlene Jean deBastrop Fontana lay curled before him now and in her and through her and with her, Billy Wayne would shape the family that had, through the will and wisdom of God, been thus far denied him. And at that moment of epiphany, Billy Wayne knew that he loved Earlene, if love was this adrenaline that pumped blood to the loins and hope to the heart. He determined to make love to her when she awoke, this time with his eyes open and the lights on.

He sat shivering with goodwill, frantic with benevolence, and hearing again the whimpering out back, decided he would find out what made the crying man behind the motel so sad. Semis tooled by on the Dixie Overland Highway and not one of the drivers knew that just twenty feet from his cab a terrible history ate at an exile's heart. Billy Wayne checked his watch. He'd been sitting nearly three minutes. He lowered the setting on the air conditioner and patted his pocket for the key. He opened the door. The shock of sun and heat was like being hit on the forehead with a shovel.

GEORGE BINWADDIE LOUNGED on a torn, beige vinyl front seat out of a Dodge pickup there in the middle of his backyard beside a cement birdbath that he had lined with tinfoil and heaped with charred chicken parts. He licked his fingers, called for Mr. Fontana to join him, and scooted over to the passenger side to make room. Billy Wayne sat, fit his backbone into a vertical tear in the upholstery. They ate quietly, tossed the gray bones at the crawfish chimneys over by the toolshed, shared sweet iced tea from a steel thermos, and sucked their teeth. Billy Wayne slipped a calico handkerchief from his back pocket, wiped his mouth and chin, and offered it to his host.

He said, "You were crying earlier."

And so as they ate, and as they finished with eating, as they started in on Binwaddie's fifth of Fighting Cock, and as they watched the sun descend over the metal roof of Papineau's Tire Center, George Binwaddie told Billy Wayne Fontana the story of his long passage from his home in the northern highlands of Pakistan (a country that Billy Wayne was honestly unable, though he tried, to distinguish from any of the other "——istans" that rattled about his head; what came to him were turbans, sand, veiled women, kneeling, beating wet saffron garments on rocks, and Englishmen in pith helmets and short khaki pants) to the marshy cottonlands of northeast Louisiana. How the night before he left Rahwalpindi on the train to Islamabad, sixty-seven of his relatives gathered at his cousin Hassan's courtyard and roasted Uncle Akbar's goat, danced, sang poems, and prayed for his prosperity. How he was put off a steamer on the Gulf of Aden, was set upon by Berber thieves in Morocco. How he washed plates in a Chinese restaurant in Liverpool for three months and two days, and how he finally arrived in New York, New York, USA, and saw snow fall for the first time and watched how it veiled the skyline, heard how it silenced the great city like harsh news from God. How he walked to New Jersey. How two hemp-smoking beatniks drove him to New Orleans in a stolen school bus. How he caught a Greyhound to Monroe.

He arrived with $1300 in Thomas Cook Traveller's Checks and used all of that money to put a down payment on the Palms. He signed the papers at 10:00 A.M. in the Pelican S&L office on Louisville and then walked the six or seven miles to the motel, jingling his bag full of keys, opened the office door, stepped into the tomblike must, sat on the littered floor, and cried.

Oh, there might be a Bass Masters Tournament on the Ouachita every couple of years or a tractor pull out to the Fairgrounds and then George Binwaddie will fill most of his twenty rooms. Fact is, however, that the Palms has never fulfilled George Binwaddie's dreams or his bank account. The only thing that kept the motel solvent in all its lean years was that Pelican S&L did not want the albatross rehung about its neck and chose instead to allow its Pakistani client to fall behind in payments, to watch the interest and penalties accrue. Binwaddie thought at first this was a strange and wonderful nation where the rich moneylenders do so much for the miserable and hopeless like himself.

"Why Monroe?" Billy Wayne asked.

"My father told me to make for a city that you have named for a considerable president. That would be an important city, he thought."

"Monroe was named for a steamboat."

"Yes. I am sure now that my father was thinking of Washington or Lincoln."

Binwaddie allowed as to how it was now clear to him that he would never reach Washington or Nebraska and would never see his family again. He had been five years in America and the great promise of that first month when he had purchased the motel, enrolled with the Better Business Bureau, ordered matchbooks and postcards, had gone unfulfilled. He had shamed his family, those now living in Pakistan and Kashmir who remembered the dancing and the taste of goat and who told their children how one day their cousin George Gordon Lord Byron Binwaddie would return from America with gold and automobiles and restore the family to the prominence it had enjoyed under the viceroys; shamed those unborn who will be told the story of their Uncle George who boarded a train with the family fortune, involved himself with drugs and thieves, and disappeared into the bowels of America; disgraced most grievously his ancestors, the progenitors of the magnificent family, inventors of the Urdu language, this family that traced its lineage back before Buddha, before Christ, before even names were used and people knew one another by scent the way lizards do. Were he ever to return, disgraced and vanquished, Binwaddie was certain that he would be hung in an iron cage from the banyan tree at the crossroads three miles east of Rahwalpindi and starved to death.

When Billy Wayne intimated that Binwaddie's fears might be exaggerated, that the family, Uncle Akbar himself, might welcome him home as the father in the parable had embraced his prodigal son, Binwaddie told him this was not the Bible, it was real life, and that he would indeed deserve to be caged, mocked, starved, and abandoned to vultures. He would insist upon it. He explained that once when Alexander the Great had marched six hundred foot soldiers across his great, great, etc.-grandfather's millet field, had bivouacked near the family's village, and had let it be known by messenger—a messenger whose tunic smelled of clove and saffron, whose eyelids were dyed with indigo, and whose hair was oiled and hennaed—that he and his officers intended to partake of the sexual favors of the village boys, Gak, the great, great, etc.-grandfather, ordered that all males between seven and eighteen be summarily gelded, and the boys submitted cheerfully. Honor was no trivial matter to this family.

"Yes, I can see that," Billy Wayne said.

Yes, even during the occasional outbreak of poverty, disease, even in the depths of famine and depression, the family understood its destiny, realized that it would once again claim its historic rank as one of the two or three preeminent families in the universe. His was, Binwaddie explained, a tribe of rulers, prophets, bankers, and demigods, and always when the family fortunes wavered, a savior was chosen to redeem and restore them through personal sacrifice, enormous courage, supernatural cunning, or astounding luck. This millennium George Binwaddie had been selected.

"Why you, George?"

Perhaps, Binwaddie explained, it was his miraculous birth. I was born during an eclipse when nothing else existed. When I cried, the sun's light returned. Uncle Akbar explained the birth then as divinely ordained and managed to convince most of the Binwaddies. The trances persuaded the doubters. At irregular but frequent intervals, beginning when he was twelve, Binwaddie suffered seizures of euphoria in which he spasmed and trembled with beatific presence. "Uncle Akbar called it ecstasy, but you call it epilepsy. I am no longer visited," Binwaddie told Billy Wayne. "Medication. And so I was sent to this hell, and I cannot save myself, Mr. Fontana."

"Billy Wayne."

"And so I cry when I cook and smell the curry and remember my city, my friends, what I have lost."

As it grew dark Billy Wayne watched the sheet lightning pale the southern sky. He wondered if there might be a message for him in those night lights. Billy Wayne, who knew so little about his own family, knew less, perhaps, than did any other adult in Monroe about the Fontanas, did know that he was the last, did realize that he stood between the Fontanas, whoever they were, and oblivion, did feel the weight of legacy and the shadow of history.

"A family can be a terrible thing, Billy Wayne, my friend." Binwaddie passed the bottle to his companion.

He had come prepared to help, but now Billy Wayne sat

devastated with fatigue. He had listened to his new and only friend but his zeal had been struck dumb. He fantasized about Earlene, about what he and she would accomplish this night, imagined the future that he hoped would issue from her loins. He smiled, stretched his legs, moved his head to Binwaddie's shoulder. He slept.

5

The Substance of Things Hoped for, the Evidence of Things Not Seen

*E*arlene awoke, smelled an unfamiliar musk on the bed linen, and thought for a moment, Where am I? "Billy Wayne?" she whispered into the darkness of the room. Outside, beneath her window, a baby wailed inconsolably, belligerently. Or more likely, some pitiful cat in heat, Earlene thought. A door closed, the crying stopped. Earlene raised herself on her elbows and allowed her eyes to lighten the gloom. Then she got up, turned off the air conditioner, and listened. She parted two slats of the venetian blinds and peered out into the ocher light of the motel lot. She heard their voices, thought maybe Billy Wayne said something about a steamboat or maybe dreamboat.

Whenever she discovered herself alone, Earlene became

uneasy. She switched the air conditioner to high and then turned on the television set on the dresser. She sat at the edge of the bed and watched. This black transvestite bragged about his boyfriend, "Killer," and an audience of handsome white families laughed their heads off at him. She changed channels and let some police show drone along just so's someone would be talking in the room. She had found herself in these peculiar, often sad places before, and it was those times that her present loneliness conjured.

When she was eleven, Earlene and her grandmother were taking a bus back home from Cousin Neva Wossman's in Minden. Grandma talked about what a trashy no-account Neva's boy Herbert turned out to be. Earlene learned that this cousin she'd never met had robbed a filling station in Ozona, Texas, and made the attendant lie down by the pumps. Then Herbert drenched the boy with ethyl and lit him on fire. So now Herbert's in prison till you-know-what freezes over and that poor deformed child he burned spent two years at the Shriners Hospital and now is so hideous to look at he wears a mask all the time, like the Lone Ranger.

Grandma lit another Kent, turned to Earlene, and Grandma had this look on her face like she was fourteen again, not fifty-seven, and in the embrace of some lovely boy, astonished that he would make such advances on her honor. She stiffened in her seat as if to protest what she knew must be inevitable, closed her eyes, and gave herself up to the caress of death. Her head dropped. Smoke drifted from her nostrils. Earlene let the cigarette burn until it blackened Grandma's fingers and spread a hole in her best crepe-de-chine housedress.

One time Earlene had run away from Bawcomville with a dark-haired man she met at the Mohawk Tavern. She was fifteen then, looked maybe eighteen, told the guy she was twenty-one. They stayed in a motel like this one. She still had the matches somewhere. The Magnolia—that was it—in Hammond. They drove to New Orleans in his pickup, drank some half dozen shots of Jägermeister and then bought some mescaline from the hippies at Jackson Square. The last thing Earlene remembers about that night was buying two Lucky Dogs from this fat guy dressed as a pirate on St. Peter Street. When she woke up in the motel room, the walls were breathing and her friend was not. She opened his wallet, found his license and a snapshot of two children and Santa Claus. His name was not Mike at all. It was Kirby Pruitt. She took the fifty dollars and the change from Kirby's overalls, phoned a cab, and waited out by the curb for it. She thought she recognized Dolly Parton over at the ice machine. Must be the drugs. At least Billy Wayne was not dead, she thought, just missing in action.

Earlene showered, splashed on some Ambush, penciled in her eyeliner, and put on the new black teddy she'd bought just for this night at Zelvateen's Fashion Extra. She admired herself in the full-length mirror on the bathroom door. She sat on the bed with her makeup bag and did her lips and smoothed in some Blush-on. She allowed herself to speculate on what she might be doing a year from now, to wonder what a child of hers and Billy Wayne's would look like. She could imagine it crying all right, could almost feel it in her arms, smell its sour breath. One thing about a child, she knew, they're so helpless, they can't leave you.

No, this was not good, thinking like this. Earlene found the Gideon Bible in the dresser drawer with the phone book. Funny thing was the Book of Job, all seventeen pages of it, was missing. It had been neatly exorcised, probably with a pen knife. Grandma had always told Earlene if you want to know what God's thinking for you, pick up the Bible and open it blindly. So maybe this lack of Job was the message. Maybe not. That would be awful subtle, hardly like a burning bush at all. More than likely, some soul-weary old boy whose girlfriend had just gone back to her husband stayed in this room and found his likeness in Job, realized how good men have ever been unfairly vexed. This old boy was maybe on his way back to Crossett, Arkansas, to see if he might could patch it up with the wife and get to know the twins a little better. Earlene knew the type.

Earlene found what she was looking for in Solomon. "I sleep but my heart waketh," she read. "It is the voice of my beloved that knocketh, saying, Open to me my sister, my love, my dove, my undefiled." She read that over again. My undefiled. "I opened to my beloved; but my beloved had withdrawn himself, and was gone." Even on your wedding night, Earlene realized, you take care of yourself. You're alone, more alone this night for what is missing. She just knew that if she even thought of a certain Patsy Cline song, she could let herself cry. But she didn't want to cry just yet, not before she gave her love to Billy Wayne. She was truly grateful to whatever power it was that had delivered Billy Wayne to her. She closed her eyes and saw him again as on that first night, in black, hair feathered over his forehead, sweating, earnest. Billy Wayne was her savior, plain and simple. He had rescued her from a life of squalor and grime, from a future as bleak as her past.

The talking head on the television began to roll. Blue light flickered in the room. Earlene looked at this new band on her finger and felt like a movie star. She closed her eyes and saw what she would do with Billy Wayne when he came to her. She smiled and slept.

6

Sweet and
Voluble Discourse

Sometimes you tell a story for its own sake, keep it alive so it will grow, mature, you hope, consider its own being and its place in a grander scheme of things, perhaps even wander onto some fundamental truth or other. Your story, after all, is a consciousness that, like the rest of us, given time and tenacity, can begin to find out what it means. As you tell the story, you trust it will not be one of those tales that refuses to look below the surface of its own behavior, examine its values and motives, ask, "Why?" Possibly, said story discerns that the cause of our apprehension and its own misfortune is the enfeebled and transient condition we share. When we afford mortality all of our attention, no benevolence, tenderness, or beauty can console us.

There are always a few people, some of them right here in Monroe, who wonder if all this verbal effort, all this talk of the Fontanas, is worth it. Folks who covet distraction, not revelation. They believe there is no wretchedness so intolerable as a man without diversion and rejoice in platitudes like "a God-fearing life is a virtuous life." And who can begrudge them this redemptive act of faith? They distract themselves so assiduously with amusements that at times it seems our whole parish, our country maybe, is sucking on a sugar tit.

They ask you, Okay, why the Fontanas? What are the sorry lives of this benighted passel of swampers going to teach us about life? Is it sins of the fathers? Is it the way we're raised? Is it poverty? ignorance? Is it fate? Is it genes? Is it a sun so hot it drives us crazy? Is it, like Moon Pie, Billy Wayne's younger boy, once explained to his brother, Duane, some deranged God compensating for his insecurities the way He did in Eden? Or is it, like the philosopher said, that we just can't sit quietly in a room, alone, television off, book closed, sit there and face what there is to our lives?

SO WHERE ARE we? We've got Earlene curled up asleep on a motel bed. We've got Billy Wayne, his head on George Binwaddie's bony shoulder, dreaming of the voice in the window. We'll get to him and to Dencil Currence, who, at the moment of Billy Wayne's nuptials, stood on the entrance ramp to I-75 in Alachua, Florida, hitching a ride to Monroe, drawn here by the presence of his wife, Hazel, who, at the time, lives in Room #1 at the Palms with twin boys, age five, who are not Dencil's and not Angelo Candela's, Angelo being the mayor's nephew, married nephew, who sees Hazel Currence "on the side," as he puts it, and not George Binwaddie's, George having waived Hazel's rent for the occasional sexual favor. We'll get to Dencil, to Angelo, and to the redoubtable Fox Ledbetter, all in an effort to tell the story of this gene or curse or whatever we decide it is that afflicts this family. Or maybe afflicts us all.

Seems folks have always talked about the Fontanas. Generations of friends have traded Fontana anecdotes over bottles of Jax at the Blue Light Cafe or under hair dryers at D'Vonne's Golden Comb. Parents have been relating Fontana bedtime stories to their children since before the First World War. However, as with other forms of gossip, oral history embellishes as it ages, making it, at times, difficult to know precisely just which are the facts, which the fancies. A case in point: Most everyone hereabouts can tell you that when the Fontana tribe began its forty-year meander in the Delta in 1864, Mangham, Peregrine's firstborn by twenty-one minutes, fashioned for each of the original twenty-five pilgrims a cucullus, a kind of conical hood designed to keep off the soaking rains, to cool the head, and we like to think, to invest the wearer with a druidic mystique. Each hood came with an attached veil that could be dropped down to cover the face in case of mosquitoes, or in pink-eyed Bosco and Mangham's cases, strong sunlight.

That part of the legend is public knowledge. Fontanas regularly wore the cuculli on their market trips to Tallulah until 1880 or so. There's even a report of a trapper's encounter with "some kind of monks or other" which appeared in the New Orleans daily along with a drawing of the "holy men." What is not verifiable, however, is that one retired CSA Major General Nathan Bedford Forrest adopted the cowl for his brotherhood of vigilantes, who then became known as the Cucullus Clan and then the you-know-what.

With so much problematic intelligence, it's best to stick with what is known to be true, or at least factual, or to that which is too intriguing to omit. The matter of Winchester Fontana's immaculate conception fits both criteria. It's what first caught the attention of people in this part of the state to the family. The Fontanas laid claim to being the only family in northeast Louisiana to have borne a child without the mess and turbulence of the sexual act. This would be the birth of Bosco and Mangham's half brother in the spring of 1864. Peregrine, you see, had gone smitten with a Miss Twyla Whatley, a seventeen-or-so-year-old schoolteacher in Madison Parish. Peregrine, whose woman, Velma Littlejohn, the twins' momma, was just then ailish with the slows, found himself setting his traps closer and then closer still to Miss Twyla's lodgings south of Young's Point.

It came to pass that Peregrine carried Miss Twyla and her few students, in a farm cart he had borrowed, to Vicksburg to watch the battle then taking place. Along about lunch Miss Twyla stood in the bed of the wagon, tooted into her pitch pipe, and the children on the grass below sang "The Bonnie Blue Flag" and "I Wish I Were in Dixie's Land." Peregrine cupped a morsel of cornbread in his hands. He straightened up as nonchalantly as he could and turned to see if Miss Twyla or the choir had spied him sneaking the food they had brought along. That's when it happened.

Dr. Tyson Bordelon, from the Memphis City Hospital, summoned to Richmond to care for Twyla Whatley, wrote the whole thing up in the *Journal of Southern Medicine* (vol. 20, no. 2, Fall 1864): A soft lead fragment from a chance bullet fired from a fifteen-shot Henry repeating rifle, discharged by a Union soldier, caused a tibial fracture in Mr. Fontana's left leg and then carried away his left testicle, carried it away from his groin and toward the abdomen of Miss Twyla W. where it penetrated the skin, the muscle, the membrane of her womb. In other words, Dr. Bordelon explained, and improbable as it might sound, spermatazoa gained access to the uterus via the bullet. More peculiar still, the spent projectile was removed from the scrotum of the baby by Dr. Bordelon after the birth.

What happened to Winchester, though, that's another story altogether, and we've got our own sleeping couple to deal with.

7

In a Dark Time
the Eye Begins
to See

*W*hen Billy Wayne was startled awake by the blast of an air horn from a passing trailer truck on the highway, he felt, then saw what he assumed was a leech, but was, in fact, a garden slug sliming its milky way up his left arm, perhaps driven mad by the pungent and penetrating vapors of the curried chicken. But where on earth was he? Billy Wayne wondered. And that was when Billy Wayne felt a weight in his trousers pocket and reached in, took out a key and saw the number fifteen written on the attached metal disk, turned it over and saw the legend "Palms Motel, Your Oasis in a Lodger's Desert." If this were a dream, he'd wake up now, frantic; he'd see Earlene's barley-colored hair inches from his face. He looked at his watch and wondered if it meant six forty-five at night or in the morning, and then he remembered. Billy Wayne blanched, broke into a sweat, stood, let the nausea pass, ran to Room #15, and found the door open and the room vacant. But the plaid suitcase sat on the bed.

Billy Wayne ran across the parking lot to the woman in the robe and slippers sitting on a beach chair in front of Room #1 and smoking a brown cigarette. "Excuse me, have you seen a young woman come by here this morning?"

"What she look like?" The woman flipped the hem of her robe over her knees.

"She's about yea high," he said, "with blondish hair. Real thin."

"My name's Hazel," the woman said. She inhaled her cigarette.

Billy Wayne nodded. "Billy Wayne Fontana."

"Blondish hair, you say?"

Where had he heard that voice?

"Greenish eyes?"

"You told me about Binwaddie, didn't you? You're the voice in the window."

"Calls herself Earlene?"

"That's her."

Hazel smiled, raised her eyebrows.

"Can you tell me which way she went?"

Hazel sized up Billy Wayne. Suddenly a television from inside her room blasted on. Woody Woodpecker was doing that frightening laugh. Hazel rapped on the window over her chair and yelled, "Turn that goddam thing down." She waited, then looked up at the window and hollered, "If I have to get up off this chair and come in there, you'll be two sorry little fuckers." The TV lowered. She said to Billy Wayne, "You look like a cop."

"I'm Earlene's husband."

Hazel smiled. "Oh look, here's Sweet Martha Lorraine," Hazel said just as a sleek tortoiseshell cat leaped onto her lap. "How you, sugar?" she said. She rubbed behind the cat's ears and the cat collapsed, purring, eyes closed tightly, arching her back against Hazel's strokes. "She'll stay like this all day," Hazel told Billy Wayne.

"Do you know where she is?"

Hazel said, "Heading toward town."

"How long ago?"

"Fifteen minutes. Maybe less."

Billy Wayne started down the highway. In a half a mile or so he came to a guy in a Mexican hat selling flowers out of the back of his station wagon.

"Excuse me, amigo," Billy Wayne said.

"Yes, sir, carnations or mums?"

"Have you seen a woman walk by here in the last few minutes?"

The man nodded. "Looked like she was crying."

"Why don't you give me a dozen of those pinks. No, the reds."

Billy Wayne saw Earlene and another woman sitting in Marianna's Cafe, at a table by the far wall under a photograph of the college football team. Marianna's was cloudy with cigarette smoke.

Billy Wayne stood by the table, flowers in hand. Earlene ignored him.

"Sweetheart?" he said.

"A tad late with the love candy, aren't we, Romeo?" the woman said.

"Pardon me?"

She put down her fork and wiped her hand on her apron. She extended her cleaned hand to Billy Wayne. "Ronnie Flacy," she said. "I'll be your waitress this morning."

They shook hands and Ronnie invited Billy Wayne to join

them. Billy Wayne placed the carnations on the chair beside Earlene and sat across the table alongside Ronnie.

Earlene said, "Ronnie, tell this here customer that I have nothing to say to him."

"Can I get you something, doll?" Ronnie said. She picked up her pencil and receipt pad.

"Just a coffee, thanks," Billy Wayne said.

"Plan to eat the flowers, do you?" Ronnie got up and walked to the coffee station.

Billy Wayne saw other waitresses turn toward him and smile. He said, "That's great, Earlene. Just spread our private business all over Monroe, why don't you."

Earlene ignored him. She buttered her grits and smiled at Ronnie.

Ronnie filled Billy Wayne's cup and freshened Earlene's coffee and her own. She set the pot in the middle of the table and sat. She told the gentleman in the mint green leisure suit at the next table that he'd already had enough coffee. He should get his self back to work is what he should do.

"Ronnie, do you think we could have a little privacy here?" Billy Wayne said.

"I can take a hint," Ronnie said. She took the saucer from under her cup and covered her coffee. "That'll keep it warm."

"Thank you, Ronnie," Billy Wayne said.

"Damn you, Billy Wayne Fontana. Even at your first breakfast as a married man, you spend more time talking to strangers—no offense, Ronnie—than to your bride," Earlene said. She was crying and biting her napkin.

"Look what you've done now," Ronnie said. She held Earlene's shoulder, rubbed a circle on her back. She looked at Billy Wayne. "Say, you're no Nancy-boy, are you, hon?"

Billy Wayne poured half-and-half into his coffee and put down the steel creamer.

"You all right, sugar?" she asked Earlene.

Earlene nodded. She took a deep breath.

"You got some napkin stuck to your lip there, hon," Ronnie said. "Let me get it."

Ronnie went away. Billy Wayne looked into his cup. He told Earlene he was heartily sorry for having neglected her, that he detested his behavior because he feared the loss of her but mostly because it offended her who was all good and deserving of all his love, and he resolved, with her help, to avoid that kind of behavior in the future. Said it just like the Act of Contrition, and he meant it, and it worked. Earlene stopped her crying, reached across the table, and stroked Billy Wayne's cheek. She smiled at him. I hope you mean it, she said.

Billy Wayne said, "Earlene, we should get back to the Palms."

Earlene blushed.

"I'll get you a ride," Ronnie said.

Billy Wayne jumped. "You scared me."

Ronnie removed the saucer from her coffee and sipped. "See that fellow by the window?" she said.

"Which one?"

"With the pocky face and the shades."

"Kind of looks like Roy Orbison," Earlene said.

"Yeah, he is cute, isn't he?" Ronnie said.

"Yeah, I see him," Billy Wayne said.

"That's Mr. Hotson Taylor. Owns the At Your Service Cab Company."

"We're all set then," Billy Wayne said. "What do we owe you, Ronnie?" Earlene rubbed Billy Wayne's leg with her foot.

"No charge," Ronnie said.

8

The End of Mirth
Is Heaviness

*N*ow that we've got up a moderate head of narrative steam, and now that Hotson has flipped up his meter and is making an illegal U-turn in front of Marianna's, we'll wait to fill you in on Dencil Currence's progress toward Monroe. Just let's say he's right then sitting spraddle legged on a toolbox in the bed of a pickup heading through downtown—what there is of it—Andalusia, Alabama. On the cab window just beside Dencil's right shoulder is a bumper sticker that says. "We Don't Give a Damn How You Did It Up North." In fact, we'll just delete Dencil's journey altogether. The next time we see him, he'll be in Monroe, and we'll come to that whenever there's an appropriate break in our causal sequence of events. That said, and the traffic light in front of You-All Rental turning green, let's get back into Hotson's Checker.

Hotson said, "You folks see the paper this morning all about Angelo Candela?"

"What did he do now?" Billy Wayne said. "Our war hero you're talking about?"

Hotson nodded, pushed in the cigarette lighter on the dash, and pulled down a pack of Lucky Strikes from the visor. Hotson checked his rearview mirror, saw the newlyweds kissing, and did not offer them a cigarette. He lit his own. "Seems Angelo was playing fetch with that hound of his. Sorry, don't mean to laugh. He's tossing a branch into the bayou and having old Blue leap in after it. On the third toss, suddenly that old Catahoula goes under, and then the water where he was starts to roil, and then up pops Blue's butt, but just for a second, and then it's sucked under, and the water's just as black and smooth as sin."

"Alligator," Earlene said.

"I hope so. Hate to think there's some bass that large and feisty down there. Anyway, that's not all. Angelo is so furious or whatever that he spends all last night on his bass boat with lights and a 12-gauge Remington hunting that thing. That's how come it's in the paper. He fired off enough shots to get the deputies out to his house." Hotson looked at his cigarette, tossed it out the window. "I got to quit."

George Binwaddie was pacing the sidewalk in front of the Palms when the Time Machine, the name stenciled on the front doors of Hotson's cab, pulled up, and he was so elated when he saw the young couple cooing in the backseat that he wept. He had not destroyed their marriage after all. Binwaddie insisted that the couple stay at the Palms for two nights as his wedding gift. And you will have a proper wedding reception right here at the motel this afternoon, he told them. He would arrange everything.

"George Binwaddie," Billy Wayne said, "my wife Earlene deBastrop Fontana."

"Honored to meet you."

"Likewise," Earlene said.

Hotson said he'd love to come to the reception, and, sure, he could stop by the hospital to see if Sister Helen could attend.

"I forgot them," Earlene said.

"What's that?" Billy Wayne said.

"Your flowers. I left them at Marianna's."

"I'll call Ronnie and have her bring them on out," Hotson said.

"Tell her she's invited to the party," Earlene said.

Earlene sent Billy Wayne to the Howard's on Louisville Avenue to buy himself a long-sleeved, white shirt, khaki chinos, and a cranberry tie. Then she retired to their room to luxuriate in a warm, scented bubble bath. Binwaddie set to work on the backyard. He hauled off the truck seat, hosed down the birdbath, raked up chicken parts, mowed the grass, and then with Hazel's help set up chairs and tables that they had scrounged from the vacant rooms. Binwaddie called Cajun Brothers Seafood and had them deliver two sacks of Grand Isle oysters, twenty pounds of boiled crawfish, and ten pounds of andouille. Then he rang up Tribal Spirits and had them send out three cases of Jax, a bottle of domestic champagne, and a gallon of Bombay gin. He ordered a wedding cake from Ludivine's Bake Shop.

At two o'clock, under the threat of a thunderstorm, the reception began with a toast by George Binwaddie who wished the couple as many progeny as there were stars in the sky, fish in the ocean, dreams in the hearts of men. This was not the shaded El-Song Gardens of the Bible Research Center or the manicured backyard of a River Oaks neurosurgeon, so neither the *Citizen* nor the *News-Star-World* bothered to dispatch a society reporter to cover the Fontana wedding reception. Had the *Citizen* sent Susie Bingham Breville and ruined her Saturday golf date at Riverside Country Club, she might have included a paragraph in her Sunday "Susie Says" column. Susie would have scoffed down some wedding cake, sipped a gin-and-tonic, checked her watch, realized she could still get in nine holes at the club, put another gin-and-tonic, in a go-cup, and left. And she would have missed all the excitement.

Billy Wayne and Sister Helen walked to the A&P for horse-radish and lemons, and on the way back got their first real chance to chat since Billy Wayne had excused himself from the supper table and had gone across to the hospital's North Wing on the evening he fell in love. Sister Helen said, "I guess you know that folks say your family is cursed."

"I've heard that," he said. "I don't believe in hereditary bad luck."

"Maybe it has nothing to do with luck. It might be that having children is a burden you will not wish to bear," she said. "Something unfortunate has befallen the Fontanas every generation."

"There's nothing wrong with me."

"Nobody said 'wrong,' Billy Wayne, just peculiar."

"So what do you think, Sister?"

"I'm worried that maybe you've relinquished your vocation. If you were called by God and haven't answered, well, that's a grievous matter. This is forever, Billy Wayne. This is not pretend. You've made a solemn choice."

"I know that, Sister."

"The marriage is sanctified, Billy Wayne. It might have been a civil ceremony, but all the same, God blessed it."

"It's natural, isn't it, Sister, to want a family, not to want to wind up old and alone."

Sister Helen took Billy Wayne's arm and stopped him. A Cajun Brothers refrigerated truck passed them. When its noise had faded, Sister Helen said, "It doesn't make any difference, Billy Wayne, if you marry or if you don't, have children or not, you will end up alone. That is not the point at all. The point is how much misery you will suffer before you end up alone."

"Look, I'm sorry for running away like that, for letting you and everyone down."

Billy Wayne recognized the look Sister gave him. He'd seen that arched eyebrow and that disconcerting half-smile before. The look that unnerved him, that said, Don't play ignorant with me, Billy Wayne Fontana. He felt unbalanced and needed to hold on to something solid. He said, "You're all I've got from my history now, you and the Fontana name."

"Stop this, Billy Wayne."

He said, "What? Stop what?" and knew as soon as he did that the lie this time was sentimentality. Well, maybe it wasn't a lie—he *was* sorry for his impulsive, inconsiderate behavior, wasn't he?—but it certainly did obscure the deeper truth here, whatever that was.

"Do you understand what you've done, Billy Wayne? Do you realize that you've made a decision that you cannot rescind?"

When Billy Wayne did not respond, Sister Helen said that who he was now had nothing to do with who he was a week ago, who he had been all his life.

"You're angry," he said.

"I'm worried," she said. "And you should be."

When they arrived back at the Palms, as they walked past the office, Sister Helen told Billy Wayne that he looked handsome. He thanked her. She said she'd pray for him. She squeezed his hand.

. . .

GEORGE BINWADDIE AND Ronnie Flacy sat at one table. Binwaddie wore a black neoprene glove on his left hand and sat shucking oysters as fast as he could, while Ronnie lemoned and sauced them and Hazel's boys, Webb and Ferlin, carried the trays of prepared oysters to the food table in the middle of the yard and set them beside the bowl of mudbugs and the platters of grilled andouille and rice. There were three or four conversations going on. Hotson Taylor was asking Sister Helen about working conditions at the hospital and she was saying how they could be better. Binwaddie and Ronnie were fantasizing possible fatal accidents that could befall Angelo. He could get bitten by a moccasin while out harvesting his marijuana crop in the Tensas swamps. Except he wraps those damn window screens all up his legs, Ronnie remembered. Someone could easily drain the brake fluid from his Mustang, but then that wouldn't exactly be an accident, now would it? And so on like that. Billy Wayne was telling Earlene that maybe she should go easy on the gin because they had a big night ahead of them, and he smiled and so did she. Hazel told Angelo how she had this premonition of disaster.

"My horoscope said the next few days would be difficult for me emotionally and financially."

"Not that crap again."

"Said I would be getting a visitor."

"I got your little visitor right here," he told her.

"I'm serious. My neck aches and that always means trouble."

Angelo swallowed an oyster, sliding it off the shell into his mouth and down his gullet. "It's the oysters, honey. Don't you know what oysters do for a person?"

And so on. And, of course, everyone in the yard could hear him because Angelo had one of those disconcertingly loud voices that can fill a restaurant or empty a room. The next thing he said to Hazel was, "You just eat the tail and suck the head, child. Easy as that." As if she didn't know already how to dispatch a crawfish.

The effect of Angelo's volume, calculated or not, was to draw attention to himself. The guests found themsleves regarding Angelo and wishing they were not. Angelo sensed the scrutiny but did not realize that the onlookers were simply awaiting his next awkward remark. He assumed that they expected an announcement. Such is the disease of politicians. He cleared his throat and announced that he was running for the State Senate. Angelo looked into the stunned faces of each and every voter and knew that he was working his first crowd, that the campaign was under way. He felt exhilarated and told his audience he didn't see how he could lose. He had the support of his uncle's local Democratic machine and his wife's modest fortune. And, of course, he was himself a young, handsome, charismatic winner of the Purple Heart, a genuine Vietnam War hero. The only thing that could keep him from office would be to get caught in bed with a dead woman or a live boy. He laughed.

"Hero, my ass," Hotson said. In general, Hotson could keep his mouth shut, but he was belligerent about a few subjects. The war was one of the big ones. Today, with five cans of Jax already under his belt, Hotson did not feel constrained by logic and reason.

"Are you questioning my patriotism?" Angelo said. He held on to Hazel's hand as he imagined he would hold his wife, Patricia's, hand on stage at the victory party on primary night at campaign headquarters.

"People are making a lot of money on this war."

"Sounds to me," Angelo said more to the crowd than to his adversary, "that you've been reading the liberal East Coast press." He smiled now.

"The Vietnamese are fighting for survival. That's why they'll win. The people who pushed your button are going to make money win or lose. They just need to keep the war going as long as they can."

Sister Helen said, "Gentlemen, we're at a wedding!"

That seemed to calm things for a moment. Everyone took a breath. Billy Wayne tried to get the reception back on its festive course. "Hey, come on, you all, there's plenty of food left."

But George, who disliked Angelo for personal, not political, reasons, for the way he treated Hazel and Hazel's boys, would have none of that. "Angelo, is it true that the Vietnamese just love dog meat?"

"Keep it up, needledick, and you'll be one sorry son of a bitch," Angelo said.

Ronnie said. "Earlene, you ever notice how some men just can't hold their liquor?"

Earlene wasn't sure, but she thought she had.

"You feeling okay, doll?"

Earlene looked at Ronnie, took a huge breath, but couldn't answer.

"I'm going to get you to your room. You maybe could use a little nap."

By this time Webb and Ferlin, who had grown tired of pearl hunting through the trash, were getting whiny. First Hazel threatened them, then she told them they weren't too old to get their bottoms warmed, and now she was telling them they'd get no television if they didn't act like human beings.

George started barking and Angelo charged him and got his hands around his throat and might have actually killed him had not George acted quickly and stabbed Angelo in the arm with the oyster knife. That's when Hotson and Billy Wayne pulled Angelo off George. And suddenly they heard the wind ruffle through the Rose of Sharon and saw this blossoming wound and the knife with a drop of blood on the blade.

The cut was not so deep, but Sister Helen said he would need a tetanus shot. She, Angelo, and Hazel drove off in the Mustang to the hospital. When he could talk again, George volunteered to watch the boys and get them ready for bed. "I don't want Hazel to suffer for that asshole," he said.

"You were quite the asshole yourself, George," Billy Wayne told him.

"Thank you."

Ronnie came out of Room #15 and told Billy Wayne that Earlene had been sick all over. She's in bed now. She'll need to sleep. Ronnie asked Hotson for a ride home. They grabbed a six-pack and left in the Time Machine. Billy Wayne and George Binwaddie sat in the yard in the slanted sunlight of late afternoon. The storm had passed without rain.

"He was hurting me," Binwaddie said.

"Don't worry about it."

Now as he sat, Billy Wayne wished he had thanked Sister Helen for coming, thanked everyone for that matter. What was happening to his manners? To his life? Well, he was a husband now. It did feel more complicated. But he wouldn't have to be a father necessarily. Married life wouldn't have to be that much different from the single life. Just that now he'd have someone to share his happiness with. He'd have to talk with Earlene about this child business. He hadn't even gotten a chance to tell Sister Helen good-bye. Maybe he'd have Sister over to the house for supper. What house? What food? Jesus!

9

Be Sure Your Sin
Will Find You Out

*U*nder the rosy opening fingers of dawn, Earlene, whose fitful sleep had been both dreamless and tortured, stirred, and then stirred Billy Wayne beside her. Earlene felt a stab in her right eye and a pain that arced across her brain and exploded at the base of her skull. She was unwilling to move her head, unable to writhe out of the bed to hunt through her purse for aspirin. She resented the subtle but unequivocal intrusion of gray light, knowing she would soon lose even the simple solace of blackness, and knowing that the surest way to survive was to deprive the senses as thoroughly as possible and to etherize, as it were, the brain. Billy Wayne snored. He tossed. Earlene accepted the futility of her struggle to shut out the world, and she surrendered to her nausea. The day, she knew, was lost to her.

About that time, Dencil Currence walked up Old Nachitoches Road to Cypress Street and then crossed the Ouachita at Louisville and went into Willis's Rise 'n' Dine. He ordered a #2 Breakfast with double link sausages and then ate the sausages and dipped his Texas toast in the runny yolks of his eggs. He asked Tenille Suzenau, the waitress, if he could have a job. Tenille told him she sure could use someone in the kitchen on this eleven-to-seven shift, but said she wasn't the boss.

"Who is?"

"Willis Huckaby."

"When can I catch him?"

"Comes on at three."

"I'll have some coffee."

Tenille poured the coffee and placed two little plastic cruets of nondairy creamer alongside the saucer. "You're Dencil, ain't you?"

Dencil smiled and stared at Tenille. "Do I know you?"

"Nuh-uh."

"How'd you know my name?"

"The tattoo."

When Dencil was still in high school at Ouachita Christian here in Monroe, his lavaliered sweetheart Maribeth Kindris was found partially naked and fully dead in a car on Lovers' Lane along with her friend Hazel Guidry's father. They evidently fell asleep with the car's engine running and carbon monoxide rising through the rusted floorboards. Dencil took his first drink that weekend, got on a Greyhound bus, slept off the alcohol, and woke up in Atlanta. That's where he had the teardrops tattooed on his face. There's one just at the corner of his right eye and another on his cheekbone and one by his mouth. That was eight years ago.

"Your old lady know you're in town?"

"Not yet."

"She'll be surprised."

"Won't she."

Hazel Guidry is the beforementioned Hazel Currence. After the tragedy, it seemed natural that she and Dencil would find comfort in each other, as it were. They married before Dencil could graduate, and while Hazel was still a junior. They quit school and rented an old and neglected twenty-two-foot houseboat docked on the river at Forsythe Park. Hazel waited tables at Boudreau's Dinner Bell, and Dencil fished off his house. He sold what gar, goo, buffalo, carp, and cat they couldn't eat to Bayles Landing Fish Market, and they got by. Dencil, however, was tormented by thoughts that he had been responsible for the deaths of two people. At first he didn't know what he could have done that drove Maribeth into Jim Guidry's arms (and legs, and so on). Maybe it was something he hadn't done. What he had all along thought of as trust, Maribeth must have understood as apathy. He might just as well have been indifferent to Maribeth for all the vigilance he had invested in their love affair. What else was Maribeth to think but that Dencil, who never pried into her personal matters, wanted her in the arms of another. His was, he concluded, the sin of ignorance.

One steamy afternoon, Dencil saw a dozen or so red-headed vultures perched on the brittle limbs of a toothache tree not twenty yards from the deck of the houseboat. He knew this was a sign. It may have been a divine warning or it may have been his own conscience at work. It didn't matter which. The rheumy-eyed buzzards had come for him. What he knew was that vultures cannot feast on what is not dead and that they will not light on a moving target. He bought some fuel, unhooked his sanitary and electrical lines, left a note for Hazel nailed to a post on the dock, started the engine, and embarked for, he hoped, the Mississippi. The engine quit almost immediately, and the houseboat, the *Regina Mare*, drifted a few miles until it ran aground on a sandbar off Lazarre Park. Dencil abandoned ship and set off on the road. He knew enough of the Bible to remember that wandering absolves sin. Now seven years later, sitting in the Rise 'n' Dine, he knew that he might still be wanted in Monroe for stealing and wrecking a house, but that he was probably not wanted by his wife Hazel.

"You know where I might find Hazel these days?" Dencil asked Tenille.

Tenille loaded packets of Sweet'n Low into their plastic containers. "You might try the Palms Motel. You know it?"

"Sure do." Dencil took a five out of his T-shirt pocket, unfolded it, and slipped it beneath the edge of his plate. "Keep the change," he said.

"Thank you, Dencil."

"You tell Willis Huckaby I'll be along about three o'clock."

"I will," Tenille said. "You can catch the bus right across the street. The #1 will bring you out real close."

"I'll walk," Dencil told her. He picked up his canvas bag and smiled. For a moment as he walked up DeSiard, Dencil considered his prospects—a new job, an old wife—and thought that perhaps he could resume a normal life after so many years of depravity and deprivation.

When Dencil had hoofed it out of Monroe some seven years earlier, he first made for New Orleans where he pretty much stayed drunk for a year, eating at a Tulane Avenue mission, sleeping mostly in City Park, and finally getting jailed when he and two of his mission buddies tried to hold up a tamale vendor on Carrollton. After thirteen months in the city jail, he got released, hitched to Florida, stayed intoxicated, and slept in the jungles alongside I-95 in Broward County. Then he tried to rob a 7-Eleven, got caught, and was back in jail. This time he stayed in for nearly six years.

In prison Dencil kept to himself. He didn't buy alcohol or drugs from the guards or get himself involved in prisoners' industries. He just punched out auto tags and watched television in the lounge. He felt better, didn't have that pain under his ribs all the time for one thing. Of course, he realized that without alcohol, he had very little to do. He also understood that when they threw him out of prison, he'd have to get his own meals, find his own shelter. He knew one day he'd have to go home, face Hazel, the vultures, the memories. Would have to be reborn was how he looked at it. (Dencil's cellmate was a politician who had just found Jesus and was all the time dropping to his chubby knees, crying, and claiming that he had accepted Jesus Christ as his personal Lord and Savior. Some of his imagery had rubbed off on Dencil.)

Dencil entered the office of the Palms Motel and rang the bell on the desk. George Binwaddie entered through a beaded curtain from his apartment in the rear. He smiled.

"I'd like a room," Dencil said.

"Single?"

"Well, separated, I guess you'd say."

Binwaddie paused. "Are you staying alone?"

"Yes, sir."

"Eight dollars," Binwaddie said.

Dencil signed the register as Buster Lowery which was the born-again politician's name.

"Number 11, Mr. Lowery."

"Thanks. Say, do you have a Hazel Currence registered here?"

"Yes, uh-huh. We do, sir."

Dencil looked out the window to the lot and saw a man in a white shirt and jeans sitting on a green tulip chair. Someone who looked familiar. "Who's that?" he asked Binwaddie.

"Billy Wayne Fontana."

"I know that name. Was he ever in prison, do you know?"

10

How Light and Portable My Pain

The next thing you know George Binwaddie has been jailed for attempted murder and Angelo has drilled two bullets into his wife's forehead, and, naturally, that makes the front page of the papers, and it's the lead story on the ten o'clock news. KNOE has a tape of Angelo weeping in the sheriff's cruiser, his face in his hands, and there's his uncle, Mayor Tommy Candela, saying what a tragic accident this was and how he'll always remember his little Patty fondly, but, no, he didn't think it was time for gun legislation, and so on.

Angelo was questioned, booked on a manslaughter charge, then released on his personal recognizance. A few days later, he held a press conference at the Holidome and, despite his lawyer's protestations, explained how he had come home about 2:00 A.M. from a campaign fund-raiser at Danny Bonderant's Fish Camp—a huge success, by the way, thanks to the citizens of Calhoun—and heard some commotion coming from the back bedroom. He explained to the assembled press how he then tiptoed down the carpeted hall and heard what could have been a scuffle or could have been—and here he paused and brought a finger to the corner of his eye. He tried the knob, he said. The door was locked. He kicked it open. Angelo held up a yellow receipt from Affordable Windows and Doors. It cost him $247.52 to install a replacement. Solid walnut. What he saw in the bedroom was an Afro-American male, buck naked, wrestling with Patty at the foot of the canopied bed. Patty was screaming, "Oh, my God! Oh, my God!"

"I could see his beady little armadillo eyes like they was frozen in my headlights," Angelo said. "And then the boy starts moving, you know, real slow, well, not slow but jerky like a squirrel, and he snatches his clothes that are lying by him in a pile, and I tell him 'Don't move!' and I take out my revolver and I hold it like this." Angelo made a gun with his thumb and index finger and held it, loaded and cocked, beside his face. "I let him see it, but he don't stop. I ask him how he got into my house. He won't tell me, but I notice the window is not closed all the way. Patty's meanwhile hysterical, but she ain't moved from under this guy. I say, 'You okay, sugar?' but she's just crying."

Angelo reached into his sports coat pocket and took out an index card and a handkerchief. He placed the card on the podium and then blew his nose. Claudia Simmons, a reporter for the Channel 4 news, sat in the front row talking to herself and rolling her eyes. This was no doubt disconcerting to Angelo, but he continued.

"Then he reached into his pile of clothes, and I saw something shiny." Angelo explained how he wasn't sure why, if it was agent orange or what, but suddenly he was back in Nam and under siege, so he shot out the light, dropped to his knees, and fired at the figure in front of him.

Here Angelo paused to weep as cameras clicked and Claudia Simmons bit her lip and shook her head. Then she smiled and jotted something in her notebook.

"Ladies and gentlemen," Angelo said, "my home was invaded by a professional criminal, a man who wore gloves, who took advantage of my darling wife, and I did what any self-respecting citizen and property owner would do." Angelo's attorney, Price McKeithen, stepped to the podium. Angelo said, "He got out the window. I mean, he fired shots, I played dead, and he got out the window. I guess." Price whispered to Angelo. Angelo nodded. "I called my Uncle Tommy after that."

A reporter from the *Citizen* asked Angelo if he would be dropping out of the senate race. He said, on the contrary, he planned to redouble his efforts, to win this one for Patty. Now that his wife was gone, he said, politics was all he had, and he would use it to make the country safe for homeowners.

Claudia Simmons stood.

"Yes, ma'am. The lady in the front row."

"Mr. Candela," Claudia said, "can you explain why the Sheriff's Department has been unable to confirm the presence of any person other than you and your wife in that room?"

"No, ma'am. I only know what I saw. You'll have to ask Sheriff Tidwell about the other."

"Isn't it true, Mr. Candela, that in the army you were an expert marksman?"

"The best shot in my outfit."

"That as a child you won the junior sharpshooter award at the Cheniere Brake Rod and Gun Club?"

"Yes, ma'am."

"Would you say, Mr. Candela, that you could knock a gnat off a buzzard's tail at a hundred yards?"

Angelo smiled. "I reckon I could do that, yes, ma'am."

"And yet you couldn't hit a six-foot man at seven feet?"

"Well, now, hold on there. I never said the guy was no six feet."

"There was no man, was there, Mr. Candela? You've made this all up."

Price McKeithen leaned into the microphone and asked Claudia how to spell her name, and he wrote it down and said he thought her questions were impertinent and inappropriate and that Angelo would not answer them. But Angelo, more concerned, it seemed, with the campaign than with the upcoming trial, aware of the bright lights of the TV cameras and the voters watching at home, said he would be happy to address the question.

"As I said, young lady, there was this six foot . . . no, you said that. There was a black man in my house, fooling with my wife, and I did what every American man would do. I defended my family and my home with the same courage that I displayed in the jungles of Vietnam. When the sheriff catches this guy, you'll see. It'll be his word against mine. The word of common scum against the word of a war hero and state senator. Who do you think the jury will believe?"

"But what if he's not found?" Claudia Simmons asked.

Angelo smiled. "It's still my word against his."

"What did this alleged burglar look like?"

"I told you. Black."

Price McKeithen put his hand over the microphone. He said something to Angelo, then to the press. "That's all, ladies and gentlemen. This has been a difficult time. Mr. Candela needs to be alone. Thank you for coming. We'll have a complete press release for you tomorrow. Good night."

Angelo drove to the Palms after the press conference and knocked on Hazel's door and walked in. He saw Hazel sitting at the table with a man he did not recognize, saw the boys asleep in their cots. "Who's this?"

Hazel said, "Angelo, this here's Buster Lowery. Buster, Angelo Candela. He's running for state senate. Buster and me went to school together. Ain't it a small world?"

Angelo shook hands with Buster. "Lowery, huh?"

"Pleased to meet you," Dencil said.

"Don't know no Lowerys 'round Monroe."

Someone rapped at the door. Hazel said, "Come on in. It's like a Greyhound Station in here now."

Billy Wayne stepped inside and asked could he just speak with Angelo a moment outside. "Hi there . . . Dencil, isn't it?"

"Dencil?" Angelo said.

Billy Wayne saw Hazel shake her head and knew that something was up though he did not know what. He heard Hazel say, "Pencil. We used to call Bubba 'Pencil' on account of how thin he was."

"You mean 'Buster'?"

"That's what I said."

"No, you said 'Bubba.' "

"Just five minutes," Billy Wayne interrupted.

"What is it?" Angelo said.

"Outside." Billy Wayne held his arm out for Angelo. "Don't want to wake the children."

On the sidewalk Billy Wayne said, "You know Hotson, of course."

"What's going on here?"

Hotson sat on the hood of his Checker smoking a cigarette. "We just want to talk with you is all."

"Shoot."

Hotson smiled at Angelo's verb. Billy Wayne said, "George is in jail."

"The man tried to kill me."

"You know he didn't," Billy Wayne said. "Why don't you just drop the charges?"

"You're going to be spending enough time in court as it is," Hotson said.

"Very funny."

"Let him answer, Hotson."

Angelo put his hand on Billy Wayne's shoulder and said, "These people have to be taught a lesson."

Hotson laughed. Billy Wayne asked Angelo what he was talking about. "What people? Motel owners?"

"Don't play naive, Billy Wayne," Angelo said.

"We're not talking about people," Billy Wayne said. "We're talking about George Binwaddie. He's wasting in jail. He doesn't belong in there, and you know it. He's already had one seizure. This is serious."

"He pitched a fit?"

"He's epileptic."

"I didn't know he was crazy, too."

"Sick, not crazy."

Hotson said, "Don't you see, Billy Wayne? What our sharpshooter is saying is that we have to teach people of color a lesson. Good campaign strategy, too. Ain't that right, Angelo?" Hotson snapped his cigarette at Angelo's feet.

Angelo smiled. "Only savages attack people with knives."

"Civilized folks use guns," Hotson said.

"Angelo, I know you're under a lot of stress. I realize that," Billy Wayne said. "The dog, the wife, the election. I know. I'm just asking you to think about George for a minute. Look, you got a little cut. What's the big deal? Drop the charges. It's the right thing. You'll feel better about yourself and you'd have one less worry."

Angelo looked to the ground and shook his head. He leaned back against the motel wall, lifted his right leg, and brushed his shoe. "I'm a man of principle, Billy Wayne. I believe in this country."

"Save that shit for the Young Democrats," Hotson said.

Angelo ignored him. "I believe in our judicial system. So let's just leave that system take its course. I'm sure if he's innocent, and I ain't saying he is, he'll be released."

"You know he's innocent."

"But I ain't the judge."

Hotson said, "Man scratches someone with an oyster knife, and the court won't set bail. Another man kills his wife, and he's out with his girlfriend at a motel . . ."

"Excuse me, gents," Dencil said. He stepped outside.

Angelo stared at him. "I don't like your face."

"Where you off to?" Hotson asked him.

"Work," Dencil said.

"The circus open at night?" Angelo said.

"You're working for Willis Huckaby now, right?" Hotson said. "Come on, I'll drive you. Let's go, Billy Wayne. Let's get something to eat. Then I'll get you home to your bride."

LATER ON, AT home, Billy Wayne woke Earlene who had fallen asleep on the couch. He reached over and turned off the radio and told Earlene how it was Hotson's idea that they should all lie about the party in court, under oath, on the depositions, whatever. Say that we never heard George taunt Angelo. What do you think, Earlene? Hotson said he and Ronnie would do it. Hotson said he even talked with Sister Helen, and she agreed to say she was playing poison tag with Webb and Ferlin. I can't believe she'd do that. What I think, Billy Wayne went on, is if we tell the truth, tell it exactly like it happened, tell it slowly, in detail, and show it all, then the judge and jury and everyone's got to see what's the truth of the matter.

Earlene looked at her husband and tousled his hair. She smiled. "You're so cute when you're earnest."

"The truth's important, Earlene. It's all we've got in the end."

"What if it comes down to the truth or your friend? What's worth more?"

"It doesn't have to be one or the other. We have to trust that reasonable people will honor the truth, don't we?"

Earlene shook her head. "Are all you Catholic boys this naive? Come here," she said. Earlene took Billy Wayne's hands and placed them on her breasts and guided them. "Put your earnestness to work, Billy Wayne Fontana," she told him.

Earlene smelled like soil, like sweet, damp clay. George is in jail and truth is all we have. Billy Wayne drew his tongue along Earlene's neck, to her ear. He wanted to say, What do you mean by "naive," Earlene? but all he could manage was a yelp.

So at long last, there on the plaid couch in the living room of their first apartment, Earlene and Billy Wayne, consummated their legal marriage swiftly, joyfully, effortlessly. Billy Wayne felt imparadised. They slept soundly and dreamlessly until morning.

11

There Is Light within a Man of Light

*B*illy Wayne had gotten Fox Ledbetter's name and address from Hotson and now sat in Ledbetter's office on a white plastic lawn chair and waited for an answer. He watched Ledbetter study the American cockroach that climbed the side of his typewriter and then disappeared inside the works. Fox took a bite from the corner of his barbecued pork sandwich, swallowed, and wiped a drop of sauce from his chin with his hanky. "I'll take your man's case," he said. Fox put the hanky in his jacket pocket and the sandwich atop the typewriter, wiped the palms of his hands on the thighs of his seersucker trousers, and reached across to shake hands with Billy Wayne. "First thing we ought to do is truck down to the jail and speak with Mr. Binwaddie."

Fox Ledbetter slipped on his sneakers. He opened a desk drawer and took out a set of keys and a cassette tape. He picked up the sandwich. "You like barbecue, Billy Wayne?"

"I'm not hungry just now."

Fox wrapped the remains of the sandwich in a sheet of typing paper and put it in his jacket pocket.

Mr. Fox Ruston Ledbetter, Esquire, was the most notorious, if not the most sought after, barrister in Ouachita Parish. He had recently made something of a name for himself by winning the freedom of a prostitute whose fingerprints were on the pistol used to first deter, then dispatch, the husband of a U.S. representative from downstate in a spicy trial that you all may have read about. There was a TV preacher involved. Fox's success, however, did not endear him to the moneyed gentry in Monroe, the late gentleman having had kin on several of our banks' boards of directors. Of course, Fox neither needed nor solicited their business, being the sole heir, as he was, to the considerable Ledbetter fortune, the Ledbetters being one of the first families of Monroe.

Fox's truck was a 1965 GMC Vandura that said Kachedorian's Market on the driver's side door and smelled of lamb inside the cab. Fox rolled down his window and handed Billy Wayne a pair of pliers to roll down his.

"Do you think of your feet when you dance?" Fox said.

"Excuse me?"

"I do. I think about my feet, and so I can't dance. Not a lick." Fox reached under his seat and pulled out a small tape player.

"You know, I've never even danced," Billy Wayne said.

"Get out of town!"

Billy Wayne thought. He scratched his nose. "Maybe as a kid, but I doubt it."

Fox snapped the cassette tape into the player. "I got something here you might like to listen to." Fox started the truck, let it idle a minute while he rewound the tape. "Now this here's your mayor talking, Billy Wayne."

At first there was music, a tenor saxophone that cut off in mid-riff, and then the mayor's voice: "Of course he did it. He said he did." You could hear a fork being scraped against a plate. "Maybe he shot her on purpose even. How the hell should I know? Maybe she was diddling this black guy, maybe not. Maybe there was no black guy." The voice paused. "He can be a vicious little idiot, Angelo can. He was like that before the war. Even as a child he was hurtful, spiteful sometimes. Other times sweet as Karo syrup." Billy Wayne remembered when he drank a jar of syrup straight and felt sick before the bottle left his lips. He must have been seven or eight. "So what if he did? Kill her like you say. What am I supposed to do? Send my nephew to the electric chair? Waste another life? He's family, goddamit. He's all I got. Don't family mean nothing to you, girl? Patty's dead and I'm sad and I wish it hadn't happened, but it did, and there's nothing you, me, or God can do about that. Let's leave her rest in peace."

Fox snapped the player off. "Claudia Simmons gave me this. Of course, it's off the record. The machine was in her purse. Can't use it in court or anything."

Fox ejected the tape and put it in his shirt pocket. "What I hear is the D.A.'s about to drop the charges. Find the death accidental. Angelo'll cop a misdemeaner plea like reckless discharge of a firearm or something like that."

"And he's running for office."

"And he's going to win."

"You think?"

"Oh shoot. I missed the turn," Fox said.

"Stubbs should take us down to Third," Billy Wayne said.

Fox took a right. "Does the term *kakistocracy* mean anything to you, Billy Wayne?"

"Is the truck supposed to whistle like that?"

"Just around corners. *Kakistocracy* means 'government by the worst.' And that's what we've got us here in this country. Maybe it's the price we pay for capitalism. I don't know." Fox turned onto Second.

"Fox, this here's a one-way street."

"Sure is. Damn." He stopped. "I can't back this sucker up, Billy Wayne. Can you?"

"Don't have my license yet."

"You some kind of Luddite or something?"

"Say again?"

"Hell, we'll just have to take our chances then." Fox drove on down Second Street. "I mean, think about it now. You tell some old boy you're going to pay him a damn good salary to sit around a clubhouse with some other bottom feeders and decide what to do with your money. That's a sucker bet, Billy Wayne. I mean, do you think any person with an ounce of integrity is going to accept money for behaving with integrity?"

"You're a cynic, Fox Ledbetter."

"You scrape the bottom of the pond, you get scum." Fox laughed. "You don't think much of my theory, do you, Billy Wayne?"

"You might could pull right in here and we'll walk."

"Only two more blocks. I got another."

"What's that?"

"Theory."

"Which is?"

"Sex."

"Sex what?"

"What drives a person to politics." Fox studied the space between two pickup trucks, looked at Billy Wayne. "I'll just park it over by the fence." Fox put the recorder under his seat. "You see, it's like needing to get stroked, needing to dominate by doing favors, pulling strings, and like that. I

don't know how to explain it. Maybe it's control." Fox raised
an eyebrow. "True or false: Politicians are people who need
to assert themselves sexually because they've got nothing else
to assert."

"Not very scientific."

"Either way, money or sex, your politician is motivated by
self-interest. That's why we have no men or women of vision
in the government." Fox thought about his own words a moment. "Take it back. They have vision only it just extends to
their wallets and their little widgets."

"Fox, that ain't true. Folks wouldn't elect a guy who was
only looking out for himself."

Fox looked at Billy Wayne and shook his head. "Damned
if you ain't hanging on to that childhood." Fox tilted the side-
view mirror so he could check his hair. He mussed it up with
his fingers. "Americans admire self-interest above all other
motivation. We all want to be robber barons so we can give a
little away, buy our way into heaven and history."

"And Angelo?"

"Maybe he'll make president." Fox opened his door. "Shall
we?"

Billy Wayne followed Fox into the parish jail, down a flight
of stairs to the basement where they registered with a deputy
sheriff and were searched. Fox turned over his half-eaten
sandwich. They waited for Binwaddie in a windowless seven-
foot room with a humming fluorescent light, two straight-
backed wooden chairs, and a small gray cafe table. "Must be
a hundred degrees in here," Billy Wayne said. "Jesus."

Binwaddie entered wearing an orange jumpsuit and white
sneakers. Billy Wayne introduced him to Fox.

Fox said, "How are you, George?"

"I am disgraced."

Billy Wayne put a hand on George's shoulder. "Don't
worry. It's a big mistake. We'll get you out of this."

Fox motioned for George to sit. He opened the door which startled the guard outside. "Could you fetch us a pitcher of water, Co'cola, or something?" Fox pulled a ten-dollar bill from his pocket. "Here."

"I ain't supposed to leave."

"Keep the change."

"Be right back."

Fox sat down opposite George. He looked at Billy Wayne. "It's not a mistake," he said. "Just like the war is not a mistake."

"But he's innocent, Fox," Billy Wayne said.

"Ain't none of us innocent. We've all done something. Guilt or innocence is not the issue."

Billy Wayne leaned back against the wall. He understood. Guilt was as natural to him as gravity. He thought about Monsignor Pargoud, how he would always give Billy Wayne a dime after each Latin lesson. Tell him to go buy himself a perique cigar. He thought about Earlene who was home now probably putting that shelving paper in the cupboards all by herself. He thought about his family and saw the featureless faces that he knew from his dreams.

Just then the guard knocked, handed Billy Wayne a pitcher of water and three paper cups with two ice cubes in each. He told them five minutes.

Fox said, "From what Billy Wayne tells me, I can't see any basis for indictment. But, of course, I'll have to study the case, talk with the D.A.'s office, sift through the evidence, and so on. I'll see if I can get you released on bond."

"Thank you."

"I want you to write down for me everything that happened to you that day. And I want to know everything about your history with Mr. Candela. Every conversation you've ever had. And your relationship with . . ." Fox turned to Billy Wayne. "What was her name?"

"Hazel Currence."

"With Hazel. Okay, George?"

"Yes."

"I'll be back tomorrow. We'll talk. Can I bring you anything?

George shook his head.

"Are you taking your pills, George?" Billy Wayne said.

George shook his head.

"You'll have another seizure."

"It's the only good thing that's happened to me in here."

12

Someone Else's Story

$\mathcal{B}$illy Wayne and Earlene rented themselves a reasonably priced and semifurnished apartment in a cozy, unadorned brick duplex at 323½ Concordia just behind the Piggly Wiggly. (At least in 1972 it was a Piggly Wiggly, though since then it's been Bobby Hao's Cajun Pagoda restaurant, then a Good Life Ministries church, a karate studio, and now it's Fuqua's Discount Office Supply, and that looks to be going out of business.) Their duplex was built in a minimalist ranch style, functional, inoffensive, with a low-pitched roof, aluminum screen doors and rain gutters. Out front stood a single vine-throttled mimosa at the end of the walk by the drainage ditch, and in the backyard, between the carport and the supermarket parking lot, were two massive pecans and a brushy persimmon.

Our newlyweds shared the house with the landlady, Nettie McCaskill, who was ninety-two and remembered when all the land north of DeSiard was cotton fields and folks called Monroe the "Egypt of the South"; Nettie's daughter, Big Mary Elizabeth, retired after forty-five years with the Monroe Department of Public Works; her daughter, Little Mary Elizabeth, an unemployed nurse's aid; Little Mary Elizabeth's five towheaded children, Tiffany, Star, Diamond, Crystal, and Paul; Little Mary Elizabeth's boyfriend, Eddie Pettis, and his own little girl, Myrtice; six hounds, and a dozen or so, it was hard to tell, black-and-white cats, one of which scooted along quite smartly on just the three legs. When Billy Wayne and Earlene sat in their living room, they could hear the Greater McCaskill Family through the walls laughing to beat the band at some TV program. Earlene told Billy Wayne how it gave her the shivers to think about it. She just knew, she said, that all the lights were out over there and that none of the children had brushed their teeth. And she would sooner, she whispered, not even speculate as to the sleeping arrangements in that apartment.

The morning after they moved in, Billy Wayne walked down to Delta Pawn and Gun and bought a used window air conditioning unit, took it home on the bus, and installed it in the bedroom. He had to cut a piece of plywood to fit the gap below the window and hold it there with duct tape, but now the unit cooled just fine. Earlene had gone off to Carol's Home and Hobby for some window shades and a roll of contact paper, something to match the kitchen paneling. Billy Wayne made himself a cup of instant coffee and sat out on the carport on one of the two aluminum lawn chairs he had bought at K&B Drugs, reading a volume of gnostic gospels.

He thought about what Hotson had said to him over iced

teas at Marianna's—that some truth was so noble, no not noble, he said. Hotson had propped his sunglasses on his forehead, shut his eyes a moment. Sublime, he said. Yes, there's
a truth so sublime and so . . . so solemn that if there's a god,
and if that god should turn his back on the truth, then what
do you do, Billy Wayne? Do you ignore the truth and trust in
your simple faith or do you honor the truth and release your
god?

Billy Wayne had looked past Hotson to a photo of the
college football team on the wall and then down at his sweating
glass. He lifted it and slipped a napkin beneath the base. He
would have to think about what Hotson asked. Billy Wayne
knew he was not possessed of a ready wit. He came to understanding at a dead plod. Nor was he contentious by nature.
Arguments unsettled him. The two had started out talking
about George Binwaddie and how the truth was that he was
innocent, and everyone knew it. They agreed on that and on
the treachery of Angelo. But here was George in jail and
Angelo on the loose. And now George could hardly even talk
or keep down food he was so distraught. Billy Wayne said
how he was praying for George and even for Angelo because
there's good in every man. That's when Hotson laughed,
nearly choked really, coughed tea into his napkin, regained
his voice, and started in about the truth.

Billy Wayne watched a red-bellied woodpecker spiral up
the scaly pecan trunk and thought about his new job exterminating pests, about his new life. He'd talk with Sister Helen
about the truth. She'd have an answer he could carry back to
Hotson.

To think that just three months earlier, Billy Wayne had
understood precisely, and without a doubt, what his purpose
was, what life meant. If this had been exactly three months ago
on a Saturday morning at—Billy Wayne checked his watch—
eleven o'clock, he would have already said matins and lauds in

the chapel, eaten oatmeal bread with boysenberry preserves, weeded the melon garden, taken confession, studied for an hour, and now he'd be at his seat in the abbey library reading the sermons of Meister Eckhart. Billy Wayne smiled. He missed those reassuring rituals and wondered now if he would be able to tolerate a life without benign routine. That's when he heard his name being called from the front of the house. He got up and went through the kitchen and living room and told Dencil to come on in.

"Is it 'Dencil' or 'Buster' today?"

Dencil smiled. "Excuse me for all that 'Buster' business back at the motel. Like I told you in the cab, trying not to stir nothing up for Hazel, you understand."

"Have a seat." Billy Wayne motioned for Dencil to sit on the sofa and when he did, the cushion sighed as though it had been waiting all morning long for the weighty relief of a body.

"I recognized you right off, of course," Billy Wayne said.

"First I thought you were this guy I met in the Broward County Jail. Busted for smoking pot."

"Can I get you something to drink, Dencil? We got tea, Barq's, I think, water, orangeade."

"No thank you. Used to have us lamps like this on the houseboat," Dencil said. "Only ours weren't two . . . what do you call these?"

"Matadors."

"Right. Ours were black with like lacy gold pajamas. One was a Nubian, the other a Nubianette. Bought them at Roy's Trading Post for fifty cents each."

Billy Wayne sat on the sofa.

"They went down in the wreck," Dencil said. He unfolded the newspaper he had tucked under his arm. He handed it to Billy Wayne. "Page five," he said.

Billy Wayne opened the paper and saw the ad. There was

a photo of Angelo in a suit and tie, hunkered down at the end of his dock, an empty chair and an empty wicker doggie bed beside him. He looked as though he was trying to remember where he had left his keys. Beneath the photo and the words "Candela for State Senate" and the slogan "Send a Straight Shooter to Baton Rouge" was a list of Angelo's accomplishments (having earned a Purple Heart with the U.S. Army in Vietnam), his educational qualifications, and his affiliations—sporting, social, political, and religious.

"Where is this National College of Technology, Incorporated?" Billy Wayne said.

"Bossier City. You know, out by the Downs."

Billy Wayne nodded. "I hear their ad on the radio."

"George is getting out this morning."

"That's great. Have you seen him?"

"Nuh-uh. Claudia Simmons, you know, from the TV, she posted bond, but I suspect it's Fox's doing."

"Well, let's go to the Palms and welcome him home."

"He'll be with Fox all day. But anyhow, we'll see him tomorrow at the affair."

Billy Wayne tried to think. "What's tomorrow?"

"Oh, right. That's why I came. Fox said to give you this." Dencil took a small envelope from his shirt pocket and gave it to Billy Wayne. It was an invitation to the carp-fishing tournament. "Tomorrow at noon till whenever at Fox's."

"Carp?"

"He does this every year. Only this time it's a welcome-back party for George, too."

Billy Wayne looked at the envelope. "I hope George is okay."

Dencil looked around, nodded his head. "You've got a nice place here, Billy Wayne. You got you a job, a good job I hear, and you married your first love."

Billy Wayne didn't know what to say.

"Hotson tells me you're a smart one. Yes, sir, you got yourself a future. You got it all if you think about it."

Billy Wayne realized that he did have everything he needed, everything he wanted. The future—he could feel it even. Time was this river flowing through his body, and he was the dynamo.

"You're the last Fontana, ain't you?"

Billy Wayne smiled. Maybe not for long, he thought.

"I even know about your great-great-great-whatever grandfather Pelican."

"Peregrine."

"Right. I know all about how he got ambushed by that regiment of Yankees and how he killed—what was it?—fifteen of them before they hanged him."

"He was a spy for Kirby Smith's what I heard. Got caught by Union boys at the Frisbee mansion on the Tensas. They took him out and shot him."

"Anyhow, he died a hero," Dencil said. "My daddy always told me Fontana stories, you know, kind of like a you-think-you-got-it-bad-look-at-what-fell-on-this-family sort of thing. No offense, Billy Wayne."

"None taken."

"You got to admit it, some sorry waters have washed over your kin."

"You probably know more about it than I do, Dencil."

Dencil scratched his stubbly cheek. "You know about your Uncle Ott?"

"One of Saturn's boys?"

"I believe so. You know about him and Collett Everman Woolman?"

"Sure don't."

So Dencil told Billy Wayne how this Mr. C. E. Woolman, whom his daddy had described as blue eyed, burly, and resolutely cordial, hit on the bright idea as to how the Delta farmers could save their cotton crops from the boll weevil. Everyone knew that calcium arsenate would do the job all right, but no one had come up with a method for spreading the chemical over hundreds of acres of plants. Mr. Woolman's brainstorm was to release the insecticide from an airplane. When he said this to the farmers, well, it was like a cold wind blew down Louisville Avenue. The farmers outside the post office looked up, and you could imagine what they saw, this malevolent rain pouring down from a deep blue sky. You could see the notion wasn't one they wanted to contemplate. They looked at one another, then down at the sidewalk. Did they have a choice? Well, they said, that sounded fine to them, now if only we had us an airplane and someone to fly it.

Well, that's when Mr. Woolman went to work and convinced a New York company to loan him a plane, a Huff Daland Puffer, and took out an ad in the papers saying how they needed some old boy who could fly their plane. And that's when your Uncle Ott showed up at Smoot Field with a leather cap and goggles. He figured if it had a motor and wheels, he could operate it. Mr. Woolman, inspired no doubt by the absence of other applicants, figured he would just go ahead and train Ott for the job, especially since the latter had agreed to work without pay, for the promise of shares in the new company. So while Ott Fontana sat in the cockpit, Mr. Woolman stood on the wing and read to him from the manual.

"You know the Union Oil Mill on the river?" Dencil said.

"Sure."

"Well, your uncle's maiden flight terminated when he banked into the storage tank and exploded."

"I think I've heard something about that," Billy Wayne said. "Wasn't there a flood or something?"

"Twenty thousand gallons of cottonseed oil spilled from the ruptured tank and washed down Trenton Street, destroyed fourteen businesses, killed six horses and one leather goods salesman from Memphis," Dencil said.

"My God."

Dencil leaned forward on the sofa. "Mr. Woolman was not deterred. He got himself a second plane, hired him a licensed pilot from Ohio, and killed every damn weevil in Ouachita, Madison, and Tensas parishes. Huff Daland Dusters became Delta Air Lines and everyone involved became a millionaire."

"I'll be damned."

"Right this morning you and Uncle Ott could be sporting around Atlanta in your Tony Lama snakeskin boots on your way to some golfing course or something."

"Not likely, Dencil. They'd have found someway to keep it from him, or Ott would have lost it someway."

"You sound a little sour, Billy Wayne."

"I do, don't I?"

"Anyway, it's just a story. Some say the plane wasn't built right. Said it wasn't Ott's fault."

"But we'll never know the truth."

Dencil thought about how your life becomes someone else's story soon as you die. He stood, shook down the cuffs of his jeans. "I'll see you tomorrow then, Billy Wayne."

Billy Wayne walked Dencil out the back door to the carport. "And thanks for the invitation." Billy Wayne held up the envelope. He watched Dencil cross the parking lot, turn, and wave. He sat on a lawn chair, sipped his cold coffee, and read the note: Billy Wayne and Earlene, You all come to the Carp-Fishing Derby, you hear? Tomorrow, noon, my place. If you need info, call me. Fox.

13

That Odd Fork
in Being's Road

*W*e present, without remark or annotation, if you can believe that, the text of the souvenir program for Fox Ledbetter's Fifth Annual Carp-Fishing Derby and Possible Fish Fry. Fox had printed a hundred-and-some-odd copies at Dixie Duplicators and handed them out to his arriving guests. Each program was a single sheet of 8½″ × 11″, twenty-pound bond, powder blue paper, folded in half so as to make a four-page booklet not unlike the Sunday Bulletin over to St. Paschal's Catholic Church. On the cover, Fox, had drawn a rather hefty and self-satisfied carp. Beneath the fish, this inscrutable motto: "Pleasure Is Never Enough." The remaining pages read as follows:

EXTRACTS
(Supplied by Shirlene T., Assistant Sublibrarian,
Delta Center for Piscatology
and Library of Aquaculture, Belzoni, Mississippi)

And on his feet a paire of spores sharpe.
In felowsshipe wel coude she cooke the carpe.
—Geoffrey Chaucer, "Prologue,"
The Canterbury Tales (first draft)

Well, you wiggle like an eel, baby
And you bite just like a shark.
Well, you wiggle like an eel, baby
And you bite just like a shark.
You may look like a troutfish, Mama,
But you taste just like a carp.
—Sin-Killer Johnson, "Fishingman's Blues"

What the carp in Zell Straughten's pond have been known to eat: Holsum hot dog rolls, pecans, chicken gizzards, red wigglers, blood bait, buttermilk biscuits, okra, Elmer's glue, Chef Boyardee spaghetti, dirty rice from Boudreau's Dinner Bell, Ivory soap, caramel, shelled peanuts, sugarcane, dough balls, marbles, souse, castor beans, mint leaves, Moon Pies, shrimp, Lucky Strike cigarettes, Blackened Carp in Peanuts, Cabbage and Charred Red Peppers from Bobby Hao's Bayou Restaurant, corn bread, honey, poke sallet, pralines, watermelon rinds and seeds, pan gravy, Wheaties, crowder peas, collards, Vicks Vaporub, crawfish heads, andouille, cracklings, fried tomatoes, millet, crabmeat salad, chess pie, scrambled eggs, Doctor Crepeau's lemon lozenges, Jell-O, sweet gherkins, Goo-Goo Clusters, Chip Straughten's 1968 Ouachita Parish High School class ring, doughnuts, Sonic burgers, curly fries, barbecued goat, grits, popcorn, toothpicks, fortune cookies, Krewe of Bacchus doubloons, paper clips, and Velveeta. Will not eat oysters.

—*The Carpmasters' Handbook*

Well, it's funny, really, how I caught my first twenty-pound iron gray mud carp (*cirrhinus molitorella*), a particularly rank variety, by the way, which feeds on the feces of the black carp. I was fishing alone down at the Yocona River. I baited this #2 Eagle Claw hook with a dough ball that I'd soaked overnight in chicken's blood. I was using ten-pound test line, no leader. (Pause.) Maybe I just remember it as ten-pound test, and maybe it was eight, and maybe it was a #3 hook and the dough was dipped in lard. I don't know. It was the Yocona River. I'm sure of that. Or the Tallahatchie. Anyway, I set the cork at five feet, dropped the plug into the eelgrass, poured myself a shot of Jim Beam, rolled a cigarette, and wrote the first six pages of "A Rose for Emily." And then she hit.

—William Faulkner, interview in the *Tensas Review*

Fox greeted Billy Wayne and Earlene as they came around the corner of the carriage house and into the backyard. "How you coming, Earlene?" He shook her hand. "Billy Wayne." He nodded.

Billy Wayne looked past Fox toward the guests, most of whom were dressed in tuxedos or calf-length strapless gowns. "I didn't know this was a formal affair."

"If you'll follow me, I'll show you inside to the dressing rooms. We have every size and every out-of-style gown or tux you can imagine."

"I don't get it, Fox. Your pool's full of fish."

Fox said he didn't swim, so when his mother died he had the pool pumped with Ouachita River water and took up aquaculture. Ordered three dozen Japanese carp from an import company in Houston. Turns out they're so prolific we have this yearly harvest.

Earlene said, "You're an interesting man for a lawyer, Fox Ledbetter."

"Where's George?" Billy Wayne said.

"I suspect he's in the shower again. He's taken, oh, fifteen since last evening." Fox led them quietly across the yard, amid the tables, chairs, and guests to the double doors at the back of the house. He pointed to a curious twist of cypress knee sculpture. "It really belongs to you more than to me. Fashioned by your arboreal kin. Fontana cypress art was all the rage in the thirties. Something Mother bought off Speed Masur years ago. You want it?"

Billy Wayne looked it up and down. "Earlene?" he said.

"What's it called?" Earlene said to Fox.

" 'Children Born of Unlawful Slumbers.' "

"I think you should keep it," Earlene said.

"Looks more like what's-his-name, that Trojan and his two boys being crushed by snakes. You know who I mean?"

"Laocoon," Fox said.

"I think so." Billy Wayne walked around the sculpture, all the while shaking his head. "You can make out three people."

"Yes. 'Blessed Trinity' would have been a better name."

Billy Wayne followed Fox and Earlene to Fox's living room. He kissed Earlene on the cheek. She said she was going in to find her a proper wedding dress. Billy Wayne turned and noticed at the head of the staircase a portrait of a large, red-bearded man in a Confederate uniform.

"That's my grandfather's grandfather," Fox said. "Colonel Aaron Ledbetter. Killed at Vicksburg."

"A hero?"

"In a manner of speaking. The colonel was struck and, shall we say, discharged, by a minie ball while he was *in flagrante delicto* with an itinerant *nymph du monde* in the cemetery of the First Baptist Church."

"Damn."

"I like to think there was that instant of percussion when the colonel must have marveled at such a piercing climax."

Billy Wayne was uncomfortable with sex-as-death figures of speech. He wanted to change the subject. Billy Wayne and Fox entered the dining room. Fox sat at the oak dining table and fiddled with an alligator nutcracker. Billy Wayne slipped out of his sneakers and into a pair of brown shoes. He said, "I don't remember my daddy. Don't remember the swamp or my family. None of that."

"Do you want to?"

"Who wouldn't want to recollect who he is?" Billy Wayne stood in front of the ebony-framed mirror over the sideboard. "First thing I remember was when I was . . . must have been four, five. I don't know. I'm sitting on Monsignor Pargoud's lap and we're on an armless rocker on the front gallery of the rectory and he's telling me about eternity." Billy Wayne sat down opposite Fox. "Actually, I was six, I remember now. I was was going to start First Communion lessons. How come I can't recall anything about those first five years?"

"Just lucky."

Billy Wayne chewed his thumbnail.

"So tell me," Fox said.

"What?"

"What the monsignor told you about eternity."

"He said, 'Billy Wayne, you think about a grain of sand on Grand Isle beach. Picture it. Think of how tiny that is. Small enough to pass through the eye of a needle.' Then he showed me a needle, and I held it, looked into its eye. 'Now imagine,' he said, 'that every thousand years a boat-tailed grackle lands on the beach, picks up a single grain of that sand, and carries it away. How many eons would it take for that grackle to remove just the grains of sand that stick between the toes of your right foot when you come out of the water? And then the sand on your side of the blanket? In your sand castle? Then the whole beach down to ten feet deep? Then Biloxi Beach? Gulf Shores? And then all the beaches in all the world, even the beaches in Red China?' I told him, 'A zillion billion trillion years, Father.' He smiled and rocked us. He said, 'And when that grackle has finally finished carrying away each and every grain of sand from God's earth, then eternity is only beginning."

"Steady-state theology," Fox said.

"I remember he produced this thin, white hanky from the sleeve of his cassock, and very gently, deliberately coughed into it, then wiped around the circumference of his mouth. Monsignor had a thinnish, reedy, almost nonexistent upper lip and had a crack exactly in the middle of his lower lip that was always raw. 'That's a long time to be broiling in hellfire, isn't it, Billy Wayne?' He tucked the hanky up his sleeve. 'Yes, Father,' I told him.

"Billy Wayne," Fox said, "have you told this to anyone before? Like a shrink or someone?"

"That's not the end. Monsignor said if I wanted to experience hell for one second, I could dip my pinky in boiling oil the next time the sisters fried catfish. I must have made a face because he said, 'Of course it will hurt. And you'll cry, and the blisters will swell on your skin and burst and get raw and infected.' Then he looked me in the eyes. 'Now just imagine the devil himself frying you in a vat of boiling oil, without a second's relief for all eternity.' He hugged me and whispered, 'Sinners will pay a terrible price for their wickedness, Billy Wayne.' And then he rocked me to sleep."

14

The Light of
Other Days

*B*illy Wayne sat on the pedestal that had once anchored a diving board to the deep end of the pool. He took off his bow tie and put it in his pocket. He watched a guest in a maroon dinner jacket, shiny black slacks, and a Tulane University baseball cap hold up a foot-long carp by its chin and tail in front of his face. The man kissed the fish while a woman with a cap like his own took their picture. The man laid the fish, not golden now, but straw colored, on the tiled apron of the pool and pressed its body with one hand and drew a fillet knife from his inside pocket with the other. Billy Wayne saw the fish raise its dorsal fin, arch its tail. He saw the gill cover lift once slowly and close. He saw the unveiled eye, obvious and vulnerable, that did not shudder, not when the knife's tip entered the anal vent, and the blood, pink as lipstick, leaked out, not when the blade sliced into the ovary and fatty tissue, carved through gristle and organ, and all that terrible, damp business slid out, the intestines, stomach, gall bladder, the yellowy velvet belt of eggs, all of it spilled to the sunlight. That eye reminded Billy Wayne of something. And with this stirring came a fear he couldn't fix.

"She has no secrets now," George Binwaddie said of the fish.

Billy Wayne turned and smiled. He took George by the shoulders. "How are you, George?"

George raised his eyebrows, shrugged. "I feel soiled, my friend."

"Well, the worst is over. Fox says that Angelo will drop the charges."

"And did he also tell you I will lose my motel?"

They watched the man in the maroon dinner jacket scoop the slippery viscera into his hands and splash the glop into the pool. They saw fish rise to the feast.

"You won't lose the Palms. Dencil's been watching it for you. Had three truckers stay over this weekend."

"Angelo intends to have the mayor's bank foreclose on the Palms."

Billy Wayne felt a chill as if he'd been suddenly cast in shadow. "You know maybe that would be the best thing, George. It really hasn't made you money, you know. Hasn't made you happy."

"This is all my fault, and my heart aches."

"Let's have a drink."

George shook his head, said he wanted to go in and lie down. "Where is your bride, Billy Wayne?"

"Fox is giving her a tour of the house."

George said, "Billy Wayne, what am I going to do with my life?"

Billy Wayne and George walked into the house. Fox was on the telephone, listening, not talking, nodding his head, rolling his eyes. Earlene and Sister Helen chatted in the doorway. Billy Wayne smiled at them. Fox hung up the phone, bowed deeply at the waist, said to Earlene, "And now may I show you my library?" He offered Earlene his arm. Fox turned to Billy Wayne, Sister Helen, and George. "You will excuse us, please." He ushered Earlene across the living room.

"And excuse me," George said. "I must lie down."

"Anything we can do, George?" Billy Wayne said.

"Change the past."

"Not even God can do that, George," Sister Helen said.

"My family must know by now that I've failed them," George said.

Billy Wayne said, "How could they?"

"I'm so tired," George said.

BILLY WAYNE CARRIED his drink and Sister Helen's to the table by the cabana. They watched the guests fishing with cane poles in the pool. He placed the tumblers onto the pebbled glass tabletop and slid out his chair.

"Did you put rum in this cola?" Sister Helen said.

"No."

"Would you mind?"

Billy Wayne picked up Sister's drink and smiled. "Of course." He shifted his weight and said, " 'Deghost your soul.' That's what Hotson said. Let me see if I can remember. He said we're just the one of us, not two entities, not body and soul." Billy Wayne thought over what he said. "Does that make any sense?"

"He's right."

"He is?" Billy Wayne said. "I'll get your drink."

Billy Wayne returned. Now there were two straws in Sister's drink. He sat facing Sister Helen with his back to the pool.

Sister held the glass in one hand, a straw in the other, and sipped her drink. She made a face. "The incomprehensible does not cease to exist."

"But we should make an effort to understand everything. God, death, Republicans, disease."

"We'll never understand Republicans, Billy Wayne."

"Maybe you shouldn't drink so fast, Sister."

"Nonsense," Sister said. She thought for a second. "You need light to see, but too much light blinds. You need reason to think, but too much reason makes you, uh, unreasonable. Too much thinking makes you dumb. That's what I'm trying to say. Don't think so hard."

Billy Wayne looked at her and offered a toast. "To friends," he said.

The conversation got back around to George and how he needed their prayers and their company, too. Yes, we need the solace of friends, Sister said. But comfort is not enough. We shouldn't forget that. When Billy Wayne suggested that maybe she was being overly grim, Sister said we're all of us wretched and alone. But then she thought about what she said and laughed. "Perhaps I have been drinking too quickly." And then they got around to Jesus.

Billy Wayne said, "I like the Jesus who suffered and died, who couldn't save himself."

Sister Helen said, "What's your point?"

"That it's the man in Jesus that makes him noble. Not the miracle worker."

"He's more heroic that way. But he's not God then, is he?"

"What difference does that make? He's still Jesus, and he preached love and tolerance."

Sister said, "If your Jesus told you to murder your child for him, would you?"

"Of course not."

"Well, that's the difference."

Earlene and Fox returned. Earlene had Fox in stitches with some joke she was telling. Billy Wayne never knew this about Earlene, that she could make people laugh. He wondered what else he didn't know about her, what surprises lay ahead.

Sister Helen called Hotson for a ride back to St. Francis. Billy Wayne and Earlene said they'd walk. They said good-bye to Fox, said no they'd as soon not stay for the carp fry, thanks. They told Fox to tell George so long.

On the way home, Billy Wayne told Earlene about his memory. Or what he thought might be a memory, he wasn't sure. It had to do with that fish eye. What he remembered is a man in a green vinyl seat who would never look at Billy Wayne no matter what. Even when he talked to me, Billy Wayne said, even then. His eyes were pearly. Earlene took his hand as they walked. Billy Wayne wondered to Earlene why he had never remembered the man and the eye before. The man must be my daddy, Pee Dubya. Billy Wayne got this puzzled look on his face. He wondered what else he didn't know about himself. Earlene squeezed his hand.

Billy Wayne wondered if, as you change, as you grow, your memories change too. And so might the ways of remembering. And as he wondered he became convinced that this was indeed so.

That night in bed, Billy Wayne heard sirens coming from the television over at the McCaskill's. He lay awake trying to convince himself he was changing, preparing himself for the reception of more lost memories. He wondered what his life held for him. The future was ripe with uncertainty. Anything could happen. Might move to New Orleans for all he knew. Might make supervisor at Haddad's. Might land a job finally at LP&L. Billy Wayne hadn't thought about that sun with its bolts of energy in a while. The light of God's countenance. Is that what it still meant to him? When God said "Let there be light" and there was light, what did He see? There was no firmament, was there? Not yet.

He thought about his past, and Earlene's, just as chancy and exciting as the future. He might soon remember the scent of his mother's breast. He might discover that his daddy told him a family secret. And if he did what might that secret be? He might see that fish eye again, see it in a smear of blood on a cleaning stone back there in the Bottom. He might crawl over to it, pick it up in his baby fingers, mouth it, suck on it, swallow it like a cough drop.

II

Power and Light

How it is I'm left alone
And why the house is cold
And why he's silent when he's home
And·how I'm feeling old—
I'll try to figure as I write
'Louisiana Power & Light.'

—Earlene Fontana and Lurleen Dooley
"Louisiana Power & Light"

1

Sometimes a
Light Surprises

*B*illy Wayne sits wearing his blue Haddad
Pest Control jumpsuit on the couch in
the living room. He's down to the one job, exterminating.
It's seven in the morning, there's a box of Krispy Kreme
doughnuts on his lap. He's licking the sticky stuff off a finger
and looking at Earlene. The radio's on and the newscaster says
how a pickup full of high-school kids went off the causeway at
Fish Hatchery Road and how the three in the cab are still
there at the bottom of Bayou DeSiard. Earlene, who is anxious
about her doctor's appointment later that day, stands at the
window and opens the blinds. She sees someone new on the
front lawn, a plastic Mexican, a tan one about three feet tall
with a red sombrero and a green serape. This Mexican has

his head down like he's depressed or ashamed, maybe, and he's leading a squat, tired-looking, brownish burro.

Earlene is alarmed. She wonders what this apparition might mean. Earlene believes in signs. Earlene understands the future to be a place, a landscape, and knows that coming events cast their shadows before them into the present. If it isn't natural, it must be a sign. The appearance of a comet is not a sign, just a superstition that should have died a hundred years ago. A comet is a natural phenomenon. So is an eclipse. An eclipse is a symbol, not a sign. A symbol of ignorance. Darkness has nothing to tell us. A dog walking on its hind legs across the stage of the "Ed Sullivan Show" is a sign. If barnyard animals started talking like in the Bible stories, that would be a sign. A tornado, no. Orange snow, yes. A phone call from a cousin you've never met who lives in, say, Meadville, Pennsylvania, no. A plastic Mexican on the front lawn, yes. That was indeed a sign.

WERE GOING TO leave Earlene just now, but only briefly. Leave her as she tries to divine what this polystyrene visitor and his beast of burden have to say about her impending visit to the gynecologist. Leave Billy Wayne too as he imagines three bodies, two cans of Pabst Blue Ribbon, and a single black sneaker bobbing against a cracked windshield. Leave because this seems like an opportune moment to mention this other Fontana who believed in signs and who may have been in the back of Earlene's mind given the portentous nature of his birth. This would be Tennis (nee Tennyson) Fontana, though he would later change his name to Legion Fontana to reflect his multiple personalities, but would always pronounce it Frenchly, so it sounded like "Legend."

Tennis's momma was given as much Co'-Cola as she could swallow, but still this was a difficult birth. Etta Fontana was in labor some fifty-four hours giving birth to Tennis, and he was born with a caul, an amniotic veil, and so everyone in the Bottom knew right off this little boy could see the future. Tennis spoke his first words at six months old and even at that it seemed he'd been holding back awhile not wanting, perhaps, to unnerve his elders. His first words were a sentence: "We want milk." He said this to his daddy, Lamar. Lamar dropped his fishcake. "I ain't got none," he said. "Then get Ma."

At the time of the flood, Huey Long sent Gilroy Passman up a tupelo to retrieve Tennis who was nestled on a branch twenty feet above the water, clutching his daddy's crystal radio. Tennis loved the wireless. He especially enjoyed W. K. Henderson's program on KWKH in Shreveport. It was while the Fontanas were bivouacked at Monroe High School that the school-board people got wind of Tennis's precocity. Here he was, seven years old, not a minute's worth of school or Bible study, and he was smarter even, they found out, than Mayor Walton Suggs. Before the water had receded enough for the clan to return to the Bottom, Tennis had learned to read, write, and cipher. It came natural to him like fleas to a dog.

For the next decade we did not see or hear much from or about Tennis. Fontanas kept him out there in the Bottom busy doing who knows what. Occasionally, Cotton Fontana would show up at City Hall and ask to speak with Mayor Suggs. He'd tell the Mayor that Tennis says you all should stockpile some lime. A mountain of lime. And then, wouldn't you know it, seems like every fish in the Ouachita goes belly-up overnight, and suddenly the slough along Riverside Drive is congested with hundreds of thousands of rotting fish bodies. Some folks began to regard Tennis as a prophet, but not enough folks. The town never did act on Tennis's counsel. He told us there'd be a weevil infestation in '32, and there was. A nasty one. He predicted the drought in '34. He said how waterfowl would drop from the sky by the hundreds and they did. Tennis sent a letter to Earl Powdermaker at the Monroe *Daily Star* telling him that Tulane would beat Temple 20–14 in the Sugar Bowl. They did. When Huey Long lay on the operating table in Baton Rouge, an aide found an unopened and blood-drenched letter from Tennis Fontana in the breast pocket of Huey's suit coat.

Then, the way Lamar would explain it later, it was like some spring snapped loose in his boy's head and all the works just took off in their own directions. Tennis could no longer control his thoughts; he had too many of them, and they hurt his head unless he talked about them and set them free. He was no longer one person, but many, and all of them babbling away a mile a minute. He did not have a usable past, one to keep him anchored in the present, because he had a myriad of pasts. Worst of all, the future was gone, or at least he could no longer recognize it. Tennis began to drift into town on his own. Began to tell his stories. He might say to you, "I feel so much lighter now that they've taken some organs out. Now I can fly to my mother in the fifteenth century. Who needs a colon to fly?" Or he might say, "I see by that cross burned into your forehead that you're not here on vacation." When he told Addie D'Anemour, our postmaster, that his, Tennis's, teeth were like a radio and on them he received messages from God's violin, why Addie took Tennis over to St. Francis and had Dr. Lyle speak with the boy.

First off Tennis seemed fine. He explained himself to Doc Lyle by quoting Einstein: "Time and space," he said, "are modes by which we think and not conditions in which we live."

Doc Lyle looked at Tennis over the tops of his reading glasses. He shook his head. "Who's this fool Einstein, Tennis?" he wanted to know.

Then Tennis confessed that he had conceived and borne a

daughter whose name would have to remain a secret and that this daughter would do anything for him. I'm her ma and her pa, he would say. She's got nothing, no one but me. Tennis was admitted to the mental ward. Over the course of the next month, Doc Lyle realized that Tennis, by now Legion, had no sense of self, smart as he was. He might introduce himself as Telemaches Petitjean one minute and claim to be Emma Bovary the next. He said he'd seen huge bakeries where people were cooked in ovens, and not on Venus, right here on earth, he said. Said he had been a passenger pigeon and had gotten shot out of the sky in Ohio. You were there, he told Doc Lyle. I saw you. He had buried seven sisters, his mother and father on their island in the Mississippi. They'd all gotten malaria. He knew that now, he said, not then. At the time all he could think about was topping the graves with stones, building a raft, and leaving before the spirits got him.

Doc Lyle and Addie D'Anemour talked about what all this meant. If each of us is the total of our past, Doc said, what does that make Tennis-Legion who seems to have everyone's past mixed up with his own? Whatever Tennis made up or heard on the radio or read in a book was as real a past to him as anything that may have actually occurred. Damned if I know, Addie said. Looks like the Fontana's brightest star is burning himself up. Even when those people get it right, they get it wrong.

Then Legion stopped talking. At first he seemed angry and then threw tantrums whenever Lamar or Etta or another of the Fontanas visited. After a week or so in restraints and in cold-water baths, he grew sad, cried himself to sleep night after night. Then calm. He said he knew what he had to do. And what he did, he told Doc Lyle the next morning, was he killed his little girl. Sacrificed her. That was the tune God had played on my teeth, he explained. His rhapsody is my command. That's when Doc Lyle called the East Louisiana

State Hospital for Mental Diseases in Jackson and said he had a commitment for them. Without his child, Legion, just a child himself in most ways (he was seventeen in 1937), grew distraught. Not medication or baths or threats or promises could calm his hysteria.

On the day he left Monroe, the day he would die leaping through the train window and off the railroad bridge and into the Mississippi River at Baton Rouge, straightjacket and all, Legion looked over to Lamar and Doc Lyle waiting there at the depot with him and the guards, waiting for the Illinois Central, and smiled his gummy grin. He had battered out his teeth, most of them anyway, on the iron rail of his hospital bed. He closed his eyes and said to them, "I look fifty years ahead and you are not there, Doctor Lyle, and neither are the Fontanas."

To EARLENE IT was all too very clear and uncomfortable. The burro's burden was the curse of the Fontanas, the curse she had told Billy Wayne could not exist. Here they have been trying to conceive a child, boy or girl, who cares, for weeks, months now, and on the day of her appointment at the Ouachita Women's and Infertility Clinic this spectacle comes to light outside her window.

"So what you think, Earlene?" Billy Wayne said.

"What's that?"

"About Pepino there. On the lawn."

"Pepino?"

"Eddie Pettis named it after someone on a TV show." Billy Wayne put the box of doughnuts on the coffee table, took a sip of his coffee. "He set it up last night."

Earlene turned from Billy Wayne and looked out again at this Pepino and burro. "Why do you suppose he put a Mexican on the lawn?"

"Maybe he's trying to scare someone off?" Billy Wayne laughed.

"I think it's creepy," Earlene said.

"Oh, come on, Earlene. It's just a statue. It's like art."

"Is that what you think?"

Billy Wayne got up and walked over to Earlene. "I know what's going on," he said. "You're worried about the checkup." He hugged her from behind. "Look, no matter what, we still have each other. We always will."

Earlene said, "Two's not a family, Billy Wayne, and you know it."

Billy Wayne didn't say anything. He just squeezed Earlene a bit, looked past her shoulder to the Mexican and his burro. Just then one of the McCaskill dogs, this rangy, blue-eyed mutt, walked up to Pepino, sniffed his polymer trousers, and pissed on his feet.

"You don't want to be the last Fontana, do you, Billy Wayne?"

2

Modern Age Motel

 *E*arlene disliked being gripped and probed, especially by this new doctor with his irrelevant silk tie and his manicured fingernails. She felt like a device or something, like an appliance with a flaw in its works. Earlene looked up at the dropped ceiling, at the bent edge of a tile, and then back over her head at a painting on the wall. She saw trees hanging from the earth down into the sky. She made up lists to distract herself. What she'd name the baby: Elvis, Johnny, Django, Clint, Zane. If it's a girl: not Earlene, that's for sure; Marilyn, Esther, like in the Bible, Tracy, Marsha (or Marcia), Antoinette. The more she thought about Esther, the more she liked it. Esther Anne Fontana. Esther Anne deBastrop Fontana. She'd try it out on Billy Wayne, see what he thought. She catalogued her favorite smells: gasoline, only not too much of it; fresh bread, especially the way it smells in the parking lot of the Ideal Sunbeam Bakery; laundered clothes hanging on the line, Billy Wayne's flannel shirts the most; pears, how they smell so wispy, unearthly, delicate, and how the dusty taste is always a disappointment; the scent of older women, musky and warm, almost resinous, and how it always makes her want to close her eyes, cuddle, and sleep. Funny, she thought, that she couldn't smell women, or much of anything for that matter, in this examining room, not even Naugahyde or whatever this is she's lying on. Just some trace of gladiolus and mint.

When she left the clinic, Earlene took the bus downtown and treated herself to an oyster po' boy at Panthieux's Cafe. She sat at the small formica table there by the window and watched the traffic drift up Third. The lines came into her head out of nowhere. "Oh, we're going through changes, we live in a motel." She wrote it down on a napkin. Now what was that all about? Maybe Russell Sikes would know. After lunch, she bought herself a new dress, an electric blue mini, at J.J.'s. She deserved it. It felt like silk, but, of course, it couldn't be.

Earlene stopped at the post office and called Billy Wayne at Haddad's and asked him if they could maybe go out to dinner, say, Wednesday. Wednesday was when the clinic would call with the results of the fertility workup. So they could celebrate, she figured, or she could at least be distracted if, you know, worse came to worse. And anyway she had this new dress and they hadn't gone out for a long time or anything. Billy Wayne thought it was a great idea. They could go to the Mohawk for crawfish etoufee.

EARLENE CHECKED OUT just fine, the clinic said. No reason why she couldn't have a child, ten children if she wanted.

Of course, Is this any kind of world to bring a child into? some of us, when we found out, might have said. But we knew this was not our place, so we held our tongues. That Wednesday at the Mohawk, Earlene and Billy Wayne ordered champagne with their meals, but had to settle for flutes of something dryish, white, and Californian.

"I made your appointment for Friday," Earlene said.

"My appointment?"

"For your sperm count. Is Friday okay? At noon?"

"The sperm count," Billy Wayne said. "Yes, Friday's fine. I'll have Hotson shoot me over on our lunch hour."

"Yes, because Dr. Whozis, I forget his name, says that knowing our plumbing's all in order will probably be just what we need to alleviate the stress, you know. That might be the problem. Stress."

Billy Wayne tore the heel off a small French loaf and wondered out loud just how they went about counting sperm anyway. Then he thought about it for a second and put down his bread.

Earlene laughed.

Billy Wayne tried to visualize the process but all he could see was this pleasant young receptionist with a bow in her hair and these perfect teeth and her taking this vial (yes, that sounds right), this vial of his you-know-what, taking it in her bare hand and thanking him for it. Thinking about what he'd have to do confused him. He was aroused, he realized, and uncomfortable. Billy Wayne slid over close to Earlene. He kissed her neck. "I'm ready for dessert," he said. He didn't usually say things like this. Corny things.

Earlene smiled. "Billy Wayne," she said, "don't you think we should eat first?" Earlene realized she hadn't felt this flush since that night with Billy Wayne at the hospital. She was happy she had bought the dress.

"You don't think I'm being stupid?"

"No."

"Well, then, Mrs. Fontana, I wonder if you would mind doing a preliminary sperm count this evening. You know, sort of an undress rehearsal."

"Crawfish etoufee," the waiter said.

"That's mine," Billy Wayne said. "Jambalaya here. And we'll have two bottles of Jax."

"Yes, sir."

BILLY WAYNE'S NUMBERS were excellent. There was no reason for his and Earlene's not conceiving a child except for the one thing she mentioned. Russell Sikes had told her about it. Russell Sikes has power, Earlene told Billy Wayne. He sees things that you and I cannot. Well, why shouldn't I believe him? Russell says that it must be the exterminating poisons you use at Haddad's that are crippling your sperm. Think about it now. That spray can kill ten thousand cockroaches in a few hours. You figure what it could do to your little bitty sperms.

Billy Wayne sat up and snapped on the light. "Earlene, I don't drink the stuff. I don't spray it down my pants. We're professional exterminators, darling."

Earlene pulled the sheet up to her neck. "That's just it. It might be the killing you do that's the fault."

"How's that?"

"Well, Russell Sikes says that we choose our metaphors according to how we want to live, even if we don't know it. He says you ought to be generating power if you want to make babies."

"Russell's the boy that says he got abducted by a spaceship, Earlene." Earlene looked at the ceiling. Billy Wayne shook his head. "What else did he say?"

"Said I should go to night school."

Billy Wayne shut off the light and snuggled up next to Earlene. "You going to take a course at the college?"

"No, something practical, I think. Something to get me ready for raising a family."

"Like?"

"I don't know. Maybe get a real estate license or something." Earlene kissed Billy Wayne on the nose. She thought about motels and about the line she wrote on the napkin, about her honeymoon, about the metaphor of life as a journey and motels as substitutes for homes and relationships and whatever else it was that Russell had said.

"Good night," Billy Wayne said.

"LP&L is hiring again. Pays $6.25 an hour to start."

"I haven't seen anything about it."

"Russell Sikes says the ad will be in Thursday's paper." Earlene said, "Billy Wayne, I want you to apply for the job."

"I will. It's damn good money."

"Good," she said.

"If there is such a job."

She squeezed Billy Wayne's arm and turned so that they would lie together like spoons.

Billy Wayne dreamed that he arrived on a call to this shingled bungalow on Grammont. He strapped his tank to his back and held the spray gun, nozzle down. The lady was in tears, said she couldn't live in this filth anymore. It's been six months, she confessed, since her last treatment. Billy Wayne opened the cabinet under the kitchen sink and saw the infestation. He aimed his gun at the carpet of roaches, and when he squeezed the trigger, not Diazinon, but light instead shot from the nozzle. He sprayed the entire house with light and told the woman, You won't be having problems for a while.

Earlene's lyrics kept her awake. "Oh, we're going through

changes, we live in a motel. Making love with strangers, we do it very well." Earlene was not happy at the cynical turn her serendipitous lines had taken. But she knew she couldn't refuse them. She would wait for the rest of the song, just like Russell said.

3

The Imagination
of Man's Heart

*T*uesday was (still is) open-mike night at Strawberry Fields, and a couple of students from the college had recited their poems about how they lost their loves but found Jesus. One of them, a heavyset, brown-haired girl, found Him, she said, on the road to Sicily Island, at a bend in Route 15 near Gilbert. Her poem was called "Damascus, Louisiana," and it made Hotson put down his beer and shake his head. The other poet, who recited his poem "Easy Does It, Jesus" from memory, and who rhymed "semester's sin" with "Sonesta Inn," found his Jesus at a twelve-step meeting in Sterlington just last month, he said.

Billy Wayne, Hotson, and Fox sat at a corner table sharing a bucket of Dixies and waiting for the election results to ap-

pear on the muted TV above the bar. Not that there would
be much suspense. The only candidate running against Angelo in the primary was Dorsey Tatum, who probably hoped
he wouldn't win for all the consternation that would bring
to a black man, but who no doubt hoped his name recogni-
tion would boost his business at Tatum's Barbecue down on
Congo Street. The three gentlemen had come out to celebrate Hotson's good news: he and Ronnie were pregnant.
Fox said he'd get Ronnie's divorce petition under way in the
morning. It shouldn't be a problem what with Darrell having
run off like he did. Hotson wondered if he should change
the name of the cab company to Hot and Tot. Fox said he
didn't think so.

Billy Wayne was thinking how that cowboy up on the stage
singing "Walking the Floor over You" looked so familiar. He
couldn't tell the hairline on account of the Stetson. The name
on the singer's guitar said "T-Bone," but that could just be a
stage name. Billy Wayne sipped his beer. Must be a stage
name, right? Who names a baby "T-Bone"? He closed his eyes
and got an image of this singer somewhere else in a white
jacket, turning toward him, smiling. He almost had it. He'd
seen this T-Bone. Where was it? At a restaurant? At the clean-
ers? Yes? No. In the doughnut shop? Seen him often, he knew
that. A nice man. Polite. When the song ended, Billy Wayne,
Fox, Hotson, the bartender, Doyle Bumpus, and a blond
woman up front by the stage applauded. T-Bone announced
that he would take requests.

Billy Wayne leaned over the table and asked Hotson if he
knew this guy.

Hotson looked over the top of his sunglasses. "Latham Taylor," he said. "No relation. Druggist at Spat's Pharmacy."

"That's right. Sure."

T-Bone thanked the lady at the front table and sang "Eighteen Yellow Roses." Then he thanked the audience and sat

down with the blond woman. He lit her cigarette and pushed the Stetson back on his head.

Billy Wayne noticed the poets off to the other side of the room at a table. Their eyes were closed and their lips moving. Billy Wayne said, "So it's official then?"

Fox said yes, the charges against George had been dropped. Then he looked at his watch, put it to his ear, tapped the crystal with his fingernail. "Dencil ought to be along here any minute," he said. "Gets off work at nine."

Billy Wayne was puzzled. "Fox, you're not acting like it's great news."

"Pelican Savings foreclosed on George and is selling the Palms to our friend Angelo."

"Get out!" Billy Wayne said.

"In thirty days George will be out of an investment and a job, not to say a home."

No one knew what to say. Billy Wayne looked over at the poets. The girl was gesturing grandly as if trying to make something large appear in the smoky air above their table while the guy nodded with his upper body. T-Bone's blond friend wrote something, no, drew something, a map, on a napkin, folded the napkin and handed it to T-Bone. T-Bone smiled, took off his Stetson, put the note in the sweatband and put the hat back on. The first election results flashed on the screen and Doyle turned up the volume. In the first precincts reporting, Angelo had grabbed a comfortable 97–2 lead. Channel 10 was not about to call the election just yet, but they did note a clear trend.

"I'm going to try George one more time," Hotson said. He went to the pay phone back by the restrooms.

"Good evening, gentlemen," Dencil said and sat down. He said work is work. He felt like a monkey dancing for peanuts and didn't really want to talk about it, but he did want a beer, several beers. He ordered another bucket of Dixies for the table and whatever T-Bone and his girl were having. And, Doyle, he said, give those two over there a round, meaning the poets.

"You ought to come with me, Friday, Dencil," Billy Wayne said. "Got an interview and test for LP&L. They're hiring. Good money, too."

"Didn't see anything about it."

"They had an ad in Thursday's paper. Meet you out front of their office at 8:45."

"Deal."

Hotson came back. "Hi, Dencil." He sat. "No answer. Anyone got a smoke?"

"I thought you were giving it up," Billy Wayne said.

"I guess I am."

"Wonder where he's at," Fox said.

"Who's that?" Dencil asked.

"George," Billy Wayne told him. "Trying to get him down here to join us for the party."

Dencil grabbed the cap of his longneck with the hem of his T-shirt and twisted it off. "I just saw him walking down 18th headed toward the park."

"Isn't Angelo's headquarters on Forsythe?" Fox said.

"It is," Hotson said. "In fact, tonight's the victory party."

Hotson figured it would take George a half hour to reach Forsythe and another ten minutes to walk north on Forsythe to the headquarters. He's about halfway there, he figured.

Billy Wayne said, "We should go after him."

"Okay, but let's take the beers," Dencil said. "Doyle, we'll get this bucket back to you, babe."

"Van's around the corner," Fox said.

IT WAS CLEAR to the four of them that they had better hustle their Pakistani friend out of the Angelo Candela for

State Senate Campaign Headquarters before matters became quite unmanageable. They looked through the window of the storefront. Angelo stood on a metal desk giving what appeared to be a victory speech. "I don't see George," Billy Wayne said.

"What if George ain't here?" Dencil said.

"We should be so lucky," Fox said.

They filed their way along the back wall behind the gathered applauders in cardboard Uncle Sam hats. The four stood by the refreshment table and listened. Angelo was talking about the integrity of neighborhoods and the freedom of choice in public education and the necessity of an armed and vigilant citizenry. Dorsey Tatum dumped a load of baby back ribs into a stainless-steel tub.

"Dorsey," Fox whispered, "what the hell are you doing here? Why aren't you at your own headquarters?"

"No party over to my headquarters," he said. "Ain't got no headquarters even. You boys, you all eat some of these ribs here."

Billy Wayne leaned over the table and asked Dorsey if he had seen George Binwaddie at all.

"Who been whattie?"

Billy Wayne shook his head. Dencil helped out. "Little guy from Pakistan. Brown skin, blue-black hair, wearing a LSU sweatshirt."

Dorsey nodded. "Yes, sir, he's somewhere up front there."

Billy Wayne looked at Dencil as if to say, We're in for it now.

While the four of them stood on their tiptoes and looked as well as possible over heads, hats, and placards, to see if they could spy George, Angelo talked about his church, his dog, his truck, his family, his friends (much applause), his gun, his trolling motor, his cigarettes, about fluoride, pornography, taxes, football, the surgeon general, homosexuals, deer hunting, gooks, draft-card and brassiere burners, the pope, and about an International Jewish-Communist conspiracy, strategic nuclear weapons, about interracial marriage, and about his personal Lord and Savior, Jesus Christ.

And then from somewhere near that metal desk came "You murdering son of a bitch. You stole everything from me," followed by a scuffle and shouting.

"That would be George," Fox said. "Excuse me." He made his way through the crowd toward the mayhem.

Billy Wayne yelled up to George to quiet down now; it's time, he yelled, that we all left. He didn't know if George could hear him or what.

Fox reached George at the same time that Buddy Tidwell did. Something about the sheriff and thoughts of returning to jail exerted a soothing effect on George. Buddy suggested to Fox that he take his client here, and you and your pals get out of these headquarters pronto or face immediate arrest and incarceration. Buddy made sure that only Fox, George, Hotson, Billy Wayne, and Dencil exited. He stood at the doorway. "Don't none of you shitkickers get any ideas," he told the assembled Democrats-for-Candela. He stood there with his arms folded across his chest until our friends pushed the van about a half block down Forsythe. When he heard the backfire and the revving engine, Buddy looked across the room to Angelo who had remained standing on the desk. "You were saying something about America for Americans, weren't you?"

"I UNDERSTAND THAT part, Billy Wayne," Earlene said. "I just don't know why he couldn't have stayed with someone else, that's all."

"He could have. Just that I insisted he stay here."

"But why, Billy Wayne? Why, when you know we need the privacy if we're going to make a child?"

Billy Wayne put his finger on Earlene's lips. "It's just for a couple of days." Billy Wayne snuggled up close to Earlene.

"You do want a baby, don't you, Billy Wayne?"

Billy Wayne said of course he did. So why had he made this occasion stressful for Earlene? He did want a baby, didn't he? He kissed her forehead, her nose, her lips, her neck.

"I can't, Billy Wayne. What if he hears us?"

He kissed her shoulder. He heard Sister Helen cautioning him. He kissed Earlene's elbow, her breast, her other breast, her stomach. He was making love not making a baby. He drew his knee up between her thighs.

"I don't suppose he'll hear us, will he, Billy Wayne?"

And George did not wake on the couch in the living room. He did not stir from his dreams. Neither stirred Billy Wayne nor Earlene, not when a McCaskill hound chased some of the dozen cats up the pecan tree, not throughout the hour's thunderstorm that shook the house and rattled the shades, not when the alarm went off at the Piggly Wiggly and clanged for seventeen minutes. They did not awake until they heard the gunshot. Billy Wayne rolled off the bed and hit the cold tile floor. "What the hell was that, Earlene? Earlene?" He reached up for her arm and pulled her down to the floor. "Stay low," he said.

"Oh, my God, Billy Wayne, what happened? What was that?"

Billy Wayne remembered George out there on the couch. He pictured his friend with the oily barrel of an automatic pistol in his mouth. Could he have been that depressed? "Stay here," Billy Wayne told Earlene. He undid her fingers from his arm and helped her slide underneath the bed. Billy Wayne stood, walked to the door, and put his ear against it. He heard the hum of the refrigerator. He quietly cracked the door a bit, waited. He whispered, "George? George, you okay?" When he got no response, he stepped out into the hall, got down again on all fours and crawled to the living room and saw what he took to be George's body prostrate on the floor. Billy Wayne reached out and touched a stockinged foot. It twitched.

"Get down," George whispered.

"Jesus, you're all right."

"But your neighbor isn't. He's gone crazy or something. He's out there with a gun."

"Who?"

"Listen."

Billy Wayne recognized the voice of Eddie Pettis saying something about the moon and about being sorry but he was only carrying out orders. "Who's he talking to?"

"Maybe you should call the police or something," George said.

Billy Wayne crawled to the window and peeked over the sill. He saw Eddie Pettis with a pistol in his hand. At his feet lay the stiff, and it seemed, noseless corpse of Pepino. Eddie Pettis raised his handgun and took aim at the donkey.

4

Russell Sikes, Charlie Weasel, and Reddy Kilowatt

*W*hen they had finished filling out their employment applications and had returned them to Miss Cole, Billy Wayne and Dencil were given plastic disks, orange ones with white numerals, 11 and 12, and told to find a seat over yonder in Room 113A and wait for their numbers to be called for the aptitude test. There were about a dozen or so metal school desks in Room 113A. Billy Wayne and Dencil took two seats in the back. Dencil checked his pockets and counted his change. He said he was going to find the canteen or a coffee machine. Cream, no sugar, Billy Wayne said.

Billy Wayne realized he was here at LP&L this morning because of Russell Sikes, a man he really didn't know at all.

Strange, isn't it? You can make all kinds of plans in your life, but still the important things seem to happen by accident. He thought about power and light as metaphors, the way Russell did. Light is illuminating and unburdening. You could be lighthearted, and that's good. But you could also be light of love. Light could be as radiant and consuming as fire, but could also be of little gravity or importance like a marshmallow or a crime novel. And there's love to the tenth power, but also power that corrupts. There's power that is vitality or virility, and power that means control and domination. He'd have to sit down with Russell Sikes and see what it was Russell had in mind.

Dencil returned with two coffees in Styrofoam cups. "Cream's in it," he told Billy Wayne. Dencil emptied six packets of sugar into his coffee and stirred it with the ballpoint pen he'd forgotten to return to Miss Cole. Billy Wayne asked Dencil about his family. Dencil told him how his mother lived in Carthage, Texas, but he didn't hear much from her anymore, how he had grown up over in Jackson, Mississippi, where his daddy, Brady Currence, worked most all his life at the state asylum. Worked in the back wards with folks that was hardly human. "He used to come home and tell me all kinds of stories about these guys. I couldn't even sleep at night wondering if this Charlie Weasel guy was going to be under my bed chewing his way up through the mattress to get to me. I bet I slept with Mama for a year when Daddy worked the graveyard. I guess they had some marital problems."

Dencil said how his daddy started staying over at the hospital. Got himself a little army cot and just camped out there. Stopped coming home. Said how they went there every two weeks to get what part of the paycheck his mama could argue his daddy out of. On these visits he began to meet the people his daddy used to talk about like General Braxton Bragg and Jesus, the Lord High Sheriff of Heaven, and Charlie Weasel himself, who turned out to be this little bitty man with a shiny bald head. He had filed all his front teeth so they looked like stained porcelain needles. Charlie wore a leash and stayed in a corner of the rec room and every once in a while gave himself a tug at the neck just to remind himself where he belonged. Dencil shook his head. "Who'd a thought madness was a catching disease?"

"What do you mean?"

"One day we went to see Daddy and his cot was gone from the hallway and he had a bed of his own in one of the rooms. He needed the support for his back, he told us. Rheumatism. Next visit he asked Mama who I was and then laughed like he knew all along when she told him. Some joke. And then we didn't see him for a while. So then Mama told me we were moving to Monroe, moving in with her sister Lisa. That's when I went alone to see Daddy. I wanted to tell him he wouldn't have to stay there 'cause we were all going to Louisiana."

Billy Wayne asked Dencil if his father recognized him this time.

"He acted like he did. At least at first. But then he started calling me 'Irene.' I'd tell him, 'Dencil,' and he'd just wink at me. We were in the rec room. I looked across the table to one of the attendants. He said my daddy was just playing with me. And he winked. What was all this winking, I wondered. Anyway, Daddy told me I was one of his cartoon wives. There were nine of us, he said. And whenever he wanted someone to talk to or needed his supper made, he'd draw one of us, either Arlene, Brigit, Colleen, Doreen, Eileen, Fiona, Grace, Helen, or me. I was the worst one to talk to, he said. I never had any jokes. And I was the second worse cook. He told me we all do what he wants us to do, just like all the others here, he said. 'Ain't that the truth, Churchill?' he said to the attendant."

"Were you scared?" Billy Wayne said.

"Shit, yes. He took my face in his hand and got up real close and he told me, 'I got the power, Irene, the power to erase you and any of these other fools anytime I want. You understand? I could blind you, decapitate you, recapitate you, grow a nettle bush out your ass, stick an eel on your forehead. Anything I want.' The attendant told Daddy to relax. Daddy said to me, 'It's a good thing for you I keep Churchill around.' He let go of my jaw and smiled. 'I'm a gentle man, Irene, as you know. Gentle until you piss me off.' I told him, 'Dencil, Daddy, I'm Dencil. Your boy, Dencil Francis Currence.'

"He picked up a pencil from this little plastic strawberry basket full of crayons and markers. He riffled through his Big Chief tablet until he found a blank page. He drew a stick man which he described to me as wearing a white T-shirt and dungarees, which is what I was wearing. And then he took this big eraser out of his pajama pocket. It was shaped like a rocket ship. He rubbed out the stick man. And then he ignored me. It was like I wasn't there. He tore the page into strips and stuffed them in his mouth. He looked at the attendant and said, 'This is delicious, Arlene, just the way I like it.' So I got up to leave. Daddy said to the attendant, 'Arlene, where did you put Charlie Weasel's leash? I'm taking him out for his dump.' Then he smiled at me and winked. He said, 'Irene, I'll get you in my dreams.' "

"Holy shit," Billy Wayne said. "Is he still in Jackson?"

"Could be. When Mama moved to Texas with Mr. Robertson, she sent a change of address to the hospital. Far as I know she hasn't heard from him.

"So what about you?" Dencil said. "You remember your daddy?"

"Sometimes I think I do. It's weird, but sometimes when I taste salt it's like I can feel him with me. Makes the hair on my arms stand up even."

"So what does he feel like?"

"Sometimes like a blanket, sometimes like a brick."

Billy Wayne thought about fathers and about the different ways of not knowing them. Was insanity as accidental as finding your future wife in a hospital room? Can you plan to go crazy? He thought about his own daddy, the man with eyes but without light. Did Pee Dubya ever realize who this child on his lap was? Did he hold the baby up to his face and smell its little belly, hug the child to his sweaty chest, kiss him all over?

"Numbers ten and eleven, please," Miss Cole said. "Right this way, please." She led Dencil and Billy Wayne down the hall to the testing room and introduced them to Mr. Mladinic who shook their hands and asked them to take the two seats across from him at the testing table. Mr. Mladinic excused himself for burping. He wore a white short-sleeved shirt and a navy blue tie with a curious, Billy Wayne thought, tie tack in the shape of a man whose body and limbs were red bolts of electricity and whose head was a lightbulb with a smaller lightbulb nose.

"I hope it won't disturb you boys if I eat while you take the test."

"That's fine," Billy Wayne said.

"You'll be taking the Minnesota Multiphasic and a personality inventory this morning. Use the Number 2 pencils provided."

"Mr. Mladinic?" Billy Wayne said.

"Yes?"

"Who's that on your tie?"

Mr. Mladinic smiled. "Reddy Kilowatt. He's the new mascot here at LP&L."

Mr. Mladinic picked up the stopwatch attached to his clipboard. "Open your books and begin."

5

We Shall Live,
and Do This,
or That

*B*illy Wayne sat in his jockey shorts and T-shirt at the kitchen table eating wheat toast, reading his LP&L manual, and sipping coffee. He had the country music station on low. Earlene had told him to listen in for the free tickets to the Willie Nelson concert. Then just be like the fifth caller or whatever, she told him. She wrote KICK's phone number on an index card and taped it to the radio. Billy Wayne heard one of the McCaskill women, maybe it was Big Mary Elizabeth, call Eddie Pettis a candy-assed, banjo-bellied tramp.

At first, Billy Wayne figured he had it all figured out. He had a new job at LP&L and the new attitude that came with the $6.25 an hour. He had his eyes on this little shotgun with a front porch and working shutters on the northside, on McKinley, just across from the levee. He had a wife, didn't he, and good friends. He had potential. Pretty soon, six months tops, he'd have a truck, a record player, television maybe. And whatever else he wanted. He'd just have to think, though, about what he wanted. He heard a *"phtt"* and knew that another cockroach had crawled into the warm toaster. He'd be glad to get out of here.

Billy Wayne tried to imagine himself in a cotton shirt and necktie, but he couldn't. He tried to picture himself on a beach somewhere, Biloxi maybe, with a nice, kind of windblown haircut, sunglasses, umbrella, cooler, looking at Earlene tanning herself on a plaid blanket. He couldn't do it. He tried to picture his retirement party from LP&L in 2010, or whenever it would be, at the Bayou Country Club. He and Dencil wearing suits. He couldn't do it. Maybe he didn't have anything figured out. Billy Wayne spooned grape jelly onto his toast and then licked the spoon.

George knocked on the screen door. "Saw your light on, thought I'd stop in."

"Come in, come in," Billy Wayne said. "Sit! Coffee?"

"No, thanks. Can't stay. You must be ready for bed, anyway."

"How was your first day at the Rise 'n' Dine?"

"Nobody liked my crunchy almond eggs."

Through the kitchen wall, they heard Nettie McCaskill shoveling dog food into her wheelbarrow. The yard dogs heard it too, and they began yelping. Then Eddie Pettis, who was probably trying to watch his television programs, hollered something about fetching his handgun out in the pickup truck and shooting the goddam hounds in their butts. The dogs didn't quiet until Nettie wheeled their dinner out to the middle of the yard and dumped it on the ground.

George said, "Listen, I'll be going. Just wanted to thank you for everything. For Fox and for talking to Willis about the job and all." George stood.

"Sure you won't stay?"

"You've got work to do. I'll give you a call."

Billy Wayne locked the back door and turned off the radio. Earlene called for him to come to bed. He sponged off the table and put away the butter and jelly, the milk and sugar. Why hadn't he tried harder to keep George here? He must have wanted to talk about something. Billy Wayne didn't like the way he was behaving. He picked up his manual, put out the kitchen light, and went to the bedroom. He lay on the bed, turned on the bedside lamp and opened the manual.

His only excuse for this self-involvement and for his recent pitiful conjugal performance was that he couldn't clear his mind of his *LP&L Tailboard Conference Manual*. He had to know the entire three hundred pages (sure, a lot of it's diagrams and photographs and it's big print and everything, but still . . .) by heart for the examination on Friday morning, everything from "Safe Operation of Stabilizer Jacks" to "Bucket Truck Dielectric Testing." And he was worried.

Earlene looked up at the wobbly ceiling fan over the bed and listened to it tick twelve times. "Well, how do you think this makes me feel, Billy Wayne?"

"I'm sorry. I don't need a curtain lecture, Earlene."

Earlene swung her legs off the bed. "You're sorry, all right."

"Where you going?" Billy Wayne held Earlene's arm.

"Kitchen."

"This test is important, Earlene. I'm still provisional. If I don't pass, it's back to cockroaches. Then we don't get our loan for the house, and . . ."

She took the manual from where it lay opened on Billy Wayne's chest. She turned the pages and shook her head.

"So you find Screw Anchor Damage Reports and Clantech Phasing Voltmeters more interesting than relations with your wife? Is that it?"

"Of course not, Earlene."

"It's been two weeks of this, Billy Wayne."

"I said I was sorry." He let go of her arm.

The McCaskills' back door slammed shut, opened, slammed shut again. The door to Eddie Pettis's pickup screaked open. Eddie and Little Mary Elizabeth argued. Earlene read from the manual. "Effects of Sling Angle on Sling Load." Several of the McCaskill dogs began to bark. "You got another woman, Billy Wayne?"

"Don't be crazy, Earlene."

"Because if you do, I want to know. You'll tell me, won't you, Billy Wayne?"

"Earlene, you are blowing this all out of proportion. I do not have a girlfriend. I just have a lot on my mind is all." Billy Wayne knelt on the bed. He held Earlene's shoulders. He wondered if he should start something.

Just then Eddie Pettis raised his voice. "I told you, god-damit. I'm going to the Legion for a couple of drinks. Period."

"Take me with you, Eddie," Little Mary Elizabeth said.

"It ain't no place for a woman. Now that's final."

"Please, Eddie."

"Idiots," Billy Wayne said.

Earlene turned to look at her husband. She stood, took her robe from the closet door, and put it on. The door of the pickup closed.

"Get your hands off the frigging truck," Eddie Pettis said. He started the engine.

"Please take me, okay, Eddie?" Little Mary Elizabeth said. And then she yelled, "Bastard!"

"You want your ass drug down the street, you just keep your fingers on that mirror, bitch."

They heard the squeal of tires and Little Mary Elizabeth shout something about all the homos at the Legion, and then they heard her sobbing, choking for breath, it seemed like. Heard her even over the yapping of the dogs.

"I'll leave you to your study, Billy Wayne."

In the kitchen, Earlene switched on the wall lamp over the table and poured herself a glass of iced tea. She sat down at the table with her pens and her tablet to await the next line to her motel song. She read the last line. "We do it very well." She noted the irony in that. She thought about her and Billy Wayne. She looked at the clock. Here she was at eleven-thirty-two in a dim and airless kitchen with an empty womb and an empty heart, trying to write words to a song. The danger is, of course, that in writing you recall what you've tried to erase. You find out, maybe, what it is you don't want to know about yourself, what you regret, what you're ashamed of. You dig up what you've buried.

Earlene remembered being pregnant at fifteen. Her friend Veola Poag told her about the doctor in Memphis. She remembered taking the Southern Continental bus alone, sitting near the back, trying to sleep, unable to eat the pimiento sandwich her grandmother had made her, wondering what Michael Hardesty was doing just then. She never told him. She did tell Grandma how she was going for an interview at the Tennessee Academy of Beauty. What's wrong with Cloyd's Beauty School? her grandma wanted to know. Three locations right here in our parish. Because, Earlene explained, there's movie stars and stuff in Memphis for one thing. And the TAB is the finest beauty school in the mid-South, everyone knows that. Nobody with any good hair lives in Monroe, Grandma. Well, there's no need to cry about it, Grandma said. You'll need some money for the trip. We'll go to the bank in the morning.

Earlene remembered the bus stopping somewhere between Alligator and Bobo, just out in the middle of nowhere. And this young woman with a straw hat, print dress, and no shoes, and her daughter, probably fifteen like Earlene, who wore no shoes, no hat, just these white shorts and a yellow T-shirt, got off the bus. The mother carried a new-looking sewing machine. They never turned to look at the bus, just walked back from where the bus had come. It was a moonless night and so dark out there that in ten yards the women had vanished.

Earlene remembered the two women and the smells of the Delta in July, the musty scent of profusion, fertility, and the cloying sweetness of decay, as if the resinous air was rank with spoilage, as if the soil itself were alive and ripening, and not just alive, but restless, predatory. She saw the lightning in the sky over Clarksdale and wished it would rain, wished the smells would wash away.

When she arrived that morning in Memphis, Earlene took the #37 city bus just the way Veola Poag had told her to, took it north till she saw the Riverview Baptist Church on her right. She put her back to the river and walked three blocks to 3220 Something-or-other Street, and there was the blue stone house. Only you could tell it used to be an Esso filling station. You could still read "Crank Case Service" through the over-coat of paint over where the service bay must have been. Three yellowed, brittle yews sat in wooden wash barrels on the cement island where the gasoline pumps had stood.

Earlene went to the refrigerator for more iced tea. She stared into the refrigerator, but forgot what she was looking for. What the doctor did didn't hurt. She remembered that much. On one wall hung a chart of the floral-colored female reproductive system. She had kept her eyes opened and focused on the ceiling until everything went snowy, and she knew if she could just stay like that, like lost in a blizzard, then she'd wake up in a while back in Monroe, and none of this would have happened. Instead the fat woman who had taken her money earlier told her to get dressed. The fat woman had a white-bread sandwich in her left hand. It had seemed like a dream then, but it felt real tonight when she could see herself so clearly, see the white gown over her body like a winding sheet, see the damp bangs clinging to her forehead, hear the whisper of air, the throaty gasp of suction.

Earlene remembered how really hot it was walking back toward the river, so hot her cotton blouse soaked through and sweat dripped from her chin, how tired she felt, dead tired, how heavy. When the men lounging on metal chairs outside the Uptown Social Club talked that nasty way to her, she was not even bothered, as if she lived in some other unreachable world from them now. Earlene filled her glass with tea, then held the glass pitcher to her forehead. She replaced it on the shelf, took a slice of lemon from a blue saucer and closed the refrigerator with her shoulder. She sat, dunked the lemon into the tea and then sucked on it.

And then she got sick at the bus terminal. A woman who said her name was Florence Nightingale, that's what she said, sat down on the bench beside Earlene, felt her forehead, helped her to the lavatory so she could be sick, and stole Earlene's backpack. Everything she had was gone. Didn't have a nickel for a phone call. Didn't have a bus ticket. If she'd had the strength, she would have walked to a police station. All she could do though was sit down outside on the sidewalk in the shade of the bus station. She tapped the pockets of her blue jeans. Didn't even have the pills the doctor gave her. She cried because she knew that all she could do now was wait for whatever would happen to happen.

She would have named the baby Martha. The Earlene on the sidewalk would have. The Earlene at the kitchen table imagined that Martha would be old enough now to talk to. She'd have wispy auburn hair and clear, dark eyes. She had never talked to anyone about it, except to the boy who drove her back home that night from Memphis. He was eighteen; his name was Dolphus Higdon; he had his own car, a 1962 Falcon, and he wouldn't mind at all driving to Louisiana. Give him a good reason to call in sick to work as a matter of fact. He told Earlene he polished cars at Bill Maggio's Downtown Auto and Detail Shop. Didn't hate it, just wasn't much of a future to it. He was fixing to go to the Shelby County Vo-Tech and learn how to repair office machines. That's the coming thing. Right in the middle of her crying there on the sidewalk, this Dolphus Higdon touched her shoulder and said to Earlene, Girl, I think you need a friend. She looked up at the boy and saw herself reflected and distorted in his mirrored sunglasses. He lifted them to his forehead. He had blue eyes. She told him what happened all in one long, breathless sentence that began with the lie to her grandmother and wound up right here on the sidewalk. You wait here, Dolphus said. I'm parked two blocks over. Be right back.

On the way out of Memphis, Dolphus pointed out where Elvis Presley lived, said he'd seen Elvis on his motorcycle, no helmet, speeding up Bellevue Boulevard about a hundred miles an hour. Cops won't stop Elvis, no way. They all know his bike. Another thing, Dolphus said, that sure wasn't Priscilla on back, I can tell you that. I seen Priscilla at a sale one time at the Beall Ladymon. The inside of the Falcon was red, Earlene remembered. The radio didn't work. Dolphus bought her a Royal Crown cola, but it only made her sick. In Mississippi, they stopped at the intersection of Highways 49 and 61 and picked up a hitchhiker, an old man who said his name was Robert Dusty. They took him about three or four miles down the road, that's all. He explained how someone had tried to poison him one time and that's how his voice got ragged like it is. Rat poison in some whiskey. Said he once had a girlfriend named Thelma in Monroe. He thanked them for the lift. You all a cute couple, he told them. You all be sweet.

Earlene smiled. She hadn't thought of that old man and his lazy eye in years.

Dolphus stopped in Cleveland and bought a sack of tamales and a jar of aspirin. Earlene had two of each. Then she fell asleep. The smell of the paper mill's what woke her up. Just take the Jonesboro Road, she told Dolphus. It was three in the morning when she arrived home. Dolphus said, no, thank you, he wouldn't stay. It was a great night for driving. Probably won't have many nights like this in my life, he said. I was happy to do it. You saved my life, she said.

Earlene bit her lip and shook her head. Dolphus Higdon was like an angel. But, of course, he was no angel at all, just a boy from Memphis who was kind to someone he didn't know. That's the miracle of it. And here she was, what, seven years later, and he was still making her feel alive, important, legitimate. That's an odd word, Earlene thought. But the right one. Legitimate. She wondered about Dolphus. What he might be doing now. I could find him, she thought. How many Dolphus Higdons could there be in Memphis? Would he even remember me? Would he remember Robert Dusty?

Earlene heard Eddie Pettis's pickup scatter gravel in the driveway. Heard Eddie cut the engine. Waited for the door to screak open. She heard, "Is that you, Eddie?"

Earlene checked on Billy Wayne. He was asleep. The manual was opened on the bed. She closed it, covered him, cut off the light. She went back to the kitchen. She took a clean, white sheet of paper. She recited the chorus she had already written over and over until she could hear the music, kind of a country dirge. And then she wrote down what she heard next:

> *We're all changing places*
> *We live in a motel*
> *So many different faces*
> *We just think it's swell.*

Everyone's so suave and cool
That you can hardly tell
The foolers from the fooled
In the Modern Age Motel.

Earlene fell asleep at the table. *In her dream she's sewing a dress for the little girl. First it's a dress, then it's a shroud. Billy Wayne's there in her grandma's parlor eating a sandwich, some kind of skink-green meat. Earlene says to him, "Dolphus, what's crazy about your eye?"* When Earlene woke up, she looked at the lyrics on the tablet. She saw it was light outside and crossed the kitchen to the door. When she opened it, the McCaskill hounds began to bark. Little Mary Elizabeth stuck her head up in the frame of the pickup window.

6

The Future of
an Illusion

*S*hug Johnson's seizure of enlightenment
came on quite dramatically during a Great
Books discussion of *The Interpretation of Dreams*. That's when
Shug felt his brain stem shudder. He felt his neck and then
felt nothing, saw nothing, heard nothing, tasted a familiar but
unrecognizable nectar at the back of his mouth, smelled ozone
like at the start of a rain shower, and the smell set off an airy
massaging of his gray matter, and he was, he understood,
experiencing a moment of spectacular and transcendent intuition, an immediate and profound apprehension of one of the
essential philosophical problems in Western culture, only he
couldn't, not just yet anyway, articulate said problem itself,
but he could, he knew (and this caused him to smile broadly),

explain quite lucidly, elegantly, engagingly, the solution to this mystery of man's existence, and it all had to do, the solution that is, with the concept of bungled action, Cartesian linguistics, the Swedenborgian idea of divinity (why hadn't he thought of that before?), and, not surprisingly, the metaphor of making bread. But he would have to talk quickly, he knew, before the insight faded, while he still grasped this ontological tiger by its tail. Shug inhaled deeply and held the edge of the table with both hands to steady himself against the imminent surge of illumination, and began. "Okay," he said, "let's start with the idea that the universe is Will. Are you with me?" And that's when Margaret Grimes intruded. She was full up to here, and she just had to say it: Sigmund Freud was a lunatic. Shug looked at her. He shook his head as if trying to rattle something free. He closed his eyes. Nothing. He had been detranced by Margaret Grimes. As suddenly as it had descended, the revelation was gone. Maybe a man gets one, if he's lucky, one of these luminous moments in his lifetime, and Shug knew he had squandered his. His nose was bleeding.

Margaret went on. "This Freud person was nothing more than a lecher and a ranting, muddlepated maniac. I mean what kind of decent man has *that* on his mind all of the time?" Margaret looked around the seminar table. None of the men, she noted, met her gaze. "Suppose we all just went around fulfilling our wishes on everyone else. Wouldn't we all be in a fix? No, it's exactly because we sublimated our desires that we were able to build civilization and a culture." And that's all she had to say, and that's final. The end. Period. Shug, disheartened, deflated, disturbed at the *intuitus interruptus*, excused himself and walked outside to the library loading dock and smoked a cigarette.

Royal Landry, who was a salesman at Danny Edwards's Dodge-Chrysler and so considered psychology his "bailiwick," as he put it, said, "We all do things we don't want other people to know about, don't we?"

"Are you saying we're all as nuts as Sigmund Freud?"

"I'm just making a point, Margaret. We don't want people to know what we're really like because maybe then they'd lock us up or they wouldn't like us if they knew what we did when we're alone." Ted Muto's eyes were closed and his mouth was opened. Ted was here because he thought Great Books groups were the second-best place to pick up women. Church was first. No one bothered to tap him awake. "Maybe," Royal said, "that means we do some things that we don't understand ourselves, don't want to understand, that we can't forgive."

Cicero Wittlief, overcome perhaps by the confessional muse, said, one crazy thing he did, or used to do that is, he hasn't done it for probably a year, seven months anyway, six months, whatever, well, let's see, five months, was that he wrote letters to this actress on a television program. No, not Mary Tyler Moore, he said, and I ain't telling you who.

Chiquita Deal, sitting next to Cicero, cleared her throat. She said, well, I still suck my thumb. Ted Muto opened an eye, wiped a bit of drool from his chin. Thirty-five and I still suck my thumb. Tommie Nash confessed to locking her doors and windows six times every night, to chewing each bite of food twenty-seven times, to never buying chicken because you can never get all the little hairs off.

"Suzanne Pleshette," Cicero said.

"What?" Royal said.

"The actress."

Then Bobby Sistrunk explained how he didn't know if this was crazy or just peculiar or maybe even it's normal, but anyway, he has eaten the exact same food every day for the last five years. For breakfast, one soft-boiled egg, cooked three minutes and thirty seconds; two rashers of bacon; one slice of white toast with oleo and Welch's grape jelly; six ounces of orange juice; a cup of Néscafé with a level teaspoon of Cremora. Lunch: an apple, two carrots, iced tea. Supper: spaghetti with oleo and ketchup; a side of Van Camp's Mexi-beans; a can of Barq's. And then he has a Little Debbie snack cake and a glass of skim milk before bed.

Royal said he didn't think it was crazy at all. "Them Chinese eat rice every day of their sad little lives," he said. "And, Bobby, look at me, we don't think any the less of you, boy." What he had meant by "crazy" was, anyway, the things we wouldn't talk about. "The stuff you all are forcing out of your mind right now. Know what I mean?" He saw the Van Veckhoven twins, Cindy and Sandy, sneak a look at each other, smile.

Ted Muto said, "I thought we were here to talk about Freud. Isn't that what we're here for?"

Shug returned to the room and took his seat.

Royal quoted Kierkegaard: "The specific character of insanity is precisely this: it is unaware of being insanity."

"Despair," Shug said. "He was talking about despair, not insanity."

"It's all the same ball of wax, isn't it?" Royal said.

Which brings us to Billy Wayne. It was indeed true, as he had told Earlene that night in bed, that he did not have another woman, and it remained true after Billy Wayne passed his examination, rose from provisional to permanent employee at LP&L, began operating a brush hog in the Bottom so that the company could run some high-tension lines up to Junction City, true even after Billy Wayne and Earlene bought the house on McKinley with an FHA loan, and after Earlene had sent off her first batch of song lyrics to Paula Records in Shreveport and to Cousins Music in Nashville. Billy Wayne did not have another woman. He was not a liar. What he did consider, however, was the possibility of another woman. And in that way, he was, if not crazy, then reckless. He allowed himself to entertain that notion, to be hospitable toward this stranger. Gradually, unconsciously, Billy Wayne let himself flirt with the prospect of being new to someone (as if he were somehow old to his wife of a year) and to feel the excitement of that.

Just how much this allowance was calculated, how much this susceptibility was spontaneous, Billy Wayne was unsure. He did think that there must be more to life than being, more to marriage than the daily round of work and quiet suppers, of chit-chat and movie going, of resolute but requisite sex, of have-a-good-day and kiss-kiss-good night. It was no one's fault that he found himself restless and unsatisfied. This is the working world. That's the way life is, and that's how it feels sometimes—stale, common, predictable. He didn't understand it, he hoped it was temporary, but he accepted it. He was being mature. He told himself when the baby came, then the spark would return to his life and would rekindle his marital ardor. But the heart can't wait sometimes. The heart needs to burn now, and it finds its own combustion.

Tami Lynne Curry sold the house on McKinley to Earlene and Billy Wayne. Two years earlier she had bought the house with her boyfriend, but they never got the chance to live in it long. He got drafted, shipped up north to Fort Dix, then to Vietnam. While he was away, Tami Lynne painted the four rooms, sanded the hardwood floors, and even spackled the spidery cracks in the bathroom ceiling. Did all the work herself. She planted a border of laurel out in front. Private Boyfriend (that's how Billy Wayne thought of him; no disrespect intended, he just didn't care to know his name) died at Hamburger Hill. Tami Lynne no longer wished to live with the memories, or rather, without the memories.

Royal Landry always says you don't sell the product, you sell yourself. Perhaps that's what Tami Lynne did—sold herself to

Billy Wayne. At first, Billy Wayne just wanted to inspect the
house thoroughly, you know, before he put his money down.
He was over to Tami Lynne's three or four Saturdays in a
row. And then after he and Earlene bought the house and
moved in, Billy Wayne was forever finding things in the yard
or way in back on a closet shelf that he was sure Tami Lynne
needed, and he would walk through the park over to her
apartment on Downey and hand her a pair of pinking shears
or an index card with a recipe for tuna noodle casserole, and
she would tell him it wasn't hers, but thank you just the same.
And maybe she'd invite him to stay for a cup of coffee, and
while he was there he might offer to hang a framed print
(Peter Max) over the couch or tighten that loose hinge on the
kitchen cabinet door. And so, in Billy Wayne's mind, this
casual acquaintance became someone he knew and then became a friend (men can have women friends, of course) and
then a good friend, a close friend, someone he could talk to.
What he saw himself doing, nurturing and cultivating this
relationship, he found surprising and exciting, but not at all
crazy. In fact, he thought of himself as at least mildly sophisti-
cated.

Soon Billy Wayne was stopping by Twin City Office Supply,
where Tami Lynne worked, just to say hello and to buy
Earlene some pens, tablets, typewriter ribbon or something.
He didn't see anything wrong with that. So when Dencil mentioned to him that people might could get the wrong impres-
sion, you know, think that maybe you and Tami Lynne are
stepping out or whatever, well, Billy Wayne just thought Dencil was crazy. Of course Billy Wayne understood the difference
still between innocence and discretion. If Dencil could misin-
terpret his harmless behavior, it might be best not to say much
to Earlene.

It wasn't until after Fox called Billy Wayne at home that
Billy Wayne began to admit that maybe the way things appear

to be are the way things are. Fox said, Billy Wayne, I noticed you and Miss Curry at the Dinner Bell at lunch today. No, you wouldn't have seen me, Billy Wayne, because you never lifted your eyes from your companion. Fox said, Is everything all right at home? Billy Wayne told him, Of course. He and Earlene were happy enough, he supposed. Maybe there was not the excitement there used to be, but that's normal, that's marriage. The important thing is they enjoyed each other. Sure, maybe they didn't talk as much as they used to, but Earlene's all the time writing her songs and he's got the job and there's always something to do around the yard. Well, it wouldn't be long now before Earlene finally got pregnant. Everything's fine. Really. I hope so, Fox said.

Though he wasn't likely to do anything about it, Billy Wayne could no longer deny that he felt attracted to Tami Lynne, to that abundant mahogany hair, those hazel eyes, the freckles. She couldn't weigh ninety pounds, he figured. He bet he could wrap his two hands around her waist, lift her to his lips like a pitcher of cool water. She was funny, affectionate almost, in a bashful kind of way. He often noticed her looking at him out of the corner of her eye, like he might disappear if she didn't keep watch. When he'd catch her at it, she'd blush, make a face. He'd laugh. Billy Wayne found out that Tami Lynne grew up in Cleveland, Oklahoma, and had followed her late boyfriend to Monroe. He was planning to go to pharmacy school at the college. Her daddy was a welder who worked pipelines and was, she thought, somewhere in Alaska though she hadn't heard from him in years. Right then, her mother was living in a sanitarium in Georgia. She makes her living faking injuries and illnesses and collecting disability checks. She calls me once a year on her birthday, Tami Lynne said. And even this, her lack of attachment, became attractive to Billy Wayne. He liked Tami Lynne, and he liked the person he became with Tami Lynne. He was more alert, more aware of gesture and nuance. But this—what to call it?—this affiliation with Tami Lynne would remain as it was—a diversion, an adventure, and that would suit Billy Wayne, or so he imagined.

THREE DAYS LATER Billy Wayne picked up Tami Lynne at her work in his LP&L truck, and they drove out to Bayou D'Arbonne for a picnic. Billy Wayne turned onto a dirt road and drove a quarter mile or so, past a clutter of discarded stoves and refrigerators, past the mound of automobile tires, and past two old women on lawn chairs fishing with cane poles, listening to gospel music on a radio. They gave Billy Wayne a wave. Just where the road played out, Billy Wayne parked. He found a clearing among the cypresses, spread his blanket. Tami Lynne sat, opened her paper sack, asked Billy Wayne did he want a pimiento or chicken salad. Billy Wayne lay on his side propped on an elbow. Chicken salad. Tami Lynne bit into a peach.

Billy Wayne heard a splash, looked up to see a kingfisher spear a minnow. He could hear the ladies' radio, someone singing "This Little Light of Mine." He listened. Sounded like the Soul Stirrers.

"You're dripping," Billy Wayne told Tami Lynne, and before he knew it, he was wiping peach juice off her chin with his fingers, and before they could do anything about it, they were in each others' arms. They made love quickly, cautiously, with their clothes on. When they finished, Billy Wayne lay there atop Tami Lynne. Tami Lynne smelled like violets and clay. Billy Wayne wondered what time it was getting to be. He wondered if the ladies had caught any fish. He peeked into their plastic bucket, saw a pair of yellow-eyed bream, curled like fallen leaves, floating on the milky water. He thought of a bare light bulb. He didn't know why. Was he falling asleep?

He saw a bowl of corn or a bowl of teeth; he couldn't tell which. He heard the Soul Stirrers sing, "Let it shine, let it shine, let it shine."

On the drive back to town, Billy Wayne realized he could get into serious trouble, driving around town with an unauthorized passenger in his truck. He stayed off 143 as much as he could. Told himself he'd have to be more prudent in the future. Tami Lynne looked into her compact mirror, fluffed her bangs, applied lipstick. When Billy Wayne dropped her off at work, Tami Lynne smiled, said, "Thank you for the hot lunch." They laughed. "Really," she said. "Thanks."

What happened next happened when Tami Lynne called Billy Wayne at home on Saturday and asked him to meet her if he could, right now, on the levee across from the Bible Museum. He hesitated. This was very odd. He said, yes, sure, ten minutes, and wondered what this could be about. She probably shouldn't just call here, he thought. No use worrying Earlene. He'd mention it. Only wouldn't that suggest that there was something wrong with their spending time together? He wouldn't mention it.

"Morning, Billy Wayne," Tami Lynne said.

"What are you looking at?"

"You, Billy Wayne Fontana."

Billy Wayne touched his face. "Is something wrong?"

She took a deep breath. "Do you think there's something wrong?"

Billy Wayne felt clumsy. He folded his arms, unfolded them, then realized his hands were just hanging there. He looked past Tami Lynne's shoulder at the cross atop the museum. "What do you mean?"

"Have you told your wife?"

"No," he said. Why would she think I'd do that? "I haven't."

"What are your intentions?"

"Does a man have to have intentions?"

"You're a married man."

"I like you, Tami Lynne. You know that."

Tami Lynne shook her head. "I think you should buy your wife's pens at Kmart from now on. Good-bye, Billy Wayne." She turned and walked down the levee to Riverside Drive.

Billy Wayne watched her. He felt relieved it was over. When he got home he walked up behind Earlene and kissed her neck. That night he took her out to eat at Frankie and Janie's. They had crawfish and salads. He told Earlene that they were a happy couple, that they were good for each other, weren't they? You've been very distant lately, Earlene told him. He took her hand. He shrugged and apologized. I don't know, he said. Just a phase.

That's the night he told himself he was lucky, told himself he loved Earlene and never could do anything to hurt her—he'd hurt himself first. That's the night, on the walk home, that he realized he'd been missing his friends. He hadn't been paying attention to their lives lately, hadn't been hanging out with them enough. Who was that person walking out with Tami Lynne? It wasn't me, he thought. That's the night George Binwaddie stole the pistol he'd kill himself with from Eddie Pettis's pickup outside the Legion Hall.

7

In This Day of Grief and of Desperate Sorrow

*A*t 10:49 on the night of Sunday, June 24, 1973:

EARLENE FONTANA sat at her kitchen table writing a song called "Big Empty House Blues" and wondering why all of a sudden her love songs turned out so sad. She put down her pen and rubbed her itchy eyes. She blew her nose. Allergies. She dropped Murine into both eyes and closed them. Earlene picked up the pen. The only sound in the house was the hum of the fluorescent tube over the table.

. . .

IN THE RISE 'n' Dine, Sheriff Buddy Tidwell thought about light and dark. Tenille Suzenau refilled his mug with decaf. Buddy swiveled on his stool and leaned his back against the counter. In the reflection from the front windows, he watched Tenille erase the day's specials from the blackboard with a dishrag. He noticed how here inside the diner, the light seemed a part of everything. It seemed to enlarge Tenille, make her more present or something, just the way halos worked in some of those paintings at the Masur Museum. The edges of all the appliances were so clearly defined, and everything was so obviously distinct, discrete, the tile from the grout, the pane from the sash, the napkin from the dispenser. Everything. But outside you can't tell anything apart from anything else. Buddy looked at Tenille and said, "Where's Binwaddie tonight?"

TAMI LYNNE CURRY looked at her list. She had sixteen cons and only two pros. She tapped her forehead with the pencil's eraser. She saw herself in the dresser mirror, a reclining figure on a double bed. She wished she had a cat. She wrote "Touch" under pro. She shifted her back against the pillow and reached to put out the lamp.

FOX LEDBETTER DIDNT think he'd ever sleep again. He sat in the dark in his den and wondered when it had begun, at what second. How long, in other words, since he's been condemned, since everything he's planned, everything he's done, became absolutely laughable. When was it that the first cell, disturbed by something—but what?—shivered and divided? Was he eating a barbecue sandwich when this business shuddered into metastasis? And what was this guest in his brain doing right now? Did it sleep? Fox poured himself a glass of Wild Turkey and listened to Charlie Parker play "April in Paris."

FROM HIS BRIEFCASE telephone, Richard Nixon called John Dean at home. "John," he said, "do you know who this is? This is the Big Enchilada, John." John looked across the room at Maureen and nodded his head. "I want you to call this off, John."

STATE SENATOR ANGELO Candela leaned his forehead into the steering wheel of his Mustang. He couldn't think of why he was doing this, this thing with the horn. He wondered about that tap on his window and that flash of light.

LURLEEN DOOLEY, PRESIDENT of Cousins Music, looked up at the sign that welcomed her to Arkansas, saw the lights of Memphis in her rearview mirror. She tuned the radio to a station with news. Tornado watch in the Delta until midnight. She could see the glow from the grandstand at the dog track, the Ramada Inn.

SISTER HELEN LOMASNEY sat in the chapel at St. Francis asking God what she should do. On her lap, a letter she'd been reading all weekend. A letter from Aunt Katherine in Cork telling Sister that her mother, Rose, God rest her soul, had died in her sleep, with the Sacrament (Father Grady was here seven hours), in a state of grace. Our Lord provided. Aunt Katherine wrote that Rose's last words to her were, "Tell

my Helen it's time to come home and take care of Himself."
Her da needed her now, Aunt Katherine wrote. He was more
than she and her sister, Maureen, could handle. Sister Helen
lit a votive candle, made the sign of the cross.

AT THE NASSAU Coliseum on Long Island, Elvis Presley
unsnapped his minicape, wiped his forehead and throat with
a silk scarf, and sang "The Battle Hymn of the Republic."

HAZEL CURRENCE STOOD in the office of the Palms Motel, phoned Room #1, and told Webb and Ferlin it was time
to switch off the TV, cut the lights, and get to sleep, pronto.
Good night. Sleep tight. She stepped back through the beaded
curtain into her efficiency. If she started right now, she'd have
just enough time to bake the Bible cake before Angelo showed
up. She got out the ingredients and mixed two cups of Jere-
miah 6:20, one cup Genesis 4:4, and a cup of Judges 5:25.
She wiped her hands on her apron, added a pinch of Leviticus
2:13.

BILLY WAYNE FONTANA sat on the only chair in Dencil's
room, a ladder-backed rocker, and listened to his friend. Dencil sat on the linoleum floor, closed his eyes, and leaned back
against the siderail of his bed. He said, Don't act, just be.
Improvise. He snapped open his can of Jax and sipped. Don't
hope; don't even expect. You'll just be disappointed. Billy
Wayne stopped rocking. But you have to have goals, he said.
Dencil smiled. Billy Wayne said, Don't you want to work things
out with Hazel? Dencil said, It's not up to me and what I want.
Billy Wayne said, It sounds like you're just settling for what

you've got. Exactly, Dencil said. Accept or be miserable. Billy Wayne looked at his watch. I told Earlene I'd be home at ten. Got to go. I'm late.

IN NEW ORLEANS, two men came back to the Upstairs Club at Chartres and Iberville and doused the staircase and first floor with gasoline and lit the fire that killed thirty-two men. Police would find twenty of the bodies "melted together."

EDDIE PETTIS PULLED his truck out of Sonic's holding a large root beer between his thighs while he tried to light a Camel. He flicked on his brights and saw the possum skitter across 80. He braked, pulled the truck over to the curb, and reached under the seat for his pistol. The possum waddled into the cotton and headed in the direction of the A&P. Eddie reached all over. He put the truck in park and lay down on the seat to search the floor. He tried to think. Some son of a bitch is going to be real sorry, he said. And soon, real soon.

RONNIE FLACY LAUGHED. Kiwanis? she said. A baby named after a fraternal organization? I don't think so, Hotson. And if it's a girl, Hotson said, Dinette. Ronnie kissed him on the nose. She said, Let's call Johnny's Pizza and order a large Sweep-the-Kitchen. Their telephone rang once and stopped.

GEORGE BINWADDIE STEPPED back from the car. He saw a man rush out from the Legion Hall and stop at the door. The man yelled something at George. George put the barrel of the pistol in his mouth. The front sight caught on the roof of his mouth and cut him. He closed his eyes and imagined the cartridge in the chamber flush against the firing pin. He squeezed the trigger for the second time, and his world ended.

8

We Count Them
Happy Which
Endure

*S*heriff Buddy Tidwell pieced together the events of the 24th as best he could. There had been, he discovered, a single eyewitness to the suicide, one Darrell Flacy, formerly of Monroe, now of Hobbs, New Mexico, who said he was passing through town hauling produce to Atlanta and was just making a phone call, one he should not have been making he told the sheriff, but you do funny things when you've had a few drinks, you understand. The sheriff nodded, said, Go on. He was making the phone call in the anteroom of the Legion Hall when he heard a gunshot. He hung up the phone—I took the shot as a sign— opened the door and saw this nigger with a pistol. And all of a sudden it was like Nam again. I like to wet my pants, Sheriff.

But before I could do anything, the-guy-who-turns-out-not-to-be-a-real-colored-after-all slips the muzzle into his mouth and fires. He opened his eyes at the last moment. Then I realize there's a horn blowing and it's the Mustang, and then I saw it was Angelo—I knew him from high school, the service, the Legion, everywhere—and I went back to the phone and called the ambulance. Glad I was able to help. He would have bled to death, I suppose. But now, if it's okay, Sheriff, I got to get the rig on the road. Thank God, he's all right.

But, of course, Angelo was not all right. The bullet from the .22 caliber pistol (owned by a Mr. Edmund Baird Pettis of Cheniere Street in Calhoun) had entered Angelo's skull above the left eye and shattered his forehead. The missile penetrated the gray matter of the brain, boring a three-inch tunnel through Angelo's memory, imagination, self-consciousness, verbal faculties, and whatnot, before it lodged snugly in the cerebrum above his molars. Angelo was miraculously alive, breathing even, but he was decidedly not all right.

Apparently, George Binwaddie, Sheriff Tidwell surmised, stayed in his room at the Layton Castle until 3:30 P.M. when he walked up South Grand to the courthouse and used a phone in the lobby to call Tenille Suzenau who agreed to work his shift at the Rise 'n' Dine. (So that when George did not show up at six the following morning, Tenille was forced to work sixteen hours straight, Willis himself being on a fishing vacation to Toledo Bend. And not just sixteen hours, but sixteen unmerciful hours. Soon as word got out about the attempted assassination, why the Rise 'n' Dine was packed with media types and curiosity seekers [those that sit up nights with their police scanners on] and all of them hungry as wolves.) George told Tenille he needed to make changes in his life. He needed to start tonight. After calling Tenille, he bought a cherry snowball at the snack bar just to get change and made another call to the loan officer at Central Bank about a personal loan for $5,000 that he wanted. George learned that his application had been declined. He went back to his room and wrote the following note: "You cannot do this to a man—to leave him with nothing. And I cannot live with disgrace." He left the note on his bed. He evidently packed everything he owned in a trash bag and carried it to the Salvation Army Thrift Store. On his way out of his yard, he took a shot from close range at a mulberry tree and split the bark. He left another note written on the back of a Palms Motel postcard and slipped it beneath the Fontanas' back door: "I came by. You weren't home. So long. George." That would had to have been between 6:45 and 7:15 when Earlene Fontana said she walked to the Safeway for salad dressing and paper products. And then there is a gap of an hour or so in Sheriff Tidwell's reconstruction. At approximately 8:15, George turned up at the American Legion Hall, bought himself a presbyterian, chatted awhile with Bobby Tubbs, the bartender, about the Saints' chances this year (bad, Bobby thought), about the price of the new Ford pickups (outrageous), and about this Watergate business (communist-inspired). George told Bobby a joke about the meaning of life, how life was like a fountain or not like a fountain, which Bobby did not get. It must have been 8:45 or close to it when George went to the men's room and didn't come back.

On his person when he died: twelve dollars in single bills, seventy-eight cents in change (one of the pennies was steel), three keys on a metal key ring, an LP&L ballpoint pen with the company's logo and motto: "We Light Up Your Life," a package of chlorophyll gum, and a brown cowhide wallet containing a social security card, a Louisiana driver's license, Fox Ledbetter's business card, and a color photograph of a baby.

Why would anyone want to kill Angelo Candela? the Monroe *News-Star* wanted to know in its morning edition. He hasn't done anything in Baton Rouge that would offend anyone. He had voted with the party on every piece of legislation and had served the people of his district well. Well enough, anyway. He hasn't embarrassed us. The article mentioned that this was Binwaddie's second attempt on Candela's life, outlined recent financial doings regarding the Palms, and wrote off the attempted murder as another illustration of the simple, albeit profound, envy of the failure at the achievement and celebrity of the success.

The following day, the paper carried a letter to the editor written by Mr. Walker Ludy of Saw Mill Road in Holly Ridge, which pointed out a number of similarities between John Fitzgerald Kennedy and Angelo Candela. Both, of course, were Democrats and Catholics; both belonged to families with histories of political involvement; both liked dogs; both took bullets to the head; "John Fitzgerald Kennedy" has twenty-one letters, "Angelo Federico Candela" has twenty-one letters; Kennedy's mother's name was Rose, Angelo's mother's name was Lily; Kennedy was from the northeastern U.S., Angelo from northeast Louisiana; both were war heroes; J.F.K. had a girlfriend named Marilyn Monroe, A.F.C. once dated Doreen Boston; Kennedy had a secretary named Lincoln, Candela had a secretary named Carr; President Kennedy's wife watched him get shot, Senator Candela shot his wife. Coincidence? Mr. Walker Ludy asked. Perhaps.

And it did not take long for a conspiracy theory to surface. There was the matter of the weapon. Eddie Pettis of Calhoun and George Binwaddie of South Grand Street had been both frequently seen at the same Concordia Street house, Binwaddie allegedly visiting the Fontanas before they moved, Eddie Pettis the McCaskills. Maybe they were. But just maybe they had another purpose in mind. At the time of the assassination attempt on Kansas Street, Eddie Pettis was only a quarter mile away abusing the counter help at the Sonic. Now perhaps he was only hungry, but just possibly he was Binwaddie's getaway driver, a driver who panicked, a driver who abandoned his coconspirator. After all, Eddie Pettis was known to have political ambitions and was known to frequent the Legion Hall and would have known that Angelo, a creature of habit, would show up at the bar at 10:30 on Saturday nights, drink two shots of Southern Comfort, buy the house a round, shake hands, and leave. After all, this was not Mr. Pettis's first encounter with the criminal justice system. Last year Sheriff Tidwell picked up Eddie for firing off a pistol (the very same) outside his trailer at three in the morning. Eddie told Buddy then how he was trying to kill this milk snake that was trying to suckle his Golden Lab bitch. If, as Mr. Pettis claims, he did not know George Binwaddie from a horned toad, then just how did this depressed and dispirited short-order cook who had, some said, nothing left to live for, get the pistol that he fired twice that evening? Could it be possible that Eddie Pettis, disgruntled office seeker, used George Binwaddie to clear himself a path to Baton Rouge?

Certainly possible, some of our citizens thought. But, in fact, there was no way to link Eddie Pettis to the shootings. So except for a bit of unsolicited but not totally unwelcomed notoriety, the loss of a pistol impounded by the Sheriff's Department, and a boost in prestige around the McCaskill household, Eddie Pettis found his life unchanged. He wondered who the hell ever got the notion that he was interested in politics. He'd have to watch what he said when he was drinking.

What the mayor, Tommy Candela, and the county Democratic Committee (seven of whom, incidentally, had founded the White Citizen's Council some fifteen years earlier) decided to do was to leave well enough alone. Just let Angelo serve as state senator. Why this might even work out advantageously, the committee figured, but no offense, Tommy. And none taken, boys. This way, with Angelo harnessed into a wheelchair and all, the committee would know at all times where he was at, know that he'd be on the floor for all the key votes (as in "on the *Floor*," not prostrate on the floor—he'll be in that nice electrical buggy we're going to buy for him), know for certain how he'd vote. The committee was sure as hell not about to let what's-his-face, Mr. Runner-up Barbecue King of the Congo, take their legislative seat away from them. And even a special runoff election would prove costly and difficult. No, they would hire them someone to stay with the boy, dress him, direct him in and out of the state house, get a nurse or whatever to feed him through that tube deal. Someone mentioned Hazel Currence. Good idea. I'll call her, Tommy said. And, of course, Hazel will push the buttons we ask her to push.

Certainly no one in Baton Rouge could object to another enfeebled legislator. Why, Angelo was not even comatose. Someone said there was a precedent for this sort of thing. I think, he said, some Cajun from Galliano or somewhere was a certified lunatic and sat at his desk in the chambers wearing a straitjacket and leg irons. Got reelected, too. And anyway there are enough senators too drunk, half the time, to speak, stay awake, or even be counted on to hit the appropriate yea or nay. Tommy said what we'll do is we'll comb his bangs down over his forehead, cover that depression there. Won't look so gruesome on television. Yes, and you know the kids, the young voter, might even go for that look. It's mod, I think they call it.

Well, Hazel took the job and asked Dencil if he might could watch the boys for her while the legislature was in session. Baton Rouge was no place to raise a child, God knows. He could stay at the motel. No, he said, that would be too sad. I'll rent us a double-wide at the Fish Creek Trailer Park. I've seen them; they're nice. And I've got the money now.

A month after the shooting, Angelo issued a statement to

the press saying that he was fit and anxious to return to work. He couldn't talk, the statement read, and he couldn't move very many of his body parts, but his brain was as sharp and as curious as ever, and his heart, well, who could ever question his heart? And no, he wrote, it was not time for a hysterical call for gun control; after all, guns don't kill or completely paralyze and maim people, people do. Our Constitution gives us the Divine Right to own and bear arms, and he is going to work hard in the state legislature to see that that right is not infringed upon. And when he takes his seat, he'll be wearing a Smith and Wesson .44 in a shoulder holster. God bless America.

A couple of weeks after she moved with Angelo to Baton Rouge to prepare for the upcoming session, to hire a nurse, and so on, Hazel called the boys, inquired after their health and studies and asked could she speak with Dencil a minute. Webb went and fetched Dencil from the roof of the mobile home where he was installing a TV antenna. Dencil, she said, Angelo may still be a fine senator, but he's not a complete and useful man any longer. Yes, Dencil said. And he thought that maybe life could turn out sort of the way it was supposed to. I'll call you, he said.

9

High-Tension Lines

*D*own in Luna, Lonnie Mohammed has a hundred and eighty acres of buckshot planted in soybeans and another four hundred acres of sandy loam in cotton. Of that four hundred, Lonnie has six acres where the stalks grow quite nicely to about knee-high, and that by mid-May, but then begin to wilt and eventually to rot. It's been that same way five years on that same six acres. Always the same disappointing and bewildering results. Lonnie's had the extension service people out to his place a bunch of times, and they can't figure it. Shoots are hearty, soil is sweet enough, plants get dusted just like the others. What is it about this six-acre strip? The extension people shrug their shoulders, run some tests.

In Fondale, Vernon Hodge has this herd of Hampshire hogs who develop the peculiar inability to walk. They are always frisky enough piglets and robust shoats, but then before they are a year old, they begin to stumble. They can stand just fine, but they take a step and collapse. A veterinarian up from LSU told Vernon he'd never seen anything like it, but it looked to him like all the swine had contracted something along the lines of Meniere's Disease. Vernon said, All of them? How could that be, Doc? That's a good question, the vet said. My guess is that it's something genetic.

As everyone around here knows, but no one is able to explain, there has not been a frog gigged out of Coulee Creek in, it would have to be at least, seven years. And no one's as much as seen an alligator in Wall's Lake in about the same time. These same kinds of inexplicable and unsettling phenomena have been reported in Caldwell and Richland Parishes as well: yard dogs lacking all ambition; gamecocks whose beaks soften, turn oatmealy, slide off the face; clawless cats; barren layers; blind crawfish; ten thousand channel cats with hamburger gill belly up in Moon Lake. The single common factor in all these reports, we've learned, is that the anomalies have occurred directly beneath or within a hundred yards of high-voltage power lines.

Claudia Simmons did an investigative report on this business for the six o'clock news. She and Brent Madison, a public relations officer for LP&L, took a walk through Lonnie Mohammed's six acres. Brent pointed to the web of power lines above his head and looked into the camera and said how since electricity doesn't weigh anything, and knowing what we do about the law of gravity, electricity is unlikely—isn't it?—to tumble from the lines. He said this with a smile. Electricity needs a conductor, he told Claudia. So can you explain to me, Miss Simmons, how something up there, coursing through wires like blood through arteries, how something, I might add, that carries light and energy, happiness and technology, to so many people, how that force could somehow adversely affect one man's cotton, another man's cattle? No, this is not a matter of electricity, Miss Simmons. My guess is it's a matter of husbandry.

And that seemed to settle the matter for most viewers anyway, those not in danger from high-tension lines, not at play in electromagnetic fields. Some folks were more inclined to believe that crop and creature loss were God's own work. You want evidence, just look through the Bible. Plagues left and right. But God doesn't work that way anymore, our Catholics said. You saying God's some kind of humanist technocrat or something? our Baptists replied. And, well, that's a whole other matter. There were some around who believed that this business could not all be coincidental, but probably even they would be unwilling to relinquish their televisions and their central air just to save the occasionally brain-damaged squirrel. Taste the same anyway.

At any rate, none of this curious affair was on Billy Wayne's mind one Saturday morning in November 1973, as he sat at the kitchen table drinking coffee, his manual on High-Tension Lines and Rural Electrification lying open on the table to the chapter on insulators. What he was thinking then was how not so long ago he'd spent his days reading Meister Eckhart and Julian of Norwich, how not so long ago, on any morning like this one, he and Earlene would be talking, oh, maybe just gossip, but talking anyway, and not sitting silently at the same table.

Earlene tore a page off her tablet, balled it up, and dropped it with the others in a small pile in the fruit bowl. Billy Wayne watched her. He cleared his throat, but she didn't look up. He wondered what Earlene had meant back when she had told him that thing about love. About how the price of love is love. Love is not something you can understand. It is something you need. It's a knife that cuts when it's absent. Is that love? Billy Wayne exhaled audibly. Earlene looked across at him, and though he wanted to meet her gaze, his eyes dropped to the manual as if repelled. Insulators.

What makes it so hard to get to know what we want? And when we know it, to get what we want? And when we get it, to hold on to what we want? Could it simply be that our normal condition is profound ambivalence? That we are at once solo and social, reflective and spontaneous, wayfaring and planted? And when we are in love, we want our love to be both enduring and passionate.

Not so long ago, Billy Wayne had known what he wanted: a family, happiness, friends, a job, time to read, to think—a kind of normal life. And that's what he assumed everyone wanted. But now those old certitudes had surrendered to uncertainty, and Billy Wayne didn't know exactly when or how that had happened. His ignorance seemed to him a crucial flaw. Why hadn't he been paying attention? What could have been so important or so distracting that he had been unaware of the truth's slipping away? What was it that had seduced him into surrendering control of the single thing in his life he could govern: his own behavior? What could have been more important than his own life? For a moment, Billy Wayne felt the unfamiliar flush of self-pity. He had forsaken his priestly vocation for a job, a job he liked well enough, sure, but not one he wanted to be doing for the rest of his life. He had given up Tami Lynne for the sake of marriage, and yes, that had been the right thing to do. Still, he felt a kind of martyr's pride at his sacrifice.

Earlene sat at the kitchen table. Between her and Billy Wayne, a wall of books: her dictionary, synonym finder, rhyming dictionary, her Walker Evans book of photographs, her songwriter's manual, and her atlas of the United States. She looked up at Billy Wayne when she thought she heard him sigh, but his eyes only darted from hers like startled bream. He hid in his manual. "High-Tension Lines." She liked that phrase and she liked all the photos of the line towers on the page the manual was opened to. The towers looked like robots about to draw their ray guns or like a chorus line of salesmen about to lift up or set down their pairs of suitcases, but all, for the moment, frozen with indecision. She wrote down the title on the top of a blank page. "High-Tension Lines." Sometimes a song could start like that. She thought about it. She'd write a song about a utility worker, someone who installs the power lines, drives a brush hog, and about his wife and how she was being neglected. Let's see. Well, she couldn't write it just yet because, of course, she knew who these people were. She'd have to forget about real life if she were going to get anywhere, have to make up a tall and blond husband named, maybe, Carl. Yes, that was good. She could see Carl's worn jeans, dusty cowboy boots and his plaid Pendleton shirt. Sometimes the right name will do that for you.

She'll put him where? In North Dakota. She opened the atlas. In Minot. Give him a scar over his left eye, a brother Larry to drink with. And where they drink is a little saloon out by the state fairgrounds called the Cottonwood or the Upper Souris River Club. The tables in the saloon are oiled pine and deeply carved with names, initials, and hearts, arrows, crosses. And the wife has a baby, and she's tired all the time. She has light brown, almost red, hair. She dreams of planting an herb garden in the yard behind the bungalow. The wind out here is driving her crazy. Some days she presses her nails into her arm until it bleeds. Some days she puts the baby in its Snugli and walks and walks. She sings to the baby. The baby is a girl. What do you name a baby girl in North Dakota? Ruthie. The mother and child are in the kitchen. The mother, Claire, sings "I've Got Peace like a River," and Ruthie falls asleep.

Earlene looked past her husband through the sunny window to the bamboo and beyond that to the mildewed gray clapboards of the Willet house next door. "You never say you love me, Billy Wayne."

"I do too tell you."

"When was the last time?"

"I don't keep track, Earlene. I don't write everything I do down in a notebook with dates and times."

"Told me you loved me without my having to ask you to. That's what I mean."

"So if I say 'I love you' after you bring it up, the emotion is invalid? Jesus, Earlene. I love you. You're my wife."

"I'm twenty-two years old, and my marriage is in trouble. And I want to know why. So just don't treat me like an idea, Billy Wayne. I'm more important than that."

Billy Wayne thought that he should reach across the table and touch Earlene's elbow or maybe get up and go over to her, hug her, kiss her neck.

"What am I supposed to think? Either you don't love me," Earlene said, "or you take our love for granted because it's not important to you for some reason."

"That's not true."

Earlene thought, "Taking love for granite. Taking it for granite. Love as a rock. Love as a tombstone." She'd have to fool with this later. Earlene said, "Count your mercies, Billy Wayne."

"What do you mean by that?"

"Why don't you just tell me what's troubling you. What's going on?"

"It's George, I think. I want my friend back."

"What else do you want?"

Billy Wayne looked at Earlene as if trying to read the correct response. "Well, what do you want, Earlene?"

"I want your love."

"You've got it. There. Easy."

"So what do you want, really want?"

Billy Wayne knew that he couldn't repeat what Earlene had said and seem sincere. "Sometimes I want a different history. I want a child. I don't know what I want. A lot of things, I guess."

Earlene stood and put her coffee cup into the sink. "It all adds up to nothing, Billy Wayne." She leaned against the sink and looked at her husband. "Friends, history, salvation. In the end, they add up to zero. All that matters is me. You will always have me. Do you understand that? Do you? And only me." Earlene held her crotch. "This is your future, Billy Wayne, right here. You'd better grab it while it is still available to you."

"Don't talk like that, Earlene."

"Oh, don't get holy on me, Billy Wayne, just don't."

"Why? Why shouldn't a person want to be holy, like you say?"

"Because saints really put people off, you know. Don't try to be a saint. It won't work. Just try to be a human being. That's harder anyway."

" 'Holy' was your word. I'd say I'm just trying to figure things out."

"Well, you don't have to figure everything out. Just relax and be honest. Can you do that?"

"It's hard to relax."

"St. Billy Wayne of Chauvin Bottom, ex-Virgin and Martyr, Patron Saint of Uneasy Husbands." Earlene smiled. "Do you want to be married, Billy Wayne?"

"Of course I do."

"Because, you know, being a bachelor and being independent are not the same things."

"I know that. Who said they were? How do you know I even feel that way?"

"Sometimes we're the last to know."

"You're wrong, Earlene. You're saying this is what I'm feeling or thinking, but you don't have a clue, you know that? You don't believe what I tell you. You believe your—what?—intuition?"

"Billy Wayne, you're all talk and no cider." Earlene turned to the sink and took the blue sponge from beside the Joy. She wet it, squeezed it damp, and wiped the table. She sat and stood the sponge on its end. "Married got teeth, Billy Wayne. That don't mean you run from it. Don't mean you look for your fun elsewhere."

"I'm not a child, Earlene." He wondered just what she knew.

"The earth and the moon can't exist without each other. If they fall apart, that's the end of both. It's like love is gravity."

Yes, it is, Billy Wayne thought. It keeps you spinning in space. Holds you down.

"The end of both. Earth doesn't get to sing its way through the universe on a new orbit."

"I get the point."

"Is there anything I should know?"

"All you need to know, Earlene, is that I love you."

10

The Lonesomeness

*B*illy Wayne sat in the company's yellow pickup waiting for the thunderstorm to let up so he could fetch the brush hog from the cottonwood thicket and load it onto the trailer and haul it back to the Forsythe Park substation. He had the squelch turned low on the two-way radio, and, following Earlene's example and Sister Helen's advice, he was writing down his thoughts. He wrote quickly. When you write things down, he realized, you see you have more on your mind than you think.

He had started out by describing images that distressed him. But he kept on thinking of other things. So now he had the original project on the seat beside him and notes to himself on business he needed to take care of on the dashboard beside the plastic St. Christopher statue. St. Christopher himself looked out on the rain as if he wasn't sure he was going to carry any more travelers across any swollen rivers just yet. Meanwhile, in the tablet on his lap, Billy Wayne wrote: So it's not what we do that matters, but where we do it.

His working thesis, so to speak, was this: that a person's mental health is based, at least in part, on how that person behaves in public, how he conducts a conversation, meets your eye or doesn't; in general, how he comports himself as a social being. When the shades are drawn and the door is bolted, a man alone can get away with anything.

(In this context Billy Wayne might have noted, but did not, the curious behavior of his own great uncle, Mendel Fontana. By all contemporary accounts, Mendel was an astonishingly attractive young man, slim and dimpled, tall for a Fontana at nearly six feet, auburn haired, and with prominent cheekbones and eyes silvered like a timber wolf's. Like his brother Cotton, Mendel earned small money by hauling moss to the gin in West Monroe and by gathering mussels in the Ouachita and selling their shells at a nickel a bushel to the button factory on Walnut Street. But unlike his brother, Mendel enjoyed wearing his mother's clothes, enjoyed having his hair marcelled, and longed to see a real city like Memphis, or St. Louis, or New Orleans. In order to finance his journey, Mendel entered the 1925 Miss Monroe Beauty Pageant and Bathing Girl Review which was held at the old Paramount Theater. For his talent, Mendel recited the opening chapter of his favorite monograph, S. S. Hall's "The Bliss of Marriage, or How To Get a Rich Husband." Mendel finished second in talent to Theda Swanson who arched her back so that her hands and feet were both on the floor and walked up and down a flight of stairs, but he won the title anyway, accepted a fifty-dollar check, a bouquet of feral irises and a spongy kiss from Mayor Beau Hudnut, and walked down the runway as

Professor Frank Fabregas's Great Louisiana Field Artillery Brass and Reed Band played "The Louisiana Oyster Commission Waltz."

The Monroe *Daily Star* ran Mendel's photo on the front page of its Sunday edition, and that's when all the trouble started. "Mendy" Fontana was recognized, it seemed, by everyone in town who had not attended the pageant. And then the Vicksburg *Ledger* ran a feature about how the most beautiful woman in Monroe was a man. All the little papers in the Delta picked it up. And so did the city papers in New Orleans, Jackson, and even up in Cairo. And then the Monroe jokes started:

Q. What's wider and uglier than a mud fence?
A. The reception line at the Monroe Debutante Cotillion.

And like that. On his Saturday-morning radio program, the mayor told Mendel directly that he, Beau Hudnut—I'm speaking as a man not a public official, son—owned a balling iron and a castrating knife and he knew how to use them, and should you ever cross my path again, you can count on losing what you evidently don't need nohow. Of course, by that time, Mendel was in New Orleans where he found work as a stevedore and love with Ulicious Toussaint.

Billy Wayne leaned his head against the window and listened to the rain drum the roof of the cab. He thought of Earlene's song about the modern age motel, and he thought about the Palms and about George. He couldn't picture George very clearly. George was an afterimage, like the red cafe curtains in the kitchen that turn green and float in darkness when you close your eyes. The single detail of George's face that Billy Wayne now recalled was his own parabolic face looking back at him from George's pupil. Is there a difference, he wondered, between darkness and invisibility?

Why couldn't he remember George in vivid detail? He tried

to recall what was on the floor of the truck. Well, the rubber mats, some dirt. He opened his eyes. Without shifting position, he saw a Lester Lightbulb memo pad with his bootprint on the top page, an empty sandwich bag, and an oak leaf. How is it you don't see what you're looking at? Like Queen Anne's lace. He'd been looking at fields of it for years and had never noticed the purple dot in the center of the flower.

Billy Wayne stretched, yawned, put his legs on the seat, his head on the seat back. He was half asleep, he realized. He often had insights in these slumbering, semiconscious moments. If the rain stopped, would the quiet wake him up?

He tried to hear George's voice. When he had first listened to it, the voice gave him goose bumps, tingled his neck and shoulders, caused his face to relax, his eyes to close. The melody of George's voice had soothed him. When he thought of George, Billy Wayne thought of himself, his own darker, brooding, driven self. He should have known the desperation that drove George to suicide. But could he have done anything to prevent it? You can have all the light you want, but without bodies for it to illuminate, the light is useless. Billy Wayne said, George, you killed yourself. What am I going to do with you?

Billy Wayne was parked on Island Drive just where Bayou DeSiard enters the Ouachita. North, beyond the dam, lay Chauvin Bottom and across the street, the Pargoud Indian Mound. Legend has it that Ucita's daughter Wichita was buried here. Wichita had saved the life of one Juan Ortego, an officer in the Narvaez expedition. Because it was customary in such cases or because he felt grateful or guilty or because he was in love, whatever, Juan Ortego married Wichita. However, when the expedition broke camp and moved on, Ortego abandoned his wife and went away with his people. Wichita died, they say—they would—of a broken heart.

Billy Wayne wondered if Earlene had saved him? Maybe.

And maybe she was the last hope for the survival of the Fontana clan. Just maybe she was saving Billy Wayne and all those who went before him, saving them all from oblivion. She was the woman he left the priesthood for. Billy Wayne looked beyond the mound at the muddied yellow brush hog glazed with rain. I sure don't feel saved, he thought.

11

Come Close
My Dying Eye

*A*fter their supper with Earlene, Billy
Wayne and Sister Helen walked across to
Forsythe Park where in twenty minutes Hotson would pick
them up for the ride to the airport. They sat at the picnic
table near the tennis courts between the large magnolia and
the double-trunked oak, the picnic table that since Billy
Wayne's childhood they had thought of as their own. Billy
Wayne ran his fingers along the carved graffiti, his own "fiat
lux," the heart with the "JD L CC," the "Red Wuz Here," the
"Donny '59."

"Is everything all right?" Sister Helen said.

"You're leaving."

"I mean at home. You and Earlene."

"I haven't felt happy, haven't felt connected to Earlene."

"What have you done to feel that way?"

Billy Wayne had been, he realized, hoping for sympathy, sympathy that would dismiss the subject. He was disappointed.

"Are you lonely?"

Billy Wayne nodded.

"I'll miss you." Sister Helen coughed into her hand, took a deep breath, looked up into the fading light of the sky. "This is it, you know. I'll never see you again."

"Sure you will. You'll be back for a visit."

"No." Sister Helen took a tissue from the left sleeve of her habit and wiped her eyes. "I won't be able to leave again. It was too hard the first time." She blew her nose.

"I'll come visit."

"No, you won't."

"Sure I will."

"That's okay. We'll write."

"Why are you going back?"

"My da needs me. I have to." Sister Helen thought for a moment. "Are you looking for an alibi, Billy Wayne, something to blame your unhappiness on?"

"Look at my history, my family. There's some code on our DNA that shorts out or something."

"I don't believe in DNA."

"This is science, Sister."

"Just don't blame some ribbon of enzymes for what you've become." Sister Helen laughed. "Look at me, giving you a lecture instead of saying good-bye."

"Here's our ride," Billy Wayne said.

Hotson pulled up, hit the horn once and waved. Billy Wayne and Sister Helen got in the backseat. "I got your luggage from the hospital. We're all set," Hotson said. Hotson told Billy Wayne to look at the new issue of *Science*. The one with the cell on the cover. Said it had an article about how they found out that mice—you're not going to believe this one—how mice can detect genetic differences in other mice by smell.

"We were just talking about genes," Billy Wayne said.

"And another article about catfish. At Memphis State University they're breeding catfish with all male progeny. Sound familiar, Billy Wayne? Helen, take the issue of *In These Times* that I left on the seat. Good article on Liberation Theology in Latin America. And Fox says so long."

"Tell him I'm praying for him."

"I will. He'll like that."

On the way back from the airport, Billy Wayne sat up front. Hotson said, I'll just drive, and he did, down Highway 80 all the way to Quebec, forty-six miles, before anyone said anything. Hotson pulled into the dirt lot of a windowless juke joint. "Want a drink?"

Billy Wayne nodded. They sat there. Hotson took a pack of Luckies from the visor.

"Fox says he's done with chemo."

"Shit." Billy Wayne looked at Hotson. "What's he going to do?"

"Morphine. And just get on with it."

"Goddam."

"Look, I'll get us a couple of bourbons in go-cups and we'll just keep driving."

"Where does it end?"

"What's that?"

"Nothing."

12

Jazz Band on My Tailgate

ometime before dawn on October 23, 1973, Fox Ledbetter, the last of his line, died in his sleep after drifting pleasantly enough, we would like to think, in and out of his narcotic dreams, waking perhaps, that last time to hear Louis Armstrong sing "St. James Infirmary" on the cassette player. Fox died on his great-great grandmother's Victorian daybed out on the veranda. He wore blue flannel pajamas, a black silk kerchief, wool socks, cordovan slippers, and a diaper. His nurse, Tolice Heimsoth, found Fox and covered him with a quilt before she called first Dr. Von Robinson and then Mulhearn's Funeral Parlor. The quilt had been sewn by Fox's first nanny, Elzadie Jaxon, from patches of his own baby clothes some thirty years earlier. Tolice told

Benton Mulhearn that Fox looked brittle, pasty, and infantile. She said he smelled like sharp cheese.

Fox weighed less than one hundred pounds when he died and had seemed to grow, if that's the word, unmercifully younger in his last couple of months. His eyes and brow seemed larger, more prominent, his chin and nose thinner. Indeed, his head now seemed too large for the narrow shoulders, the attenuated limbs. His runny eyes fought to stay open; his mouth no longer closed over his suddenly enormous teeth.

It doesn't seem right to lose a friend and character like Fox. And, of course, it isn't right. It's not that his death was unexpected. But how do you prepare yourself for the haste and vehemence of this devastation? It would be gratifying, not to say entertaining, to have had Fox around for the duration of our story. He would have evolved before our eyes into, well, who can imagine what? Perhaps, he would have fallen in love again. He could be there this morning at his office, phone line on hold, reading *Light in August* or *Wise Blood* for the tenth time. He could look up and see the cockroach negotiate a path across his computer keyboard, climb up and into the disk drive. Fox might consider instinct and intelligence, the oldest living things and these new silicon brains. Put your money on the roach, he'd think. He might go to lunch at the Dinner Bell with Hotson, order the fried chicken special with loganberry pie, talk about Latin American politics or event horizons. Or he just might call Claudia Simmons—it's her day off—see if she might want to drive out to that catfish place on the river in Fondale. He'd ask her if she's ever been to Mardi Gras. He'd host another and then another Carp Fishing Derby. He'd finally learn to play the saxophone. So much for life imitating art.

Fox had the chance to consider his death, to deny it, to come, if that's possible, to terms with it, to plan for it. What he believed was that there was nothing more than this—one body, one time. And this, of course, was distressing. There was no heaven, no hell, no Avalon, no Nirvana, no Elysian Fields, no reincarnation, no any kind of afterlife, and though that was unfortunate and disheartening, and however much he wanted to believe in a sweet by-and-by, in life everlasting, Fox knew that to do so would be romantic, ingenuous, and perverse. He understood, or thought he did, how fear and disappointment may have first motivated man to presume divinity and paradise. He just couldn't buy it. There was no solace here. Death was not a crossing. It was nothing. But this oblivion, Fox believed, could be ennobled if it served to inspire us to explore and to cherish what is precious in life. The way he figured it, knowledge of the void is grace. That's our salvation. Of course, salvation doesn't last long.

Fox was reading a century's worth of family obituaries when Billy Wayne stopped by for what would be their last evening together. Billy Wayne carried a six-pack of Lone Star longnecks under his arm. He walked into the dining room and saw Fox in his sweatshirt and jeans, sitting at the table amid a clutter of books, photographs, maps, audiotapes, newspapers, notebooks, and a typewriter. Billy Wayne sat, handed Fox a beer, opened his own. You're looking better, buddy, Billy Wayne said. Fox said, You're not here to bullshit me, are you?

The chandelier above the table was fully illuminated. A small gray cone of patchouli incense burned in a saucer on the table. "I hate the smell in here lately," Fox said.

"How are you feeling?"

"I used to think only good things hurt."

"I'm sorry, Fox." Billy Wayne sipped his beer. "I don't know what to say."

"I'm not taking this calmly, I want you to know. Do I look calm? I might look calm, but I'm just tired." Fox put his face in his hands then looked at Billy Wayne. "I'm weak, worn out,

vulnerable. I'm trying to muster some, ah, courage, somewhere. I lost mine when my hair fell out. Can I borrow some
of yours?" He smiled.

"What little I've got."

"You want to hear something? Listen to this." Fox unfolded
a yellowed strip of newspaper and patted it flat on the table.
"My grandfather's obituary. Monroe *Evening News*, January
30, 1921." Fox put on a pair of very old, steel-rimmed reading
glasses. "These were his," he told Billy Wayne. He read: " 'Sincere and profound expressions of sorrow and regret were
heard in subdued tones from young and old alike Sunday
morning past when the sad news was dispatched that the
unequaled combat between Wallace Youngblood Ledbetter
and the great adversary of mortals was ended and that the
King of Shadows was again the victor. A righteous Christian
has gone from among us. Peace to his ashes.

'Mr. Ledbetter was a man of sweet and modest manners
who was greatly beloved by all who knew him. He was a kind
and indulgent father and husband, a courteous neighbor, and
a citizen of sterling worth. The deceased was a member of the
First Baptist Church, was a founder of the Ouachita Parish
Free Public Library, and was well known in the area for his
cultural and social philanthropies. His passing will be especially mourned by our coloreds and Fontanas who have both
been the recipients of Mr. Ledbetter's generous goodwill and
bounteous largesse.' "

"It says that?" Billy Wayne asked.

"In black and white. Now listen to this." Fox picked up a
second newspaper article. "Now this is my grandmother. I
won't read it all. 'Mrs. Ledbetter's daily life was truly a benedic-
tion and in her quiet and lovable way will be so missed by her
friends at the First Baptist Church where she had attended
services and Sabbath School for fifty-eight years. The widow
of the late Wallace Youngblood Ledbetter was surprised by

the Reaper, having been taken suddenly and desperately sick with bowel trouble the previous Thursday, and despite every effort by Dr. Claiborne, remained in that condition until death relieved her suffering. Dr. Claiborne also confirmed that Mrs. Ledbetter had been seriously, but not morbidly, ill for a year with sclerosis of the brain.' " Fox tapped his forehead with a finger. "The brain again, you see."

Billy Wayne had been wondering if maybe right now somewhere in his own body some cell weren't twitching itself into a tumor. He handed Fox a bottle, finished off his own, and opened another.

"And then there's Aunt Elizabeth," Fox said. "She killed herself. Here she was a healthy, sociable, intelligent woman, married, a mother of two. Very animated and funny. I loved her. And then suddenly, at thirty-six, she lapses into this desolating depression. She ate rat poison which severely damaged her esophagus and her stomach but did not kill her. Then she threw herself down a flight of stairs. That was thought to have been an accident. All this time, by the way, she is not talking to or looking at anyone. Then she severed an artery in her arm with a chisel."

"Jesus!"

The two men sat quietly. Fox put a tape in his player. They listened to Al Green: "Through the storm, through the night, lead me on to the light." Fox said, "Now don't you get depressed, Billy Wayne. Look at me. I'm beyond depression. I'm sad. I won't deny that. I'm pissed off. I'm . . . well, maybe I am a little depressed. This is shit, Billy Wayne. Goddamn."

"Think positive, Fox. I read somewhere it's mind over matter. You can will away your illness."

"Mind *is* matter."

"Just keep thinking, 'I'm going to beat this.' Don't give up."

"A dying man thinks with his heart. You can't fool the

heart." Fox thought about what he had just said. "You have to trust your heart at this point, Billy Wayne. That's what I'm trying to do."

"Is there anything I can do?"

"I'm living in the past." Fox leaned back in the chair, stared up at the chandelier. He closed his eyes and the image of the lights remained, drifted to his right; he followed it. "I've got no future, and really the present, no offense, is intolerable." Fox took a sweater from the floor beside his chair. "This is a bad sign. What's it? Ninety-five degrees? And I'm cold. He put the sweater on, buttoned it, pulled the cuffs down his wrists. "*Homo memor*, man the rememberer. That's me. In a way, Billy Wayne, you're more important to me, more real to me, in your absence than your presence, in your going than your coming. It's not your fault. I'm back there on the day I met you. You're sitting at my desk asking me to help your friend George Binwaddie. You're wearing a maroonish shirt buttoned to the neck, but the collar buttons are undone. Khaki chinos, black sneakers. You keep twirling the hair behind your right ear." Fox folded his arms and smiled at Billy Wayne. "Tomorrow, I'll remember how sweet it was of you to drop by today, how clean and cold this beer tasted."

"Do you need anything, Fox? Can I run any errands for you? Deliver any messages or anything?"

"I never wanted to be a lawyer. I hate lawyers. Failed archi-tects, failed musicians, failed English majors. I wanted to read. I was good at it. I figured it must be as important as making plastic lawn Mexicans. Should have worked at a library, maybe written book reviews. I should have gone off with Betty Anne Teller."

"The minister's wife?"

"I loved her. She loved me. But I thought that would have been wrong."

Billy Wayne shook his head, looked at his hands. "I don't know."

"So here I am," Fox said.

The tape player stopped with an unnerving snap. It was so quiet without the music.

13

Documents

*D*ear Earlene Fontana:

We here at Cousins Music are pleased as can be to inform you that we have accepted two (2) of your songs ("Modern Age Motel" and "All-American Boy") for publication and recording. Congratulations!

As we are a new and a small (for now) company, we cannot afford the grand payments or royalties (as the enclosed contract indicates). However, we do like to nurture talented young songwriters and expect that our initial investment will pay off handsomely in the future. Please accept our modest but encouraging offer and think of it as a down payment on a great career.

Let me say that I particularly enjoyed the sense of (would

you call it?) a kind of grace in the face of horror and desperation that you have captured. Very contemporary. We have a couple of new artists in mind for your material: a boy from Smackover, Arkansas, named Clare (we might change it) Holcombe, who if he's not the next Faron Young I don't know who is; and a sweet young thing from Ohio somewhere named Tracy Ellen Stafford who is a sort of winsome Kitty Wells, if you know what I mean.

Please sign all copies of the contract and return ASAP (as soon as possible). Please send more songs please. P.S. I will be in your area the week after next (family matters in Morehouse Parish) and will try to reach you by telephone. Perhaps we could have dinner.

Sincerely,
Lurleen Dooley, President
Cousins Music
1229 21st Avenue
Nashville, TN 37214
(Music City, USA)

October 24, 1973, Monroe, Louisiana
From the Ouachita *Citizen:* "Local Barrister, after Brief Illness"

Mr. Fox Aaron Ledbetter, Esquire, died yesterday at his home on Riverside Drive after a brief illness described by him as a "shadow on the brain." He was 36.

Mr. Ledbetter attended Neville High School in the city and was valedictorian of his 1955 graduating class. He attended Tulane University and LSU Law School. He was the son of the late Mr. and Mrs. Larkin Ledbetter and the nephew of City Solicitor Marcus Ledbetter.

In addition to his modest law practice at 137 Bres Avenue, Mr. Ledbetter was a docent at the Masur Art Museum and a member of the museum's board of directors. He also served as a trustee at St. Francis Hospital.

Funeral arrangements are being handled by Mulhearn's Funeral Parlor. There are no calling hours.

Louisiana Power & Light: Accent On Safety

Issued in the interest of accident prevention by the Safety Department, Northeast Division, Ruston, Louisiana

Location: Northeast District, Chauvin Bottom, Monroe

Injured's Classification: 3/C Lineman

Injured's Name: Dencil Currence

Type of Injury: Burns on chest and left arm. Sprained ankle and wrist.

Description of Accident—Summation

The transformer, a 25 KVA CSP, w/cutout, single bushing 13800 GRDY/7970 × 120/240 with no secondary neutral to tank strap, had been connected to the newly installed 1/0 3/c secondary cable.

All other grounds and neutrals connected to the energized transformer were disconnected causing the transformer tank to be energized at primary voltage—7970 volts. (See illustration.)

The only path to the ground for the primary connection was through the transformer hangers and the pole; therefore, the pole began to smoke and burn. Mr. Currence, who had climbed the pole was instructed by the foreman to come down. In the process of unbelting, the lineman apparently made contact with the transformer case or the secondary rack, which may also have been energized at the primary voltage, and a house service neutral, causing him to fall off the pole to the ground.

Remember: A transformer tank should *never* be disconnected from an energized transformer. Always check for the presence of a secondary neutral to tank strap on this type of transformer.

P.S.: Mr. Currence is resting comfortably at his home and is expected back to work within the week. He thanks you for your cards.

Hint of the Week: Dead lines or feeders must not be tied together.

14

When the Gates of Death Were Opened, Did You See the Darksome Doors?

*B*illy Wayne ordered the catfish basket with a side of fried dills and an iced tea. He folded the menu and handed it to the waitress. The cover read, "Everyone Comes to the Dinner Bell—A Tradition on the River Since 1936."

"Sweetened," she said, "or un-?"

"Sweet, please. Thanks."

Billy Wayne pulled a napkin from the dispenser and wiped his utensils. He nodded hello to the man two tables over, the cowboy from Spats', what's-his-name. "Doing fine thanks." Billy Wayne smiled. He rested his chin on his folded hands and looked out the window at the Ouachita. Not dead anyway, he thought.

He could just drift along like he was doing, follow the current where it carried him, keep clear of white water, wind up somewhere downstream eventually. What's so bad about that? No, he wasn't exactly happy about the quiet routine at home, but, of course, what's happiness got to do with it?

The waitress brought the tea and a straw. Ever since he could remember, Billy Wayne had been telling people, telling himself, that all he wanted out of life was to be happy. "Follow your bliss." Where had he heard that? He wondered was it too late to get a side of okra. He looked for his waitress. She was at the station smoking a cigarette, riffling through her pad of orders. He wouldn't bother her. He took out his notebook and pen from his shirt pocket. He wrote the word *happiness*. He'd make a list. He wrote, "1.) St. Francis." He closed his eyes and saw himself at three in Sister Helen's lap. They're on a rocking chair; maybe it's in his room. He's eating an orange. They play Mon Cheval where she bounces him faster and faster on her knee singing:

> *Mon cheval, allons au moulin.*
> *Doucement, tranquillement*
> *Il marche, il marche, il marche, il marche,*
> *Il trotte, il trotte, il trotte, il trotte,*
> *P'tit galop, p'tit galop, p'tit galop, p'tit galop.*

And she does it till he can't stop from laughing. He wrote down, "2.) Kentucky." All morning he heard voices praying in the chapel, smelled the starched pillowcases, saw the slotted light slanting through the blinds. Was it knowing that he did not have to rise in the cold and pad off to theology class that made him prize that moment? He remembered the jam jar of water on the bedside table and the pink paper straw in the jar and how the straw stuck to his lip when he sipped, how there were no bubbles in the water. He remembered thinking how the illness proved he was not like the others. He was a boy of almost intolerable sensitivity like St. Dominic Savio. He knew he would have to suffer for his compassion. He remembered someone, perhaps Brother Finton, placing a cool, damp wash-cloth on his forehead, muttering ejaculations. He tunneled under the blankets, snuggled back to his dreams. He even remembered the dream: He was in an oarless boat on a lake in heaven.

"Catfish basket. Dills," the waitress said.

"Thanks."

She set down the order. "Freshen that tea for you?"

"I'm all set, thanks," Billy Wayne told her. Across the room, Mayor Candela was sharing a joke with four gentlemen seated at a booth.

He'd been happy with Earlene, of course. The happiest was those first few days. Billy Wayne put down his fork a moment and wrote, "3.) Cheniere Lake." Happy not just making love. Happier than that. When they snuck out of the hospital early that first morning, they walked all the way to Bawcomville, got hold of Papaw's tent out of the garage, hiked out to Chen-iere Lake Recreation Area, and set up camp. For a day and a half they didn't eat. They could hardly untangle themselves from each other, could hardly talk fast enough about their tragic, but now insignificant pasts, their intense and noble emotions, their daring and marvelous future together. He remembered feeling confused and telling Earlene. She told him. "It's all right, Billy Wayne. You're a good person, and people know that about you. But you don't always need to do what you're told. You need to trust yourself. You're not a child anymore. You're a man now, Billy Wayne Fontana." This permission of Earlene's came as such a revelation to Billy Wayne that he wanted to cry. He held her there in the darkness of their tent, so black that he could not see her.

Billy Wayne wanted to leave now and call Earlene, tell her,

yes, he loved her. He wanted to drive right home and make love to her in the afternoon like they used to do. He was sick of worrying about the Fontana curse lurking just below the surface. Like original sin or something.

Fact is Billy Wayne was living a lie, going on pretending to Earlene that he was and always had been a faithfully monogamous husband, that he had not lived, was, indeed, not still living (how could he argue with that?—wasn't he still missing Tami Lynne, still daydreaming about her?) a double life? He was not the man she thought he was, not the man she married. No, he was instead this trifler who, every day, disgraced his wife with deception, who reinforced her shame by denying it. Billy Wayne put down his fork, wiped his mouth with a napkin.

The waitress said, "Is everything okay here?"

"Great, thanks. I'll have the ticket when you get a chance."

Billy Wayne put his notebook and pen in his shirt pocket. He checked his watch. He still had twenty minutes to get back to the Bottom. He pulled a five out of his wallet and dug in his pocket for change. Out the window, he watched a bass boat drift into the bushy thickets along the riverbank. Billy Wayne knew what to do. He would confess to Earlene, tell her everything. Billy Wayne paid his bill and went out to the truck. He started the engine. He remembered as a boy that feeling of invincibility after Confession, the way he might cross a street without looking both ways because even if he got slammed by the choir van of the Mount Giliad Missionary Baptist Church, he would go to heaven.

Billy Wayne thought about Tami Lynne, about the first time he'd stopped by her house with the used electric drill he'd bought at Delta Pawn and Gun. He was fixing to mount her traverse rods. She wore no jewelry, no makeup, a white T-shirt and dungarees. And then he saw her there in the truck beside him, her face in profile, the blue vein at her temple, the three little birthmarks on her cheek, the damp bangs pasted to her forehead. He stopped himself. He'd tell Earlene and make it soon. Maybe she knew already. Maybe she's just been waiting all this time for him to fess up. Maybe this confession would be just the proof she'd been waiting for, the proof that he loved her.

When Billy Wayne asked her out to eat, Earlene was both surprised and pleased. She wanted to tell him, I can't, I'm working on a song about a woman who buys a Ford Falcon for seventy dollars and drives it west until it breaks down which she takes as a sign that this is where her life starts over, here in Emporia, Kansas. But she didn't say that; she said, Where? The Mohawk. We always go to the Mohawk; let's go somewhere special. Billy Wayne called the Warehouse #1 for reservations.

Perry Mabry, who was their waiter that night, said that the only incident in his seventeen years at the restaurant that was a greater disaster was the foggy night in 1963 when a barge crashed into the stilts of the building and the whole restaurant listed three feet on its river side and all the tables and the diners started sliding toward the wall. You probably anticipated some ungodly scene, didn't you? Noble intentions (if that's what Billy Wayne's were) do not always effect sublime results. And sincerity does not always warrant understanding.

After they had eaten (Billy Wayne had frog legs, Earlene, fried oysters), Billy Wayne cleared his throat, fiddled with his flatware, stared into his water glass or out the window at the sunset over the Union Oil Mill, and told Earlene everything at once. He watched Earlene blanch, gag, and vomit on the table.

Billy Wayne slept in the company truck that first night, then checked himself into the Windsor World Motel on Louisville. He called Earlene every day. Finally, after two weeks, she agreed to talk with him. I've got an hour, she told him. I've got a job interview at one.

"What about your songs?"

"I'm finished with them."

"Oh, I get it, I'm responsible for that, too."

"Fuck you, Billy Wayne."

When they met over coffee at the Rise 'n' Dine, Earlene told him he could have the house. She handed him her keys. She was leaving and she had started divorce proceedings. Billy Wayne said, Wait a minute, I thought we could talk about getting back together, about going to counseling, you know. "I love you, Earlene. We can be happy again."

"It's over."

"Why does it have to be over?"

Earlene didn't care who heard it. Not Tenille who pretended to be filling ketchup bottles at the counter, not the landscaping crew in the next booth, not Margaret Grimes, sipping her coffee and doing the Jumble in the newspaper. She just told Billy Wayne, "Because right now, I hate you. And that hate is binding me to you. I don't want that, don't want to be attached to you in any way. I'm leaving you and that house and everything in that house including the Earlene Fontana who was foolish enough to live in a fantasy world, and blind enough to care about someone as deceitful and self-centered and cruel as you."

III

*F*ontana in Extremis

I'm hopeful but I wish I could be sure
And could arrange to be around when he endures
Revenge as cold as any I could plan
When the other woman finds another man.

—*Earlene Fontana and Tracy Ellen Stafford*
"When the Other Woman Finds Another Man"

1

Wonderful Power
in the Blood

*W*hen you are gossiping about someone,
what we say around here is you are syn-
dicating his name. Well, when news of the *Twin City Queen*'s
funereal voyage reached the nonboating rest of the town, why
our older citizens especially, those who had lived when scores
of Fontanas walked barefoot on our streets, traded in our
stores, and cheered like banshees for the Monroe Roustabouts
in the Cotton States Baseball League out at the old Casino
Field, those old folks began to haggle amongst themselves
about the jarring and, it would seem, climactic turn of events.
Billy Wayne Fontana's reputation was in considerable syndica-
tion all over town, at Rotary luncheons, in the lounge after
the meeting at the Barak Shrine Temple, in the parking lot

at the Woodsmen's Lodge, and just before and just after the Homemakers' Joyful Life Bible Study at the Peter Rock Baptist Church.

What folks were prattling about was all this: Earlene had disappeared, and no one, not Pawpaw even, knew where she'd gone. Russell Sikes divined that she was nearby, but he couldn't tell Billy Wayne just where exactly. But while Billy Wayne couldn't find his wife, he did find Angelo Candela and Hazel Currence living (when they weren't in Baton Rouge) with Dencil and the boys in Dencil's double-wide. That didn't make sense to Billy Wayne—having the man responsible for George's death in your house—and he said so.

Dencil explained how the boys were fond of Angelo, how he's no trouble at all, how Hazel sees he's fed through the machines, dresses him and stuff. Dencil, by the way, was feeling better, just his ankle hurt in the rain. Said he put in a bid on a new job in public relations—being Reddy Kilowatt. Just had to wear a funny red suit, attend social events, get photographed with engineers and like that. Piece of cake. No more poles and live wires.

The Binwaddie clan, sixty-seven of them including Uncle Akbar, had arrived meantime in Monroe and hired out the *Twin City Queen* for a New Year's Day memorial voyage to honor their late savior, George. They hired Dorsey Tatum to cater and Tremaine Davis to entertain, and they invited 142 guests. The family had somehow parlayed George's ownership in the Palms Motel into collateral for a loan from a CIA-backed Pakistani bank and then into a series of escalating arms deals and into a fortune. And on this trip up the Ouachita, Billy Wayne came face-to-face with his past.

He hadn't expected Tami Lynne, but there she was squeezing by him in the doorway to the lounge with her date Ted Muto, and she smelled of violets and levee grass. Billy Wayne said hello, smiled, watched her walk away. He thought about what Hotson had said—that a person can't stop loving whom he loves.

And then he saw Earlene at the rail of the first deck, wearing a long-sleeved black dress and her hair tied up in a chignon. She introduced Billy Wayne to her friend Royal Landry who excused himself. Billy Wayne told Earlene you don't get over people you love just in a few weeks. She told Billy Wayne she'd get over him just like she got over scarlet fever.

Some folks thought, well, this here impending divorce must be a sign of providential intervention, and if Billy Wayne is at all smart, and we know he is, he'll read that sign, heed its message, and maybe, we can hope, resign himself to the monastic kind of life that seemed preordained for him. It was rumored that someone had called a Father Michael Foley up in Kentucky and found out that Billy Wayne's return to the novitiate there might prove embarrassing. Satisfying, but embarrassing. On the other hand, everyone knew that seminaries all over the country were desperate for the warm bodies of good men. There was even an article about it in the *Citizen*.

Most folks, of course, did not know the couple personally, and so the discussions were seldom emotional, but rather cerebral, philosophical even. Folks looked upon the imminent childless divorce kind of like a fortuitous insurance fire. Not planned for, certainly, but not completely unexpected either. People surveying the smoldering ashes looked at one another, afraid to say anything about it, but glad to have escaped and happy to be able to start all over. What all this meant was that soon there may not be any Fontanas in Monroe. Some people, maybe even most people, had hoped for this. But then how would we define ourselves as a town without Fontanas? Sure, we were "The Pacemaker City" and we had the tallest TV tower in the state and more athletes per capita in professional sports than any other city in the country. Still, those were merely facts, not definition. Many speculative conversations took place over many a cup of washy coffee at many a restaurant about just what life might be like in the post-Fontana future. But before anyone could wax nostalgic, we received the unsettling news that Billy Wayne and Tami Lynne Curry were living together in what some would call sin. Honestly, folks were bewildered. "Does the boy understand," a lady at the cosmetics counter at Kresge's said, "that he is out there tap-dancing on the rim of nothing? Jesus Christ going to slap him down." The Reverend Dr. Jimmie Diggins said in a private conversation, "Have we been carried to the brink of relief only to be euchred by fate once again?" Our Methodists, you see, are used to substituting "Fate" for "God" when their faith has been shaken, as if not to let on what they don't want to know. We held our breath again.

One who was not flummoxed by Billy Wayne's erratic and, as far as folks in town were concerned, destructive behavior, was Russell Sikes. He told his little astrology group that before they left on their Thanksgiving trip to Machu Picchu, there would be one more Fontana on the earth. A Scorpio. Next thing we hear, Tami Lynne's in a family way. How does Russell Sikes know these things?

EARLENE HAD GONE, and there Billy Wayne was, an ex-husband-to-be at twenty-one, devoid of physical love, spiritual vocation, and emotional companionship. He did not afford himself time to think, but did the irrational thing and remarried just as soon as he could.

Nine months after she moved in with Billy Wayne, back to her old house on McKinley, to the home that she had planned to share with her first lover, Johnny Van Zell, Tami Lynne delivered her first child at St. Francis Hospital. That was November 12, 1974. They had married in June, just as soon as Billy Wayne's divorce became final. The birth was uneventful:

the boy weighed nearly eight pounds, had ears flattened to his skull in the Fontana style, screamed healthily enough and all. But the next day, a nurse discovered a problem. Turns out the child was born with a heart wired like a pinball machine. Tami Lynne phoned Billy Wayne at LP&L and told him to hurry to the hospital. "They found something the matter with the boy, Billy Wayne. I don't know what I'll do."

When he arrived at the neonatal ICU, Billy Wayne found his wife in a wheelchair staring at their baby, wrapped in tubes and tape, asleep in a glass case. Tami Lynne was crying. The unit was bright, shadowless, and cold. A nurse talked on a green wall phone. She had a finger in her other ear and was smiling. In an incubator beside Billy Wayne's son was this baby no bigger than a yellow perch.

"My God," Billy Wayne said.

"Maybe it was all that coffee I drank," Tami Lynne said.

Billy Wayne massaged her shoulders. "That's foolish, Tami Lynne," he said. "I'll talk to the nurse."

Billy Wayne learned that his son had gone from a jaundiced yellow to blue to white to pink and back again, that a specialist, a Dr. Rangaraj, had arranged for a series of tests to be run that morning, and beyond that, no one knew what the cause of the problem might be.

Billy Wayne watched the monitor attached to his son, saw how the erratic pulse suddenly and inexplicably twitched from a sedate 120 up to 275 and then jumped again to 400 as if the silver ball were jammed on a coil, He knelt on the floor by Tami Lynne. "It's my fault," he said.

"You mean that silly curse you talk about?" Tami Lynne smoothed his cowlick.

It was not what he had meant exactly, but he said, yes, the curse. "My family has had problems with this sort of thing before," he said. What really concerned Billy Wayne, however, was not the figurative sins of the father, but his own blatant transgressions. Hadn't he turned his back on his sacred vocation? And does not he that soweth the flesh reap corruption? Hadn't he also torn asunder what God had joined together? And will not this God punish such pride? Was this not the wages of his sins before him now, crying in its troubled sleep?

Tami Lynne stroked Billy Wayne's hair. "Look at me, honey," she told him. "Don't you worry none. We'll be all right, the three of us."

"I should have realized." Billy Wayne prayed. He wanted to know the boy just a little while, maybe just hold him, make him smile. That's when the monitor's alarm buzzed and the red light over the unit door flashed. The nurse, who had been on the phone again, hurried over, made sense of the monitor's paperwork, took a hypodermic syringe from her pocket, and inserted the needle into the baby's IV tube. In thirty seconds, the pulse was 150. "He's a tough little guy," she said.

"Nurse, has my boy seen a priest?" Billy Wayne said.

"No, he hasn't. Would you like me to call Father Corkery now?"

There may not be time, he thought. "No thank you. But perhaps you could help me with this."

The nurse held the top of the incubator open while Billy Wayne dripped water from an eyedropper on his son's forehead. He said, "I baptize you," and he thought, and the name came to him, "Duane Pargoud Fontana, in the name of the Father and of the Son and of the Holy Ghost. Amen."

Thus Billy Wayne, erstwhile altar boy and seminarian, reverted to his prelapsarian Catholicism and performed his one and only baptism on his dying son. But Duane survived. Doctors stabilized the heartbeat with drugs, and although optimistic, advised the parents to plan a prudent life for Duane, one that would not include, for example, midget league football, cross-country running, or anything else that might cause undue physical exertion. So distraught was the new father that he considered a vasectomy and had even scheduled himself an appointment. Tami Lynne begged him not to, showed him articles from the *Sons of Mary Newsletter* and the *Louisiana Journal of Medicine*, the latter making a correlation between vasectomies and the incidence of impotence. He canceled his appointment. He did, however, take precautions against another birth, at least until the evening, months later, after the wine, the steak Diane, and with Charlie Parker playing on the stereo, he finally succumbed to the relentless maternal pleadings of Tami Lynne.

And didn't the eyebrows lift all over town? and didn't the tongues clack? Here we had our physically corrupt evidence, as if we all needed it, our proof right off that the Fontanas were indeed unblest and bedeviled, cursed for certain, any fool could see that now. And that Billy Wayne had made a serious miscalculation in his dealings with the Almighty. We had our assurance, those who wanted it, and our entertainment, if that's not being too harsh. We had the promise of some years more of being able to witness and participate in this glorious tragedy that had so long been a part of our collective lives. There's an undeniable, if somewhat perverse, excitement in that expectation. "We can't let the nuns get their fists on this boy," is what folks were saying. "We could maybe try steering him toward a career in physical education. Coaching seems to keep them single. The whole football team's like your children is what does it. Course he's got the heart thing."

Dr. Rangaraj told the *Citizen* that Duane's difficulty was in fact a quite unspectacular malady, paroxysmal atrial tachycardia, not uncommon for some reason in first-born males, and easily treatable with Digoxin. Usually the therapy works in stabilizing the electrical signals that cause the heart to beat. It may recur at some later time when the medication is withdrawn, but normally it does not. When the patient reaches around seventeen or eighteen, he is out of danger. Yes, Dr.

Rangaraj told the reporter, he was indeed surprised to learn that for a hundred and whatever many years now, the Fontanas have sired only males. He wondered about the documentation, to be quite honest. Still at each birth, he said, despite whatever has happened in the past, the odds remain fifty-fifty that the child will be a girl. They never get any better than that. In this case, history has no bearing on the present. It will all even out over time, he said, you can be sure of that. He said he had read about a similar case in which an extended family of desert dwellers in Rajasthan had recorded 537 consecutive male births over a period of 83 years. The family insists the gender was determined by the fathers' diets.

IN A CORNER of their bedroom, Billy Wayne stood by the crib on the baby's first night at home and watched him sleep, watched the ribs expand and the legs twitch. He touched Duane's blotchy cheeks, the backs of his hands, his fuzzy hair. Now he knew that everything he had gone through, every pitiful mistake he had ever made, everything was worth it for this moment. He wanted to wake his baby up, ask him where he got the red hair. He lifted him up, carefully, holding the head still, and sat with him on the rocking chair in the dark and felt the slight weight on his arm. He stopped himself from touching the little chest.

2

I Have Begotten a Strange Son, Diverse from and Unlike Man

*I*t made all the sense in the world according to Hazel. Everyone involved stood to benefit, so why wouldn't Dencil see it? Why was he so put out by a piece of paper? That's all it is, a wedding license. Why's he so determined to canker her spirits? Nothing has to change, she tried to tell him. The plan was that Hazel would marry Angelo, and the sooner the better. This was Tommy Candela's brainstorm, and Hazel was happy to give him the credit for it. See, Hazel, by having her photo in the papers all the time wheeling Angelo to this committee hearing and that shopping center grand opening, holding his hands onto those big useless scissors they always give you to cut the ribbon, and like that, had earned herself a favorable reputation in Baton Rouge and on the home front, as a selfless, compassionate, and tireless woman, an angel of mercy. It was time, Tommy figured, to cash in on that reputation for the good of the Democratic party, the city, the entire Fifteenth District, indeed, the great and sovereign state of Louisiana.

It was becoming clear to everyone that Angelo was about to lose his usefulness. Should some local maverick decide to mount a primary campaign (and there was talk, Tommy confided to Hazel who shared it with Dencil, that that signifying parasite, Eddie Pettis, was considering just that, only we'll put the quietus on that in a hurry—set his bony ass in stir five minutes after he announces), and this candidate challenges Angelo to a debate or something, we'll be in trouble deep. It's a proven fact, Tommy explained, that your average voter likes some vigor in his politicians, likes to see some light in the eyes. Now if what Angelo had was a war wound, why he could be the Louisiana State Vegetable that he is and still win hands down. The voters reward a man who does what he's told. Unfortunately because of the damn press, everyone already knew the piddling circumstances.

So the deal was that Hazel marries Angelo in a quiet ceremony, decorous, but mildly festive, you know. Angelo's Catholic, so we'll do it over to the Little Flower of Jesus, if that's all right with you, Hazel. Tommy explained how Hazel's previous marriage to Dencil, being a JP affair was null and void as far as the Catholic Church was concerned. But, of course, Dencil recalled that it had happened, and he had the ring to prove it. Somewhere. Or had he pawned it? It may have happened historically, Hazel said, but legally the event had been expunged. Yes, Dencil, one of Tommy's colleagues took care of that little problem for us. The boys and I are Guidrys, soon to be Candelas. She gets the Candela name, and she runs for election in the fall with the support of the Candela machine. She wins the election, receives an income which is more than she's making now, not to mention the generous perquisites. Plus, she'll have the Candela apartment in Baton Rouge, the Candela house on Bayou DeSiard, a handsome slice of the Candela estate. As to the boys, well, they'll get adopted and will come into their share of the inheritance, plus, of course, they'll associate with a better class of friend, Tommy said, than that trailer park trash. Plus, if Hazel wanted them to, they could work as pages in the state house. Be good for them. A living history and civics lesson. Stand right there in the corridor where Huey Long was assassinated, something they won't soon forget.

Hazel explained all this to Dencil on the very day that he had gotten the job as Reddy Kilowatt at LP&L. The first Reddy had quit to become a weatherman/kids' cartoon show host/ clown at a TV station up in El Dorado. Dencil knew this was a job with a future. No more replacing capacitator fuses, no more installing secondary spreaders, no more bucket rides. When Hazel came in from her city hall meeting with Tommy, practically breathless with excitement, Dencil was wearing his Reddy Kilowatt costume, modeling it for the boys, who both thought it was outstanding. His ears were little white light sockets. The outfit was a red foam-rubber deal that made Dencil's arms and legs look like lightning bolts. And he wore white gloves and white boots and a white helmet shaped like a lightbulb with a little red lightbulb nose.

Hazel told Dencil they needed to talk. She sent the boys out to play. I don't care. Play catch, play Tet Offensive if you want. Just get out. She sat Dencil down at the table and spilled the plan. She assumed he was just as happy as she was until he took off his helmet, and she could see he was almost crying. He told her he thought it was a terrible idea. "It's cheap, that's what it is."

"Dencil, sometimes I just don't understand you."

"Tell me again how I'm better off in this deal."

Hazel shook her head. "Look at yourself. You satisfied to be a clown all your life? Where's your dignity, Dencil Currence?"

"All my life? I start on Monday. And I ain't a clown. I'm a symbol."

"I've made up my mind. I'm doing this for all of us. I'm going to marry that crippled man in the back room, and all you have to do is lay low for a while, Tommy says, till after the election. Then we're walking on Easy Street."

With that, Dencil hugged his helmet to his chest as if it, and not he, had been insulted, got up and took his keys from the little nail on the doorjamb, walked out the door, got into his truck, and drove away. When he didn't come home that night, Hazel called Billy Wayne and cried. Could you find him, Billy Wayne, please, and carry him home?

This was a Saturday morning. Billy Wayne called Hotson who said, sure, he'd love to go on a treasure hunt. So Tami Lynne, on her way to her seventh-month checkup at the OB/GYN clinic, dropped Billy Wayne off at Hotson's place near the college. Dencil probably hadn't gone far, Billy Wayne figured. He's got to be to work on Monday to get his publicity pictures taken. He wouldn't jeopardize his job, not after waiting for so long.

Webb and Ferlin had an idea where Dencil might be, and they told Billy Wayne when he called to check in with Hazel. Whichever one was on the phone said Dencil liked to go to this one particular place because it was so peaceful and he could think. But don't tell him we told you.

"Well, son, you haven't told me yet."

"Promise?"

"Promise."

"We're just worried."

"I know you are."

Dencil was out at Black Bayou Lake, out there in the middle, up in a duck blind. They saw his rent boat tied to a cypress, and tied their own john boat aside of it. They climbed the ladder.

"You been here all the time since last night?" Billy Wayne said.

Dencil nodded.

"You must be hungry by now," Hotson said.

Dencil pulled a paper sack out of his backpack. "I got water and a pile of palmetto hearts I cut on the way out." Dencil told them what Hazel had said, and they agreed it was a bad idea. What did he want to do about it?

"It makes me think that all she wants me for is the one thing, you know. Well, two things. Watch the boys for her, too. Jesus, I'll miss the boys if she takes them away."

They talked about their children. Hotson's little girl, Anna, was two now, and it was nice, he said, now that he and Ronnie split the cab driving that they both get to spend time with the baby. Billy Wayne said how now that Duane's found his lungs, they've had to stop going to the movies and restaurants.

Billy Wayne said, "Dencil, how do you tell those boys apart?"

"Easy. The way they walk. Webb keeps his head tilted to the left and looks down a lot. When they talk to you, Ferlin's always leaning in toward you. Besides, their teeth are altogether different. Webb's got the space in between." Dencil tapped his front teeth. "When's the baby due, Billy Wayne?"

"Two months."

Hotson said he was getting eaten alive and shouldn't they go. We'll stop at Strawberry Fields for a couple.

"I'll just tell her, 'No,' " Dencil said. "But then I'll do whatever she wants. She knows that. What else can I do? Won't be so bad, I guess."

"Thought of a name yet, Billy Wayne?" Hotson said.

"Tami Lynne's thinking of Boone if it's a boy, Kylie if it's a girl."

"And you?"

"I like pulling one out of the air."

In mid-July, the second child arrived. The unfortunate Boone Kyle was born with two tiny cartilaginous appendages resembling flippers more than legs. The doctors could offer no immediate explanation for this cruelly atavistic deformity and seemed genuinely embarrassed in the presence of this demi-child, as if they wished not to witness what they had wrought. Billy Wayne took the tragic birth as a further divine repudiation of his life and suffered guilt so overwhelming that he endured a prolonged season of lassitude, losing heart and energy for all matters connubial, familial, and financial. He only stayed on with LP&L, it seemed, because the work kept him out of the house. He was all the time brooding, one, or going through the motions. Oh, he held his child, rocked it, cleaned it, but he never gurgled at it like he had with Duane, never just stared at it, never hummed "Birdland" to soothe it to sleep.

Tami Lynne was patient with her husband, figuring he would come to terms with this child, with his life as it now stood, in his own time. She worried that he blamed her for the "tragedy," as he spoke of it. Blamed her for wanting the second child, for persuading him to have it. When she asked him about it, though, he denied it. When she said, Billy Wayne, it's not fair, you know, you're punishing me for this, and we should be grateful for our exceptional child, he said he was not trying to punish her. In bed, he would lie spooned against her, drape his arm across her waist. Tami Lynne, all she could do was stare at the clock on the bedside table, listen at the baby's snuffled breathing, imagine how it would be when someday Billy Wayne came to his senses, and they were the one big, sweet family she wanted them to be. She saw them all in a convertible wearing sunglasses, driving to Pass

Christian for a beach holiday. I mean if it's anyone's fault, she thought . . . and then the baby cried.

Duane loved his little bubba, liked to fool with him in the crib while his momma watched, liked to drive his little plastic Jeep over the baby's belly, like to tickle his pumpkin and watch him giggle, liked to wake the baby up by calling his name, only it never came out "Boone Kyle" like it was supposed to. It came out "Moon Pie." Tami Lynne decided she liked the name and began using it herself.

Billy Wayne didn't like it. He told Tami Lynne what are people going to think? They're going to think we named our baby after a snack food, think we're making a cruel joke or something.

"I don't care what people think. Not a lick. He's my baby."

"He's going to have a hard enough time as it is."

"Anyway, he loves his name, don't you, Moonie, don't you just love it? Yes, you do." She made a trilling kind of noise, and the baby laughed and moved everything he had in frantic little circles.

Billy Wayne, though, could not assuage his nettled spirits, not so long as he stayed in that shotgun on McKinley with the symbols of his perfidy, the daily reminders that he had betrayed his vocation, his first wife, and perhaps his destiny. Why was it he, who only wanted a normal kind of life, like the lives of those he saw around him, how was it he kept turning his back on that which he coveted every time it was offered to him? Billy Wayne did not understand himself. Life, he knew, would never be normal again.

3

A Flesh Clothed
with Worms and
Clods of Dust

*B*illy Wayne resolved to discover everything he possibly could about his family,
about their lives, the community out there in the Bottom that
he had never known, but had heard about all this life, and
about his familial penchant for ruination. He spent the better
part of six weeks' leisure time in the morgue of the *News-
Star* researching every reference he could uncover about any
Fontana. He read a long article that indicated Bosco Fontana
had spent time with the James Gang near Delhi. He learned
about the cypress knee sculpting enterprise that flourished in
the thirties and about his Uncle Lafayette who founded the
First Church of the Second Deluge and about chuffle-jawed
Uncle Fluellen who made bottle trees to rid the parish of evil

spirits. But most of what he read pertained to the inordinately gruesome deaths of his kin. Lonnie, Ronnie, Johnnie, and Donnie Fontana blew themselves up at Fort Polk during World War II by playing Hambone with a live grenade. Clement and Alvin Fontana jumped off the tower of the Layton Castle and landed facedown, holding hands, in the driveway. And then there was Uncle Aubrey Fontana who got into a scuffle in the Cattle Baron parking lot and got stabbed up the nostril with the aerial off a taxi cab. Aerial passed right up along into the brain.

Billy Wayne called on Grayson Berard who probably knew more Fontana stories than anyone in the parish, and who seemed to be, as he spoke with Billy Wayne there in his kitchen, sipping at the bourbon that Billy Wayne had so kindly brought along, seemed to be taking mental notes toward another.

"You look an awful lot like your great-uncle Lafayette. Anyone ever tell you that?"

"No, sir."

Grayson lifted his Haddad Hardware ball cap an inch and scratched his head, set it back down. "I remember when you was born. You was a cute little booger." He poured three fingers of bourbon into his jam jar, held the bottle up to Billy Wayne, who shook his head.

Billy Wayne asked Grayson his opinion on this curse business. Grayson said as to how that was one time the orthodox thinking, but now the idea of the supernatural embarrasses a lot of people. Of course, they are selective about that, you understand. They aren't discomforted by God, not one bit. It's just the devil, I guess, makes them blush. Prefer their Satan to be a what-do-you-call-it, a concept, not a trickster.

The way Grayson reckoned it, there were, let's see, four popular theories regarding the regrettable destiny of the Fontanas. Grayson counted them off on his fingers. First is the genetic theory, which is certainly intriguing, isn't it? he said, but remains for the most part, uninvestigated. Second, there's the sociological theory, favored by the college crowd, that blames the Fontana environment, physical and emotional and all that, for their wretched lot. Then there are those who hold that it's all been bad luck or coincidence. And last, we got the more conservative thinkers who figure all the adversity is God's retribution for what must have been one extraordinarily despicable sin. Grayson thought for a moment, looked up at the ceiling fan. I guess that's a kind of variation on the curse theory, isn't it?

Billy Wayne freshened Grayson's drink and poured himself a shot. He looked over to the luffing cafe curtains in the window above the sink. "So what do you think, Grayson? Which is it?"

"I *don't* think." Grayson smiled. "I just tell stories. Let other people figure them out."

"Of course you think."

"I just tell what happened and how it came to happen." Grayson looked at Billy Wayne. He leaned closer to the table, held its edge with both his hands. "Not what's convenient to happen, you understand. Nothing worse in telling a story than convenience. That and trying to make a point. Anyway, I don't have time to think."

Grayson Berard pulled a wooden match out of the bib pocket of his overalls and cleaned his ears with it. "I can tell you this, though," he said. "I can tell you how all this curse business, as you call it, got started."

"Well, I'd like to hear that, Grayson. I would."

Grayson and Billy Wayne carried their drinks out to the front porch and sat beside each other on the pair of armless, cane rockers. Grayson closed his eyes, cocked his head, took in a long, slow breath. "Rain tomorrow," he said.

Grayson told Billy Wayne about Aeneas Fontana, a boy so

dumb he wouldn't know enough to pour piss out of his boot with directions printed on the heel. About how Aeneas went to New Orleans, to the Quarter, down to St. Anne Street to call on Marie LeVeau's daughter Marie LeVeau, who is also a voodoo priestess like her momma. Wanted her to wash him clean of his enemy's conjuration, by which he meant his yellowy pallor and the infernal fetidness that saturated his body. Course it ain't no spell at all, it's the four years working in the sulfur mines in Calcasieu Parish, inhaling brimstone dust, rubbing it into his skin, that's rendered Aeneas sallow and noisome. They say his breath alone could knock a buzzard off a shit wagon.

Grayson told Billy Wayne how Aeneas became fascinated by a stereograph entitled "Andromache at the Bath," that he spied on Marie LeVeau's highboy there in the parlor. How he just knew if he could snap the card into a stereoscope he'd be able to see the lady's twitchet right through her diaphonous robes. How he snatched that stereograph and ran out the door and across the street to the apothecary shop where he stood staring at his two images of Andromache, one for each eye. And that's when Marie LeVeau put the wanga on that sapheaded boy who was, of course, his own enemy and had just proven it. Put it on the boy and on his whole family unto ten generations. She caused him to rise off the ground and to spin in place like a top. Grayson told Billy Wayne how when the chemist and a stock boy ran out of the shop to gaze on this gyroscopic man, Marie directed Aeneas to execute a tumbleset through the shop window.

"So from then you all have had the curse," Grayson said.

"That's a colorful story, Grayson. But I don't believe in voodoo."

"Don't think I believe it myself sometimes."

"Aeneas," Billy Wayne said. "He's the one they found dead out near the gas fields, right?"

"Exploded. Body swelled up with poisons, methane, whatever it was. By the time they found him, he had turned blue and blown up. Gators wouldn't go near what was left of him. Found a dozen dead vultures though."

"Another drink, Grayson?"

They drank awhile and rocked. Grayson said, "I ain't said there is a curse, understand. I just told how the notion got started."

Billy Wayne thanked Grayson for the story, told him to keep what was left of the bottle. He stood. Grayson reached out and stopped Billy Wayne's chair from rocking. "Bad luck," he said.

4

The True
Beginning of
Our End

*R*oyal Landry wanted to tell a joke before a recent meeting of the Great Books group got started. This was his way of easing the lingering tensions that had developed at the previous meeting (*Essays on Theodicy*), a testy session that had culminated in Shug Johnson calling Leibniz a "Pollyanna." Said if he'd have lived in Monroe, he wouldn't think this was the best of all possible worlds, would he? At one point Cicero Wittlief interrupted, said he'd been to both Atlanta and Fort Worth, and he didn't find life (". . . and I'm speaking of 'quality' now") in those centers of culture any better than what we got right here. Margaret Grimes asked Shug if he was taking his medication like he was supposed to. "You been acting sorrier than gully dirt ever since Bakunin," she told him. Ted Muto wanted to know were the twins coming, did anyone have any idea?

"So tell us your joke, Royal," Bobby Sistrunk said.

"René Descartes walks into a bar, hops up on a stool, doesn't say anything. The bartender recognizes him, figures, a philosopher, classy guy, probably drinks the best. So he goes up to Descartes, wipes the bar in front of him, and says, 'Can I get you a drink, M. Descartes? Chartreuse? B&B? A cognac, perhaps?' Descartes looks at the bartender, says, 'I think not,' and disappears."

And yes, the joke did seem to settle some nerves and did set off a flurry of variations on Descartes' most famous theme, lines like, "I think, therefore I think I can, I think I can," (The Little Engine That Could); "I think, therefore I'm Kant"; "I think I'm God, therefore I damn."

"Well," Margaret said, "we can sit here all night making lightsome conversation or we can get to work." She opened her file folder, removed several typed pages, tapped them to order on the seminar table, smoothed their edges, cleared her throat, looked at Shug across the table, and said, "I would like to start if no one objects." No one did.

The evening's topic was the Book of Genesis, and Margaret began her discussion by citing the two very different accounts of creation you get there in the first two chapters, which everyone seemed aware of (except maybe Cicero, who scrunched up his face, looked down at his King James, leaned over to see if maybe Bobby's edition was different, almost said something, but thought the better of it), but were not alarmed about the contradictory versions, as Margaret seemed to be. First, she said, we've got man and woman created at the same time by a God who is evidently both male and female. But then the book reneges and offers us Adam at the top of creation and Eve, an afterthought, at the bottom. Yes, I'm talking about that Adam's rib crap, she said.

Tommie Nash said what she thought was that Moses was just trying to be more poetical in the second telling. God breathing into the nostrils of the dirt and everything. "I think he succeeded, don't you all? That's the story we remember most vividly."

"Well, Moses ought to get his facts straight, don't you think?" Margaret said. "Was it a year or forty days? Did Noah send out a raven or a dove? take in pairs of animals or seven pairs of the clean? The man can't be trusted with details.

"Tell me this," she said. "Why were those boys, Shem and Japheth, so unhinged at their brother Ham's seeing their daddy buck naked and dead asleep? The boys had just slept with their daddy for a year on the ark. Or forty days or whatever. They all got the same equipment, right?"

That brought a smile from Ted Muto and a blush from Chiquita.

"They're all about the same cubits long, far as I know. So what could be special about Noah's rod that he had his own child's descendants cursed for the boy's looking at it?"

"What's your point, Margaret?" Shug said.

"Only reason the boys would be so alarmed, so humiliated at Noah's nakedness would be if Noah was their momma and if Ham had taken advantage of her in her drunkenness. I'm saying this is a simple tale of incest. I'm saying that the Noah, who supposedly saved humankind, was a woman."

Royal Landry hadn't heard the last five minutes. He stared out the window into the traffic on North 18th Street. His life was a mess. His wife, Sandy, was seeing another man, a widower twenty years older than she was. Nice enough fellow, sings in the First Baptist choir, sells appliances at Sears Roebuck. Royal wasn't angry about it, not devastated like he thought he was supposed to be. They didn't know that he knew, and maybe he wouldn't ever say anything. His own affair with Earlene Fontana seemed to be at an end. Now she wouldn't answer his phone calls. The irony, he thought, was appropriate.

Royal tuned back in to the discussion. He knew he'd have nothing to add. Genesis had bored him. Maybe he'd tell another joke. His customers always like a joke. Now Cicero and Shug were talking about how to tell a story. A philosophy joke. Let's see, the Zen life-is-like-a-fountain joke? No one ever gets it. A sophist, a neo-Platonist, and a Skeptic walk into a bar? Maybe. Cicero raised his voice above Shug's. This is ridiculous, he said. If you want to tell a story, you begin at the beginning and you continue on until the end and then you stop.

Would that this were true, Cicero. Consider Genesis. What was God doing before He (to use the Biblical pronoun) created the heaven and the earth? And where did He come up with that idea and why? Was it something he had mulled over awhile? (And how could that word *awhile* have any meaning before time? How could any verb exist?) We always need to know the second just before the first second in order to comprehend the first second and know the moment after the last moment if we are to understand the end. We need time before time, time after time. So we might answer Cicero by saying that all of our stories arise from obscurity, struggle at meaning, and arrive at the unknowable. And the narrator's job then, is to nudge the edges of meaning into the midst of the mystery.

We are, all of us, moving at an unthinkable speed away from the primal event, while at the same time, the what-it-is-we're-heading-for is accelerating away from us at an incomprehensibly greater speed. A story is like that, like the universe, in that it seems to expand in opposite directions, at its alpha and omega, away from its primordial order. On the one hand, there is inevitably just one more thing to explain before these other things can be explained. On the other hand, as the story moves toward its inescapable conclusion, it tends (as ours does, you'll attest) to ramble as if it had lost the will to finish. Of course, our narrators ("they who must choose") are only human, and who could blame them for wanting to live a little longer with people (some would say characters) they care about and to settle into their fictive world for life everlasting? Picture your narrator walking down some flat-out hot July two-lane highway in the Delta here, and she sees up ahead these heat snakes rising off the tarmac and sets them up as her destination. She says, When I get there, I'll rest. She sets off toward the snakes, but they are gone when she gets to them. There they are, up the rise at the next crossroads.

We've been busy telling you the story, making sure to infuse coincidence with causality, putting in an Uncle (Napoleon), leaving out another (Ezra the Vinyl Man), pointing out relationships among resemblances, seeing that curiosity is properly motivated and all that. And, of course, being as faithful to the truth of what happened to the members of this family, our Fontanas, as we know how to be. And you've been doing your part. You noticed that the water in Bayou DeSiard was sometimes gunmetal gray, other times a kind of brushy green. You've seen how Earlene does her hair. You looked so closely at Angelo's creased forehead you've noticed how the left eyebrow is notched. You've had to furnish restaurants and kitchens, see the cars parked along Louisville Avenue. And right now you've got to imagine the lights in the Boscobel Room flicking off three times. That's Maryalice Wiggins's signal to the Great Book seminarians that they have five minutes to conclude their meeting.

"Before we go," Royal said, "I want to tell you all another joke."

Shug asked Royal if he was feeling all right this evening. You've been so reticent. Royal nodded, said he was fine. Thank you for asking. He said, "Martin Heidegger and Baruch Spinoza walk into a bar, only Spinoza falls on his face because he's already intoxicated with God. Heidegger props him on a bar stool, orders himself a stinger, and sits on the stool where Descartes used to be. The seat is warm, but Heidegger feels a chill. On the bar's mirror, over the reflected Spinoza's drooping head, is a sign announcing closing time as midnight. Heidegger drinks and tells the senseless Spinoza a dirty story about Husserl and a farmer's daughter which ends with the daughter's saying 'It was phenomenological for me, too.' At eleven, the bartender makes last call. Heidegger, well into his stingers, is belligerent. He points at the mirror. '*Das* sign,' he says and looks at Spinoza's watch, *Es nicht* midnight. *Wir nicht* going,' he tells the bartender. '*Verstehen?*' "

5

Where Is That Promethean Heart That Can Thy Light Relume?

*W*hen her alleged husband Sidney Saunders died following an extravagant and, some have claimed, intentional ingestion of laudanum in 1889, Anne Livingston erected a monument at the city cemetery to his memory and as a public rebuke to the malicious gossip concerning the marital status of the couple. This granite tomb stands today at the DeSiard Street entrance near the graves of the Chinese laborers who died here building the railroad to Vicksburg. It is topped by a presumably life-sized statue of Saunders which holds in its left hand an unrolled scroll purporting to be his marriage license. It reads: "This is to certify that Sidney W. Saunders and Anne Livingston of Monroe, in the state of La., were by me joined in holy matrimony, March 25, 1875. John M. Young, justice of the peace, City of St. Louis. Witnesses: John W. Rice, Frank Gregory."

Within the vault are a now decayed bentwood chair and an oak escritoire used by Saunders during his life, its wood gone spongy, swollen, spoiled. The widow, it is said, spent hours each day for the seven remaining years of her own life in the vault, sitting beside the casket, reading Thackeray by lamplight to the ghost of her husband. Before leaving the cemetery each afternoon, Anne Livingston prayed over a child's grave, one whose headstone was ornamented with tiny granite frontlace shoes and ankle socks.

Billy Wayne Fontana did not build a monument to his former spouse. After all, Billy Wayne was not obsessed with Earlene. He never called her, did he? Never mailed her a letter. Never asked Ronnie to deliver a message, not a proper, written message anyway, not even a hello, how are you doing. He had looked Earlene up in the telephone directory one time, under Fontana, under deBastrop, "D" and "B," but couldn't find her. He did not worry about her, did not follow her around as one suitably obsessed would do, did not inquire as to her well-being. But he thought about Earlene at least once every single day.

He might go to his closet, say, put on a shirt for work, and then realize it's one that she had bought for him at Howard's. Or he might be driving down St. John Street and notice a doorway that they had ducked into one day to get out of a rain. Or he might be watching the sun set over the levee and recall the peachblow of Earlene's breast, and then he would feel that shudder in his groin, the hum at his neck, and he'd close his eyes and moan. Sometimes Billy Wayne thought he could still smell Earlene's scent, like brine and flowers, in the kitchen, and when he did he became overwhelmed by her presence and their past.

Sometimes Earlene *felt* like obsession, like when he could,

out of nowhere, hear her voice, clearly, talking about something he could not understand, saying, "What if we shifted
here to F-sharp major?" or whatever. Or he could see her, but
never her face, see her opening a door to a dark room or
trying on a pair of shoes in a store he could not recognize.
Russell Sikes told him once, It's all out there, you just have to
use your other senses to tune in.

Billy Wayne sat at the kitchen table and watched Moon Pie
draw his pictures. He smiled. Maybe he'd made his life better
somehow, better than it had been a few years ago, better than
when Moon Pie was born, for sure. He pushed that thought
out of his head. He was better off than Dencil if you thought
about it. Hazel and the boys were pretty much in Baton Rouge
full-time these days now that Webb and Ferlin were into that
private school and Hazel was majority whip in the state senate.
And here was Dencil taking care of Angelo practically full-
time.

Ever since Billy Wayne had quit the day job and gone on
nights with the company, things improved. He devoted himself to the lives of his children as only a man fueled by guilt
and liberated by imagination (his eventual reconciliation with
Earlene, sometime, somehow) truly can. He knew that his
selfless regard for their well-being would now alleviate his
suffering and understood that if he felt incomplete, well, that
was hardly important anymore.

So mornings now when he arrived home from work, he
baked, fed the boys biscuits and gravy, put the finishing
touches on Duane's arithmetic homework, made their beds.
He'd walk them to the corner, wait for the school bus and
then the van that picked up Moon Pie and took him to the
school for the acdemically gifted. He'd go home, read the
paper, brush his teeth, wake Tami Lynne, and go to sleep.
Evenings before work, while the boys watched color television,
Billy Wayne got out the ammonia and the car wax and shined

up Moon Pie's electric wheelchair. Then he plugged the battery into the charger, listened to the hum. He'd make the boys their sandwiches for school lunch, tuna for Moon Pie, egg salad for Duane.

Of course, what this arrangement also meant was that Billy Wayne seldom slept with Tami Lynne. That wasn't something he thought much about, preferring to consider their time together as an unfortunate but unavoidable victim of their economic and parental obligations. Besides, Tami Lynne seemed happy enough, didn't she? And, of course, he loved her, cared about her in his way. So he wasn't always passionate, not always obsessed with her the way she had said she wished he'd be. That didn't mean he wanted to hurt her; in fact, it meant he wouldn't have to. He was being as honest and as sanguine as he knew how to be, and the result was tranquillity in the house. The boys had never been happier so far as he could tell. Tami Lynne, even, was not so tense as she used to be and no longer competed with the boys for his attentions.

Tami Lynne was indeed happier than she had been in the days, years really, three years at least, when Billy Wayne was nearly always depressed and remote. But her current emotional state had less to do with Billy Wayne than he imagined. When he had settled into his protracted melancholia, and before he regained some of his senses, at least, and struck up a relationship with his sons, Tami Lynne, who had grown accustomed to domestic affairs and reliant on household comforts, steeled her feminine will, and finding her old job at the stationers unavailable, went to work as a checker at Safeway and found herself a lover. Found him, in fact, back in the meat department.

Whom she found was the assistant meat manager, her old friend Russell Sikes. At first, she was just glad to have someone she knew to talk with at breaks, someone whom she'd always admired, frankly. Soon, she was driving him home from work.

Sometimes they'd stop for a drink or something to eat. It was like neither one of them wanted to get home. One lunchtime at Morrison's Cafeteria, Tami Lynne let on about her unhappiness at home, about Billy Wayne's crazy talk about the family curse and his consequent frigidity and all that.

Russell's opinion was that the Fontanas just might be from Venus—the morning star, not the city in Italy.

"Those little spacemen sauté your brain, Russell?"

"Look, you don't just all of a sudden show up in history as some full-grown swamp man like they say what's-his-face did."

"Peregrine."

"Not if you were born on earth you don't. People on earth have a past. Think about it."

"I'm thinking you ought to get yourself out of the meat locker once in a while."

"I'm serious," Russell said. He used a napkin to wipe his forehead. "Just like a Capricorn to look at the truth and not see it." He told Tami Lynne that Venusians have been dumping their genetic undesirables on us for two centuries, ever since they discovered a special molecular transport process at about the time the first beaver pelts were being canoed down the Ouachita from Arkansas.

"You're so cute when you're excited, Russell." Tami Lynne smiled, checked the time on the sunburst clock on Morrison's wall. "It's two-thirty."

"Hitler was a Venusian," Russell said. "So is Jimmy Connors, the tennis player, not the stock boy in produce."

"We've got us one half hour. Maybe we could drive out to the levee before going back to work, Russell." Tami Lynne ran her tongue along her lips. "If you catch my drift."

MOON PIE SHOWED Billy Wayne his drawing of their family—four smiling stick figures holding hands. Billy Wayne, on the left, was burnt sienna, then a goldenrod Tami Lynne with a squiggle of carnation pink hair, then an olive green Duane, and an apricot Moon Pie who had no stick legs and seemed to be floating, held to the family only by the nub that was Duane's left hand. Above them all in the paperwhite sky, a tiny watermelon sun, with waves of lavender light.

"That's beautiful, Moon Pie," Billy Wayne said. "Can I keep it?"

Moon Pie said he could. Billy Wayne leaned forward and kissed his son on the cheek. He held up the drawing so Hotson could see it. Hotson had just walked in with the newspaper under his arm.

Hotson told Moon Pie the drawing was lovely and gave Billy Wayne today's *News-Star-World*. He turned the paper in Billy Wayne's hand to the bottom of the page and pointed to the story on Earlene deBastrop Fontana. And the photo. A new one, Billy Wayne thought. Her hair's so short. The story was about her trip to Nashville to watch Tom T. Hall record one of her songs. She got to meet George Jones, who is so nice, she says in the article, a real gentleman, not at all like some folks say. The article ended by saying that it didn't look like Earlene would need to be selling insurance much longer. It didn't say anything about the songs except to mention the title of the one Hall recorded, "Broke Down Car on the Linville Road," which didn't mean anything to Billy Wayne except that it couldn't have been about him. Insurance?

THAT EVENING AT dark thirty, Billy Wayne went out to sit on the porch. Tami Lynne had taken the boys to the movies or somewhere. He thought about Moon Pie and about how he, Billy Wayne, had spent the afternoon feeling sorry for himself. He took out an old family photo from his wallet, a photo of the four of them. Billy Wayne saw how much Duane favored his momma, eyes more hazel than brown. Tami Lynne had dressed the boys in new outfits the day they took the coupon down to Olan Mills and had the portrait done. None of them looked relaxed, not even the baby on Tami Lynne's lap.

You couldn't tell anything from looking at it. You couldn't tell from the way he was bundled that Moon Pie ended where Tami Lynne's lap began. Looking at the photo, you couldn't tell that Duane would sit in his crib and knock his head against the headboard for hours if you let him. You couldn't tell either that Tami Lynne, her face here rouged, her hair spritzed and full, had cried herself to sleep for three months because her husband (that's him with his hands on his boy's shoulders like he's keeping his helium-filled son from floating away) had declined to have intercourse with her. And you couldn't tell that a week before this portrait was taken, she had said to him, Okay, if that's the way you want it, and had stopped crying.

He knew he loved Moon Pie, just didn't love the idea of deformity, of something so alarming and irrefutable that it could not be overcome. Deformity, after all, was the reminder, the symbol of his sin. Just then Hotson drove up in the Time Machine. He joined Billy Wayne on the porch. Billy Wayne showed him the picture. "If only I didn't keep seeing what wasn't there," he said, meaning the rest of Moon Pie. He returned the photo to the wallet, the wallet to the pocket.

"You think you haven't been punished enough," Hotson said. "Maybe you think if your wife leaves you and takes the boys that ought to do it. Maybe you're trying to force her to leave. You know, the way you're acting."

Hotson said hi to Russell Sikes who'd come along with a Safeway sack under his arm. Said he had a couple of pounds of lean ground chuck for the Fontanas. Billy Wayne thanked him and said why don't they all go inside for a couple of cold ones. That suited Hotson and Russell just fine. Billy Wayne held the screen door open for the others and before he could close it and step into the house, a barn swallow swooped into the living room and smashed itself into the ceiling fan. The men were quiet. Then Hotson said, "Holy shit!" Russell looked into Hotson's eyes and into Billy Wayne's. "Who's going to die?" he said.

6

If There Be Any Sorrow Like Unto My Sorrow

*T*ami Lynne asked Billy Wayne to step in from the porch and to have a seat at the kitchen table. She closed the door to the boys' room and poured herself a glass of red wine. She announced that she was going to talk now and she didn't want to be interrupted until she was finished. Fair enough, Billy Wayne said. I'm listening.

Tami Lynne acknowledged her years of intermittent infidelity with Russell Sikes. She told her husband that his sexual austerity and his emotional self-indulgence had driven her to it. Your goddam obsession with your loss of innocence. No, she didn't mean that to be an excuse. What she'd done was wrong, and it was shameful. Yes, she regretted it, but the fact remains, she should never have become so desperate, so blue, as to cast her eyes outside their home. She took a breath, sipped her wine, and kept her eyes on Billy Wayne.

"I'll tell you exactly what I regret," she said. "Not telling you, and not leaving you a long time ago." Tami Lynne cried quietly. She put her head in her hands. "I just kept thinking, hoping that you'd snap out of it."

Billy Wayne stared at the wooden bowl of fruit in the middle of the table, at the orange with the rosette of white mold on its rind. What was he expected to do? His mind was imageless, unhelpful. He would eat a grape if he thought he had the energy or the will to chew it. Was this what he had wanted all along? To end this ill-fated marriage without having to be the villain, the one who fools around, walks away? Billy Wayne looked at Tami Lynne's heaving shoulders. After a minute, he asked what the boys knew about all this.

"They don't know anything yet."

Billy Wayne sat back in his chair, let his arms fall to his side. "Do you love Russell Sikes?"

Tami Lynne wiped her eyes with her thumb. "You have no right to ask, Billy Wayne." She said, No, she didn't believe in astrology and all that. "But I'll tell you what, I believe in Russell Sikes." Yes, she did. "Russell Sikes finds me stimulating. And I am, you know. And I'm funny. Yes. And smart."

Billy Wayne knew he should say something.

"You used to be so sweet, Billy Wayne. And eager. You wanted to know everything and you liked people." Tami Lynne paused. "You loved me." She realized something. She said, "Russell Sikes spends his time in the future. But at least he has a future."

"The past is important." Billy Wayne said. "Mine is anyway."

"And crowded."

Tami Lynne poured wine into her glass, listened to the squeak of bedsprings as one of her boys tossed in his sleep. "Don't you have anything to say?"

When Billy Wayne didn't respond, she said, "The marriage is over." When he still didn't say anything, Tami Lynne said, "You're not even going to try to talk me into staying, are you?" She watched him set his jaw. "Bastard!"

"Is this some kind of game, Tami Lynne? You tell me you've been unfaithful, that the marriage is finished, that I'm . . . I'm dirt, that you love someone else, and then you expect me to just rush into your arms or something? Doesn't that sound a little crazy to you?"

"Billy Wayne, I stopped expecting anything from you long ago. I'm going to bed."

"Wait a minute," Billy Wayne said. "What happens now?"

"Don't worry, Billy Wayne. We'll leave. It's your house. Too many ghosts here for me anyway."

Billy Wayne leaned his chair back. "Where will you go?"

"Now you're concerned, is that it?"

"Tami Lynne—"

"You son of a bitch. You think you're off the hook, don't you?"

"What's the use? I can't talk to you."

"Are you going to pretend the boys don't exist now?"

Tami Lynne carried her glass to the sink and emptied it. She put the wine in the fridge, walked to their bedroom, and closed the door.

Billy Wayne closed his eyes. He felt detached from his life somehow, but anchored to that kitchen. He looked at the clock. Quarter to ten. He listened for noises coming from their bedroom. He could call in sick to work. And then what would he do? Sit in this chair all night? Earlene's old writing chair, he realized. He knew that if he tilted his head in the light, he'd see the traces of her handwriting etched into the soft pine tabletop. No, he should go to work. At least he could think in the truck, in the dark.

He peeked into the boys' room. Couples get divorced all the time. The kids adjust. He was just letting this happen, wasn't he? Billy Wayne made himself a muffuletta, packed a side of crab salad in a margarine tub for his lunch. Jesus. He was going to be late for work. Billy Wayne took his keys from the nail on the doorjamb, his lunch. He snapped off the kitchen light and closed the door quietly behind him.

Near dawn, Billy Wayne parked the truck on Lennon Camp Road beside the old Dallimore farm. He'd managed to keep busy and distracted all night and to put off thinking about what to do. But in an hour or so his shift would end, and then what? Go home, kiss the boys on their foreheads, make their breakfast, pretend his wife never said those things to him last night? A strange morning. Fog on the Bottom. Lightning, thunder. The weathered clapboards on the house were the color of mink. Mrs. Dallimore, who must be ninety-five now, lived on this big old place alone. Family long gone. The shed there looked empty, its tin roof pitted, the barn empty, the house empty. A single braid of service wires ran from the power lines over Billy Wayne's head to the house. On this braid, about halfway to the house hung a single bare lightbulb, burning now over the empty, weedy chicken yard. Mrs. Dallimore's defiant gesture, Billy Wayne thought, this drop of light in an ocean of cold, dark matter.

So, let's see, he thought, Tami Lynne gets the boys, the house, the lover. And he gets to be alone somewhere. Why should she get the boys? What kind of prize mother was she carrying on like she's been with that two-faced son of a bitch Russell Sikes. Hotson was wrong. Billy Wayne knew that he didn't want to be punished. He'd already punished himself enough. Punished himself by thinking too damn much. Maybe all that ruminating was a way to avoid doing anything. What was he afraid of? It was time maybe to stop all this constant thinking and act. Do something, anything. No, not just anything. Billy Wayne slowed himself down. He could have the power, he realized, to shape his future. No one else could do that to him now.

Billy Wayne saw the clouds lighten over the Dallimore house and shed, saw the silouettes of the live oaks against the umber sky, the clumps of mistletoe, the beards of moss. He started the truck. He didn't know just yet what he was going to do, but thinking had only gotten him to the dead end he was at. He needed to be with his boys. They needed him. He felt it.

7

Lift Up the Stone and You Will Find Me There

illy Wayne and Duane were gone for a year and a half from Monroe. For the first sixteen months they just sort of drifted from one campground to another, with the occasional stay at a motel during the rains or when it was simply too hot and dangerous in the swamps. That first day they drove out of town to Black Bayou Lake, rented a boat, and motored out to Treasure Island. Billy Wayne had drawn up a pirate map with a big "x," trying to distract Duane from the obvious fact that something was desperately wrong. While Billy Wayne set up their tent on a dry mound and built a campfire, Duane looked for the treasure, but where the "x" was, fifteen paces from a clump of Spanish dagger, was spongy muck, cow-belly, and probably quicksand, Duane figured, some pirate's clever trap that he would not fall into.

By the time they set up camp in Chemin A Haut park a few days later, Billy Wayne had explained the truth to his son, that Duane's momma was leaving his daddy for Mr. Russell Sikes and that he, Billy Wayne, who loves you, he told Duane, hugged him, well, I just couldn't let her take you away is all. He told Duane the reason why he didn't take along Moon Pie was we couldn't slosh the wheelchair through muck and brush now could we. Anyway, Moon Pie's got his special needs that we could not provide for out here in this wilderness, much as we might want to. Besides, your momma would be awfully lonely without neither one of her little boys. I know she's got Russell Sikes, but that ain't the same. Billy Wayne admitted that what he was doing was not clearly thought out, was, in fact, criminal and foolish, he guessed, and they could both drive back right now and maybe everything would be forgiven. Or we could just stay together, have whatever kind of adventure we have and, you know, be pals in a way. Duane said, well, I want to stay with you, Daddy, and maybe we will so find us a treasure. Billy Wayne thanked him for that, said we'll be going back eventually. We'll know when the time's right.

The longest they stayed in one place was the nearly four months, from early June to late September, when they lived at the Admiral Benbow Inn in Jackson, Mississippi. Billy Wayne took a part-time job working the lunch shift at this fast-food place, Hushpuppies, where he had to wear baggy pants, a blousy shirt, and a straw hat with a feather in it and say things like "Would you like a fried dill or some porky beans with your catfish?" or "How about our fudge pie for dessert this afternoon?" After work Billy Wayne would take Duane to the library to do his lessons. Then they might go to a movie or to Gridley's for barbecue. Lots of nights they'd wind up back in the room talking about Moon Pie and what trouble he might be getting himself into this time. Or they'd talk about death.

When Duane was three and four years old, Billy Wayne remembered, he was all the time talking about death, which made Billy Wayne wonder if his boy had some instinctive understanding about his faulty heart or something. And now here Duane was nearly a teenager and he still wanted to talk about it. Duane would say you can't be something one second and not be something the next. And he didn't buy the notion of soul separate from body.

In late September, Billy Wayne drove them to Vicksburg, crossed the river, and headed south on an old blacktop that soon enough became sand and gravel. He told Duane he wasn't sure where they were heading. He was following his nose. Somewhere east of Somerset they came to this area that had once been an island before the river cut a new channel. Davis Island. How did Billy Wayne know this was Davis Island? He must have read about it somewhere. Jeff Davis had owned all this land in here in what was now the trans-Mississippi state of Mississippi.

Billy Wayne followed what he figured must have been an old logging road, a trackless one now, that twisted beneath a canopy of sweet gums, their starry leaves just taking on their red and yellow. The road played out in a grassy field about fifty yards from an old hunting camp that you could see hadn't been used in years, not by people at any rate. The window glass was broken, the door opened and warped. Inside you could see where the roof leaked, where the roots of a water oak had pushed through the dirt floor in places. The only human artifacts were an old table, a bit high for their camp stools, but sturdy enough, a hickory axe handle, an empty jar of Sperm Gun Oil, and a rusted, double spring beaver trap. Here was another thing then. How did Billy Wayne know this was a beaver trap, not, say, an otter trap? He'd never seen anything like it that he could recall. For some reason, the unfamiliar had chosen this day or this place to reveal itself to him. He knew that they could drive on over to Newellton, find a Jitney Jungle, buy supplies, be back in time to clean the cabin a bit, sweep out the mouse and fisher scat, nail a tarp over the doorway and cheesecloth over the window, pitch the tent, gather wood and start a fire outside, all before dark. And that's what they did.

Billy Wayne and Duane had built the campfire down near the pond, and now they sat in its glow listening to the "kick kick kick" of the cricket frogs and the occasional slap of a fish breaking water. Billy Wayne drank coffee, Duane tossed buttonballs from a sycamore into the fire and waited for them to pop. The image that came to Billy Wayne's mind was of someone standing behind him, pulling his jacket off his shoulders and down his sleeves. Only it wasn't the jacket, but his brain that was inside out. Everything exotic, like we said, seemed commonplace to Billy Wayne, and now all things familiar took on a certain strangeness. He knew the name for this phenomenon, *jamais vu*, but didn't now how he knew it. Earlier he had found himself staring at a broom, at the knot of broom corn on the neck, at the slope of the shoulder, the four rows of stitching, two blue, two red, holding the bristles in place. And now here was his son talking to him about wanting to go home pretty soon, okay, Daddy? But it was like Billy Wayne had never looked at his son before. Sure it was the firelight making Duane's face gray and orange, wasn't it? Billy Wayne said, Yes, I think we'll be going home in a while. You miss your momma, don't you? And Moon Pie, Duane said.

Hotson had told Billy Wayne many times that his worst flaw was distraction, that he allowed his mind to be too easily diverted from whatever task it was undertaking. But on the island everything drew his attention. When he looked at a foxglove or at one of the red-eared sliders sunning itself on a log, he didn't have time for the past, didn't think at all about the future. This place, Davis Island, or what he thought was Davis Island, was sacred to him somehow. He noticed himself notice everything. When he walked through the canebrakes, he would do this thing with his eyes where he would look at some distant spot on the horizon, just rest his vision there, not focus or anything, try not to look, and that way he could scatter his sight and could see anything that moved anywhere, from the ground at his feet to the sky over his head and for 180 degrees left to right. If anything at all stirred, that fleshy-headed vulture wheeling in an updraft, the aspen leaf twitching on its branch, this shamrock spider jerking at the side of her web, then Billy Wayne saw it, watched it, studied it.

About three-quarters of a mile south of their camp, near an oxbow lake, Billy Wayne and Duane came upon the remains of a fireplace and chimney for what must have been a house, a log house most likely. They found a dump out behind a holly thicket and dug up mostly blue and green glass bottles and jars, a couple of cracked earthenware bowls. Above the site, on a rise, they found a row of nine stone tablets, chalky white, moss and lichen covered. Billy Wayne knew what they must be, and the knowledge made him tremble. This is a burial ground, he told Duane. We should leave the dead here in peace. Duane said, I wonder what killed them? Billy Wayne said, Malaria probably. Duane said, I wonder who buried the last of them?

On their walk back to camp, Duane wondered why there weren't names on the stones if it was a graveyard.

"Probably couldn't write," Billy Wayne said. "Out here writing wouldn't come in so handy as talking would, or singing. You'd have to know how to read the sky, the river, the trees."

In his dream that night, Billy Wayne saw the nine tablets

of stone become nine loaves of golden bread, each with a name carved into its crust. And they were the names of the living and the dead, of Fox and George, and of Helen, Angelo and Moon Pie, of Duane, Billy Wayne, Peregrine and Pee Dubya. And the vultures descended and pecked at the eyes of the loaves and bounced, hopped, stretched, and flew away. And he saw Duane sealed in a pond of glass and Moon Pie drowning in a lake of fire, and he saw that on Moon Pie's forehead, the flames had burned Billy Wayne's own name. He tried to call out to Moon Pie to explain to him why he had gone away, but frogs leaped from his mouth instead of words. And then a great silence followed in which Billy Wayne could hear the fire say, "Because thou hast left thy first love," could hear the voice of light say to him, "I am awake in my sleep. I am the dreamer and the dream. I am the everything that is nothing, the spark of the soul, fire of the heart, ember of love. I am up and down, top and bottom, strange and charmed. I am the woman clothed with the sun and the child swaddled in darkness. I am the tissue of contradiction, the eye in the needle, the needle in the eye. I am the insubstantial and absolute idea and the hammer that shatters your skull. I am the color you have not named, the light which makes all visible except itself. I am the wave of reason, the particle of faith. I am the star in the cosmos and the atom with the universe inside. I don't seek, I find. I am the writting on the wall, the unutterable speech of the stone."

Billy Wayne believed that dreams had nothing to hide. They did not obsure, they illuminated. They were sometimes illogical, sure, in need of editing perhaps, but they were always overt and obvious and so he knew now what he had to do. He had to get back to his boy, his family, his life. And this time he would pay attention to what was out there and not just to the small voice inside. He shook Duane awake, told him we're going home. Duane said, I got to pee first.

8

The Past
Unwished for,
The Future Sure

*N*ature cannot abide that any place should be empty. Neither, evidently, could Russell Sikes. Two months after the disappearance from Monroe of Tami Lynne's husband and child, Russell Sikes had moved himself, his cleaver, his filleting, boning, carving, and ham knives, his sharpening steel, his astrology newsletter, ephemeris, his oxblood work boots, and his white coats into the Fontana shotgun. Where nothing had recently snuggled, now slept Russell Sikes. The new arrangement, however, did not please the grieving Moon Pie. Perhaps he understood this new domestic order as an affront to his hope for the reappearance of his daddy and his bubba, both of whom he missed so terribly much. Moon Pie sulked and moaned much of the day. He grew slovenly that summer vacation, would just leave the dried cat food stuck on the tread of his gray tires. The plaid blanket that covered his vestigial limbs was so sticky sometimes with spilled root beer and half-sucked candy that Scarlet, his kitten, no longer leaped up on his wheelchair to nuzzle and purr on her master's lap. Moon Pie was, we all feared, eroding, you know, the way a river cuts a bank, slowly to start, but soon— all at once.

Meanwhile, in his column for the *Twin City Shopper*, Russell Sikes predicted that Billy Wayne and Duane would be found by Thanksgiving, alive, healthy, and for Billy Wayne at least, repentent. He wrote that Billy Wayne would plead guilty to kidnapping and would serve time in Angola, but would emerge like a butterfly from a chrysalis—beautiful, cheerful, curious, and ready to taste the sweetness of life. As the holiday approached, Tami Lynne asked Russell if she should set a place for Duane at Thanksgiving dinner. And how many pounds of yams should she mash? But the pair were not found. The *Twin City Shopper*, embarrassed (it had conducted a contest as to the exact hour and day that Billy Wayne and Duane would knock on their own front door), hired a woman from Calhoun to do its horoscope from then on. Russell was let go. He was baffled and depressed, but undeterred. In early December, he placed an anonymous phone call to Sheriff Tidwell, suggesting that the Fontanas were at the bottom of Horseshoe Lake. Only, of course, it was not anonymous on account of Russell's pronounced speech impediment.

After the Police Jury authorized the search, and after nothing vaguely human was recovered from Horseshoe Lake, Sheriff Tidwell dropped in on Russell at Tami Lynne's and emphatically suggested that he make no further anonymous calls. "That lisp gives you away, son." Russell watched the front door as he whispered to the sheriff about the dream that had been plaguing him for the past two weeks.

"It's the same thing every night, Sheriff. It's eating at me."

"Do tell," Buddy said. He tipped the Stetson up a bit on his forehead, folded his arms, and listened.

"First there's Duane. He's floating on his back inside a white coffin and he's looking right at you and he's smiling. Pretty weird, huh?"

"I'd say so."

"Then you see Billy Wayne and he's being suffocated by this damp, black blanket. Then it gets stranger." Just then Russell snuck another glance at the door, took Buddy by the elbow, and led him down the steps to the walk. "There's Moon Pie and he's swimming in this river or pond, something, you don't know what. He's got these whiskers, kind of like a, like a seal, or an otter, you know, and he's diving under the afterwash of a passing houseboat."

Buddy took a breath and put his arm on Russell's shoulders. "I'm no psychiatrist," he said, "but it strikes me that just maybe there might be some guilt at work here, Russell."

"Sheriff, you got to believe me. Something's going to happen. My dreams don't lie. I'm afraid to sleep anymore."

"Am I right about the guilt, Russell?"

"Guilt is for egotists, Sheriff. We don't control our destiny."

Buddy looked at him. "I'm going to give you some free advice, son. If you can't sleep at night, get up and watch Charlie Chan on the TV. Just stay off the phone or else. Capisce?"

Later on, after all the mess, Buddy Tidwell would comment on the curious and rattling accuracy of Russell's visions, how the bodies were all discovered kind of like the way he described, and so on. Buddy found it all creepy and remarkable and was glad he didn't have to try to explain it to anyone. Of course, by that time, Russell Sikes was no longer in Monroe and so was unable, we imagine, to savor the moment of vindication. But let's not get ahead of our story.

Shortly before Christmas, then, Tami Lynne drove Moon Pie out to the new Pecanland Mall to watch Santa Claus parachute in over the parking lot. She hoped a chat with Santa might boost the boy's spirits. Santa wore a camouflage jumpsuit and landed in the bed of a Chevy pickup. Moon Pie told Santa he didn't suppose he'd find his daddy or Duane under the Christmas tree, would he? Santa stole a look at Tami Lynne and said, "That's right, Junior, so tell Santa what else you want." Moon Pie pulled a medical supply catalogue out from the knapsack looped around the hand grip of his chair and showed Santa a deluxe, long-life battery that was guaranteed to keep him motoring for a hundred miles between charges. And that's what he got for Christmas.

Now he no longer had to depend on his mother or on the unreliable Russell Sikes to charge his battery. Now he was free and independent. He bought bicycle reflectors for his spokes and for the back upholstery. He strapped a flashlight to the armrest with duct tape. Twice, the state troopers found him tooling down the breakdown lane of the interstate toward Shreveport—looking for his daddy, he told them. Tami Lynne was decidedly troubled. She indicated to her son that he'd best cease his vexatious behavior pronto or else he'd lose his battery altogether. Of course, both she and Moon Pie recognized an empty threat when they heard one. What was she supposed to do when she had to work, for one thing? Hire some unemployed cotton chopper to push the boy up the ramp at the back door after school or what? He couldn't make it up with his puny arms, now could he? So Moon Pie was again everywhere he was not supposed to be, it seemed, whirring along in his supercharged machine. One thing he liked especially, when the weather turned warm, was driving through the Zodiac Car Wash while Cecil Pilcher, the attendant, sprayed him with the pressure hose. Cecil was seventy-two years old and this was the best job he'd ever had in his life, he told Moon Pie. Cecil had no teeth to speak of and yellow eyeballs and only three fingers on his working hand. And he always wore a tan ditty-bop hat. He'd let his cigarette just dangle from his bottom lip. The pair of them would eat boiled peanuts and talk about how people looked like their cars. They'd laugh like crazy. Moon Pie'd get soaked like that, then motor into Safeway, head for the meat room and sit there icing up while Russell Sikes sawed through sides of swine.

Tami Lynne sat him up on a kitchen chair and gave him a talking to. "Honey, you're going to drive me mental if you don't stop these joyrides. Is that what you want? You want your momma in the psychopathic ward over to St. Francis?"

"No, ma'am, I don't."

"So why do you do it?"

Moon Pie tapped his flipper on the seat cushion and mumbled he didn't know why.

"Look at your momma. Don't you know I worry about you, baby? You'll get yourself killed one of these days."

Maybe Moon Pie thought, "Who cares anyway with my daddy and brother gone," but if he did, he kept it quiet.

"I've got an idea. If you're good as can be, keep to the sidewalks and all, stay in the neighborhood, I'll buy you that lizard you've had your eye on at Dr. Dolittle's."

"The chameleon?"

Apparently, Moon Pie wanted that lizard because he was extra good, even started conversing politely with Russell Sikes about particular cuts of meat. He named the lizard Duane Junior.

It had been nearly a year since the kidnapping and still not a trace of father and son. That's when Saterfiel's Dairy got in on the act and printed a red-and-white photo of Duane on its half-gallon cartons of whole milk and below it a phone number to call should you see the boy. The *Citizen* ran a feature story

marking the anniversary and printed a front-page picture of
Tami Lynne pouring Saterfiel's milk onto Moon Pie's Sugar
Pops, Tami Lynne looking wistful-like, Moon Pie crossing his
eyes like he does. Thinks it's funny. Seeing her boy's face in the
refrigerator everyday had a soothing effect on Tami Lynne. It
was rather like having her son in the house again. She'd leave
the milk carton on the table at meals and sometimes even
ask it questions. So when Saterfiel's replaced Duane with the
upcoming season's NLU football schedule on their milk cartons, Tami Lynne was devastated. She wanted Duane back
desperately, the flesh and blood Duane, and his father with
him, if that's what it took. She now accepted her own complicity in the crime that had divided her peculiar little family. Her
three men could be unsettling at times, Billy Wayne flat out
depressing, she knew, but they were hers, at least, and she
belonged with them. She became increasingly petulant with
the fourth man, Russell Sikes, the interloper, and irritated
with his predictions. She simply refused to listen any longer
to his dreams.

During all this period, Moon Pie was keeping in touch with
his daddy as best he could, by reading the stacks of Billy
Wayne's books Tami Lynne had piled in her closet. Moon Pie
could smell his father's hands on the book jackets. He'd read
first all the pages stained with coffee, all the underlined passages on all the dog-eared pages. He was looking for clues as
to where his daddy might have gone off to. Most of the books
were about religion and most of them, as far as Moon Pie
was concerned, were full of questions. What he wanted was
answers.

This one book in particular, this *Gospels of Sri Ramakrishna*,
he recognized as the stuff his teacher in the gifted program,
old Mr. Glass, was always talking about. These gospels were
all about rejecting the needs of the body. This wasn't real life
all these mystics dealt with, Moon Pie thought. Real life was

brain tumors, missing parents, paralysis. It was toothaches and diarrhea. Moon Pie did like reading about some of the saints who were obviously crazy like St. Catherine of Siena who went looking for someone to murder her. He liked Jesus. Jesus knew about infirmity and didn't try to deny or ignore it. Mr. Glass had called Jesus a great teacher, a prophet. Russell Sikes said Jesus was a very accomplished astrologer. When Moon Pie thought of Jesus he saw the man with his heart outside his body. And his heart on fire.

Russell Sikes, by the way, was no longer bothered by the Fontana Death Dream. By this time Russell was dreaming of a world in which we are all Arabs. In this world, you all had to pray at certain times. Even if you were on a bass boat, say, on Black Bayou Lake, and a storm was blowing, and it was prayer time, why you had to stop and pray. It was good, this Arab world, Russell said. Like all visionaries, he felt the compulsion to share his version of tomorrow with anyone wise and kind enough to listen. Russell printed his message on colorful leaflets and tacked them up wherever he could, at markets, bus shelters, and washeterias. The bottom of each leaflet was frayed with notches where he wrote his phone number so that people could just tear one off, stuff it in a pocket, and later when they got a minute, give him a call. No one ever did. Seems not many cotton farmers or field hands were crazy about the notion of their grandchild wearing a burnoose. Russell understood and told his cousin Johnny Ray that, after all, you had to expect people to be skeptical at first. Tami Lynne, though, went way beyond skepticism the night they had their big fight at the Sho Bar. The Sho Bar down Louisville by the bridge was their spot, Monday their night. Was hardly a soul in the place when Tami Lynne dropped a quarter in the jukebox and punched up George Jones's "If My Heart Had Windows." They sat at their corner table.

"You say his name's John?" Tami Lynne asked.

"Not his, its. They don't have sexes like we do."

Tami Lynne was thinking, You and me, Russell, we don't have sexes either if you keep this up much longer. They were discussing the chief medical officer of the spaceship that had shanghaied Johnny Ray and Russell that time. The one who had massaged a hot, redolent, vision-kindling salve onto Russell's brain. "John Alice Stansbury," Russell said. Each day, Russell remembered more and more about his abduction.

Tami Lynne stared into Russell's tiny blue eyes.

"Well," he said, "they have a right to names, don't they, sweetheart?" He told her how John Alice was with the crew that had built the pyramids in Cairo, not the Illinois one, and had supervised the Venusian hatchery at Poverty Point.

Tami Lynne fished a Tylenol from her purse and washed it down with a half inch of beer.

"Think about it now. Didn't I tell you last week they'd find a body on the levee and didn't it happen just like I said?"

"Russell, this is Monroe. They find a couple of bodies a year down by that slough."

"Wrapped in duct tape like a silver mummy?"

"Can't we ever talk about normal things? Phone bills, vacations, dental appointments?"

"Coroner said he was alive when they did it." Russell shook his head. "There's something I didn't tell you about that night on the ship."

"I don't want to hear this, Russell."

"They're fixing to come back for me shortly."

"You're talking like an imbecile, Russell."

"You all can come with me, you and Moon Pie."

"All right, that's enough." Tami Lynne stood. "I'm going for a drive now. And then I'm going home. When I get there, I want to find you reading the sports page or polishing the furniture. And I want all of those magazines gone, and the charts and the dreambooks. All of it. If we are going to stay together, Russell Sikes, it will be on this planet."

Moon Pie found the note addressed to his momma taped to the fridge. Russell wrote that it was time for him to go, that this part of his life—the butcher part—was clearly finished, that he was going to a town called Sedona, Arizona, because he'd seen it in a dream. And not to worry, he wrote, Duane and his daddy would return the *following* Thanksgiving (my mistake—had the wrong year!). Which they did.

9

Jesus Freaks

*M*oon Pie's opportunity to learn more about Jesus came that summer when Monroe hosted the annual Southern States' Bible Convention, proudly sponsored, the ad in the *Citizen* said, by the Biedenharn Bible Foundation, radio station KSIN's "Sonrise Seminar" Program, Pelican Bank's Tithing Club, and by the Coca-Cola Bottling Company of Ouachita Parish. Tami Lynne wouldn't go. She believed in God all right, but she paid as much attention to Him, she told Moon Pie, as He pays to me, and she was not about to waste her Saturday afternoon inside a civic center crawling with them holy rollers. And no sirree Bob, you cannot go by your lonesome, honey. Moon Pie's solution was simple and acceptable to Tami Lynne. He called Dencil. Dencil said sure, he'd love to go. I'll pick you up at noon.

Moon Pie had not expected this at a Bible convention. He hadn't thought that the first thing he'd see would be this big old aquarium just like the one he kept Duane Junior in at home. Only this one was full of—he counted them—five spade-headed pit vipers. A message made with that black plastic tape and pressed white letters like you might see on a goldfish tank at Dr. Dolittle's was stuck to the aquarium glass. It said, "They shall lick the dust like a serpent."

Moon Pie said he wasn't exactly sure what he wanted to see, but he'd know it when he saw it. They stopped at the Bethel Bookshop booth. The lady with the sculpted hair the color of a Dr. Crepeau's lemon lozenge kept her eye on Moon Pie all the time. Like maybe he was going to slip a copy of *How To Be the Happy Wife of an Unsaved Husband* under his lap blanket. Or maybe this one: *Maximized Manhood: A Guide for the Born-Again Single*.

They walked around awhile, stopped at the Ryre's Study Bible booth but not the Witness Panty Hose booth. At the end of the Dispensational Millennialist aisle they came to the Loaves and Fishes Food Court and found themselves an empty table. Dencil bought the corn dogs and Cokes. Dencil asked Moon Pie to remind him why they had come. I wanted to find out about Jesus, Moon Pie said.

"Maybe you aren't looking for Jesus, you know, Moon. Maybe it's solace you're after. With your daddy gone, your brother . . . Maybe you need something to take their place. Till they come back, I mean."

Dencil told Moon Pie that he had to visit the men's room, to go on ahead, and he'd catch up. He looked at his map. "If you get that far, wait for me at the Homemakers' Evangelical Missionary booth. Number 146. But don't talk to them."

The sign over Booth 120 just said, "Seal up what the seven thunders said," and the preacher, a man in a butternut-colored suit and a bad haircut, with eczema on his forehead and bloodshot eyes, was holding a Bible in his left hand, poking the air with his right, and was testifying to nobody. Moon Pie stopped.

The preacher looked at Moon Pie. "I've seen miracles. Right there in my church, the Church of the Tried Stone in Lufkin, Texas. And I feel a miracle in the firmament this afternoon." The preacher raised his head, raised a fist above his head, shut his eyes and screwed up his face like he was having maybe bowel trouble. "I've seen cataracts peeled from Alma Meadows's milky eyes. I've seen enamel put back on Savell Ockman's blackened teeth. I've seen hair restored to the balding of both sexes, seen ingrown toenails shrink right up. I've seen the palpable healing of Jesus Christ. I've seen cancer dry up and I've seen a brain-stem baby fold her hands and praise the Lord. I've seen Dale Fluetroy, who took an icepick in the eye during a domestic dispute, praise merciful Jesus, seen him rise up off the marble slab at the morgue, get dressed and walk home."

The preacher set his Bible on the card table beside his pulpit. He looked at Moon Pie, closed his eyes, smiled, nodded, looked at Moon Pie again. "Now, I don't know what you done, boy, to enrage Jesus so, or what your daddy or your grandaddy done to leave you all pitiful like you are, and I don't care." The preacher knelt down in front of Moon Pie. "Do you believe, son?"

Moon Pie didn't answer.

"Don't piss the Lord off, son." The preacher put his hands on Moon Pie's head. "Do you believe?"

"All right, I believe," he said.

"Jesus, heal thy fishboy!" the preacher said. "Shadiami kyala landalalala sayla. Shulala melalaba balalaka. Ununamaba-mamal asonodonulawawola."

Moon Pie felt the hands lift off his head and heard Dencil tell the preacher he ought to be ashamed of himself.

Moon Pie did indeed know it when he saw it. What first grabbed his attention was the framed color poster of three bald men in bathing trunks standing together in someone's weedy backyard. Each of them had a tattoo on his chest. The man on the left in the black Speedo was pointing at his. It was a bleeding heart right over where his own heart would be, and the tattoo heart was impaled by a dagger and embedded in a wreath of deeply red roses. The fellow in the middle, the only one of them smiling, his tattoo heart was run through by seven swords. The man, well, actually, the boy on the right— you could see he wasn't more than twelve or thirteen, even with his bald head and shaved eyebrows—had a squat little heart punctured by three spikes and topped by a cross. This was the something physical about Jesus that Moon Pie had been looking for. Some people might think of the heart as the soul, or might think it's a symbol for love or charity, but when Moon Pie looked at these icons, he saw something more concrete, more fragile, and he thought he understood what Jesus was telling him.

The priest or brother running the booth closed his breviary and smiled. Please, he told them, look around. There were hundreds of holy cards depicting Jesus and his disembodied Sacred Heart in poses ranging from the stark to the sentimental. In most of the depictions, Moon Pie noticed, Jesus held open his robe to display His luminous heart. In a few, He actually touched His own heart, and those were the pictures Moon Pie liked. If you can touch the heart, then it must be flesh, not shadow and light or smoke and mirrors. Moon Pie bought himself a holy card for seventy-five cents, one in which

Jesus grips the heart in His left hand; the heart itself is drenched in blood, dripping, is sizzling with fire and belted with thorns. You can see the firelight passing through the wound at the back of the hand.

That night in his, his and Duane's room, Moon Pie taped the holy card to the headboard of the bottom bunk next to the snapshot that Hotson had taken of the four of them, him, Duane, Billy Wayne, and Tami Lynne in front of the monkey house at the zoo.

Moon Pie heard his mother on the phone in the kitchen, asking to speak with Rev. Guice. "And I thought," he heard his mother say, "that since he's into God now, Jesus anyway, that maybe you could help him. Moon Pie heard his mother tell the Reverend Guice, whoever he was, that this Thursday evening would be fine.

Moon Pie slipped out of his wheelchair and into bed. He switched on the reading lamp and looked at his choices scattered on the bed. He opened his daddy's *Lives of the Saints* and read about martyrs: about St. Elmo's intestines being wound out of his abdominal cavity and onto a windlass; about St. Winifred's severed head; about St. Lawrence roasting on a gridiron, and about awls being stabbed into St. Crispin's skin.

Maybe these saints knew that Jesus loved the afflicted. The cripple at Bethesda, blind Bartimaeus. Miracles. Jesus always had time for the lame or the blind. The Centurian's servant, the woman with the issue of blood, the man with palsy. Lazarus. Both of them, the dead one and the leper. Why would Jesus bring a man back from the dead if the soul were blissfully in heaven?

Tami Lynne knocked, said it's late now, Moon Pie. Nine o'clock. She kissed him on the forehead and switched off the reading lamp. In the dark, Moon Pie pictured Jesus in a Speedo. He counted the wounds: the hole in his side, two in the hands, two in the feet, the crown of thorns. It took awhile, but Moon Pie counted eighty-seven open cuts on the forehead and scalp. Jesus turned around. Moon Pie examined the flagellated back and the legs. They never tell you about the legs. He began to count.

10

Stricken,
Smitten of God,
and Afflicted

*M*eetings of the Disabled Person's Bible Fellowship at the Grace Episcopal Church took place on Thursday evenings in the church's day-care center. The Reverend Richmond Guice met Tami Lynne and Moon Pie in the church parking lot. He didn't look like any preacher Moon Pie had ever seen. His hair was long for one thing, and uncombed. He wore these round wire-framed glasses, and he had a withered left arm that ended with a nubby hand that looked a little too much like a goat's udder to suit Moon Pie. Didn't dress much like a priest or minister or whatever they called them here, either. His short-sleeved shirt was silky-looking and lavender, and his Roman collar was loose and hung from his neck like a comma. Father Guice told Tami Lynne to pick her son up at eight-thirty. He shook hands with Moon Pie, got him out of the car and into the wheelchair, and then led him up the ramp to the day-care center. At the classroom, Father Guice switched on the fluorescent lights and told Moon Pie to come on in.

Father Guice unfolded several metal chairs and arranged them in a kind of circle in the middle of the room. "The others will be along shortly," he said. He sat in one of the chairs. "Buddy Glass tells me you're a genius," he said.

"You know Mr. Glass?"

"We're old friends. He's been on my radio show a few times. The group's actually not all that much into Bible study or anything. I don't know what your momma told you."

"Just that she thought this might do me some good."

"Sometimes the good is just the talking. Like you might want to talk about your daddy and brother and all."

Moon Pie said hello to the other five of them. Then he listened. People seemed to talk about whatever was on their minds. Murl Tedeton was twenty-three and blind. He wasn't about to go into all the gory details again for the umpteenth time, he said. But for Moon Pie's sake he explained how four years ago at work he somehow splashed chemicals into his eyes and burned his corneas, lenses, pupils, retinas, the whole shooting match. He took off his sunglasses and revealed sockets of meringue.

Teddy Faber, who could have been thirty years old or fifty, had Down's Syndrome, Moon Pie could tell. Teddy said he was hungry. Father Guice took out a stick of Juicy Fruit, unwrapped it, and gave it to Teddy.

Three years ago, when he was fourteen, Huey Rabun dove off the high board at the Forsythe Park pool and knocked his head on the cement apron, and he's been paralyzed from the neck down ever since. Shecorbia Wilson's head jerked and flopped when she spoke. Her left arm, tucked into her side, seemed useless. Her legs, Moon Pie noticed, were scissored and stiff and were probably as inconsequential to her as his flippers were to him. Shecorbia said that she would need the money from everyone who was making the Atlanta trip by next week, so she could make the motel arrangements.

You're invited, of course, Father Guice told Moon Pie. We make these pilgramages a couple of times a year. This time they were going to some little town in Georgia. The Blessed Mother appears at this farm there on the thirteenth of every month.

Moon Pie didn't know what to say. "I'll ask my momma."

Huey said, "Tell her people are being healed at this place."

Moon Pie smiled. "I don't think so," he said.

"How do you explain that people who were blind could see, who were lame could walk?" Father Guice said.

"Because I can't explain it doesn't mean it's a miracle."

Father Guice said Moon Pie was right. "It's not a question of proof. It's a question of belief. And some are called to darkness, you know, and some to light."

"Aren't you all going to make yourselves miserable waiting for something to happen that isn't going to happen?" Moon Pie said.

Father Guice smiled. "What you're telling us makes perfect sense. The thing is that we," and here he raised his withered arm and gestured to the group, "we here in this room have witnessed the miraculous."

Then Huey told Moon Pie the story of Wiley Goforth and how the Fellowship used to meet weekly in Wiley's room up at St. Francis even though Wiley was in a coma, had been for two years. How the coma happened was Wiley's home from school with the measles, not faking this time. He was watching "The Guiding Light," his momma said, when he fell asleep on the couch and just never woke up. So this one Thursday night, Father is talking, I think, or someone is, and Wiley's momma is by his bedside like she always is. Wiley opens his eyes, says out loud, "He showed me a river." At least that's what we think he said.

"Was all that prayer in the room," Murl said.

"By the next morning, he was off the machine," Father Guice said. "In a week he was walking, and pretty soon he was back to almost normal. Right now he's a security guard over to the college."

"But Wiley was sick," Moon Pie said. "If you're sick, you have a chance to get better. Disabled is permanent."

Shecorbia said Jesus put us here to know, love, and serve Him and we could all do that better if we have all our parts and had them in working order.

There was a moment of quiet, and then Father Guice cleared his throat. "Why do you think," he said, "that the few of us have been afflicted with disabilities?"

"That's a mystery," Moon Pie said.

"A mystery?" Murl said.

"Mystery is good," Moon Pie said. "You get to wonder about it, like we're doing, and imagine, think, and when you do, you get as close to God as you're likely to get. In your mind, I mean."

Father Guice nodded. "It's like prayer."

"I think so," Moon Pie said. "And that's how I'm different than my daddy. He never saw anything lovely about not having answers. I think that was the cause of his distress."

"Are you saying Jesus wants us to suffer?" Shecorbia said.

" 'As ye are partakers of the sufferings, so shall ye be also of the consolation,' " Moon Pie said. "You can do it now or you can do it later."

After the meeting, Father Guice asked Moon Pie if he wanted to come on his radio show and talk like you've been talking tonight. We're on Saturdays and holidays at six in the morning. You wouldn't miss school or anything. Could maybe get Mr. Glass to give you extra credit.

KSIN CALLED IN a reporter and a photographer from the *News-Star-World* to do a feature on its new handicapped prodigy, Moon Pie Fontana, child of sorrows, when he was invited back to do a second show. The photograph showed Moon Pie with headphones on, leaning into the microphone on the sound control console. The publicity earned Moon Pie a marked degree of local celebrity and a larger audience share for his subsequent appearances on "Sonrise Seminar." People who didn't give a second thought to God on a usual day rose early to listen in to what the little fellow had to say.

The way the program worked was Father Guice would make a point, say about the image of God. Then Moon Pie— and they didn't rehearse this—would talk about what he thought: If God is a spirit, like you say, Father, without a body or parts or passion, if He's pure being, well then God is not restricted to space and time the way we are. That makes sense, Father Guice would say. So He's omnipresent, Moon Pie would say, and eternal. He's essence and existence, light and particle. Here's some else of what he had to say:

"Jesus lost everything, didn't He? Lost His family, friends, life. And that's His message—don't hold on too tightly to what you love, what you own, because you will lose it. Now that could be your automobile or it could be your daddy."

"Jesus is the Teeth of Time."

"Jesus's message is not that we'll live forever, but that we'll die forever. He came not to show us how to live, but how to die."

"All that Jesus cares about is failure, misery, and pain. That is what evokes His compassion."

"Good health makes provincials of us. We stop thinking about others. We figure, well, we don't need braces to walk, dogs to lead us, bags to empty our waste, we don't need ramps to get us into church, and so we think nobody does."

Besides talking to Moon Pie, Father Guice took phone calls from listeners who had questions or comments for Moon Pie:

"What you said about good health, I agree one hundred and ten percent. I had one leg shorter than the other, and I prayed to Jesus to lengthen the leg because I could no longer tolerate the ache in my hip and in my lower back and the pain shooting down my sciatic nerve. And Satan made that baby leg grow two inches in front of my eyes and my husband Bobby's eyes, too. And I was fit, and I fell away from the Lord. I no longer needed Him. And I lived in sin until ten years later, which is last April, when my Bobby run off to Oklahoma with his first cousin Dessie Rae Odum, who should burn in hell, and that's when the spirit of God moved upon me, and I was saved."

"I have a buildup of pus around my lungs which I have removed monthly at St. Francis with this enormous and dreadful needle. But what I'm wondering is am I doing the right thing, you know? Should I stop having the pus sucked out? For that matter, should I start smoking again?"

"Jesus told me to call you, Moon Pie. Jesus told me you are dead right about everything you say, and he wants the people in Ouachita Parish to know the truth. Yes, sir, that's correct; He visits me. Calls me His little bride, His victim of love. Told me He was everything, and I was nothing. Love, He told me, is a killing disease."

"Moon Pie, this is Blondell, first time caller from Sterlington. Love the show. My testimony is this: My baby Weldon, when he was born, before he died, he squawked like a blue jay. And when you laid him down on the crib, he gurgled like . . . like a . . . well, kind of like a drowning cat in a burlap sack."

"Anyone want to know what real suffering is you come over to my house and crawl into my iron lung. Lie still like I did for six years. See what it feels like. I keep it in the living room to remind me how lucky I am."

AFTER THREE WEEKS, the show was doing so well for KSIN, better even than "The Prophecy Hour" on Sunday mornings, that Jerry Meachum, the station manager, flush with the prospect of total market penetration, called Moon Pie and Father Guice into his office after the show and told them how pleased he was, and how this was really only the beginning. "You know that, don't you?"

Moon Pie couldn't imagine. The beginning of what?

Jerry said, "The beginning of your ministry. 'And a little child shall lead them.' " Jerry leaned back in his swivel chair, folded his hands on his belly.

"I don't know about that," Moon Pie said.

"Sure, it's overwhelming now, but you'll get used to the idea." Jerry nudged a bowl of after-dinner mints toward Moon Pie's side of his desk. "Have a couple."

"No, thanks."

Jerry looked at Father Guice, loosened his tie. "What do you think, Reverend? You think the boy has a duty to the Lord to spread this message? Or no?"

"Well, sir, I think he's doing just fine on our show."

Jerry stood, took off his sports jacket, draped it over the back of his chair, and walked around the desk to Moon Pie. He hunkered down in front of Moon Pie and put his hands on the wheelchair. "Truth is merchandise, just like anything else. Just like antacid tablets. And if you don't advertise it, like the prophets did with the word of God, if you don't hustle the truth, ain't no one going to hear about it, ain't no one going to buy it, no matter how remarkable it is."

"I never said this was the truth, Mr. Meachum. It's just what I think. And I think it's what I believe, but I am only a kid."

Jerry Meachum tousled Moon Pie's hair. He stood, said, "I don't want to rush you into anything. You think about it. Talk to your momma. Tell her this. I think I can get you a TV appearance, maybe work into a regular show."

IT WAS MR. Glass's idea that for extra credit, Moon Pie ought to conduct tape-recorded interviews with friends and acquaintances. Mr. Glass loaned Moon Pie a small tape re-corder, said just ask them their thoughts about God. Moon Pie played the responses on the show.

Dencil C.: I wouldn't want to think that God didn't exist. We need the comfort. But He probably doesn't exist.

Hazel C.: It's funny, but I don't know anyone who thinks that God is everywhere anymore. What happened to Him, do you think?

Tami Lynne F.: God's something personal that doesn't need to be discussed in public. People get too excitable about God. Look at all your wars.

Azzie Lee O.: It might be better if we thought as hard about people as we do about God.

Hotson T.: Back when the universe was the size of a smitch on the head of a pin, God was the quantum particle that unbalanced the mix. Anyway, like Augustine said, God cre-ated the universe out of time, not in it. So we'll never know anything about God. And it doesn't matter. No pun intended.

Cecil P.: God's like what you call your sadistics, statistics, whatever. You can use Him to prove anything you want, even contrariwise things. Am I right?

ON THANKSGIVING MORNING Moon Pie talked about Jesus and his innumerable wounds and said that even before the disfigurement, Jesus the man was probably nothing much to look at, not at all like the picture on the decoupage clock here in the studio. The telephone's Line #1 blinked. Father Guice pushed the button. "Hello. Happy Thanksgiving. You're on the Mainline. Go ahead."

"Moon Pie, this is your momma. Am I on the air?"

"Hi, Momma."

"Moon Pie, honey, come on home now. Your daddy's come back to us. And your brother, Duane."

11

The Light Which
Puts Out Our Eyes

*P*erhaps on that dank and feverish night
one hundred and forty-something years
ago when Peregrine Fontana mounted his found woman on
their rude bed of damp moss and musky pelts, and groaned
and ground two lives into being, it became the cruel and
unavoidable fate of the Fontanas to endure heroically or
mindlessly a century or more of misery and affliction and to
be ultimately vanquished by this uncompromising and degen-
erate gene. Or does the responsibility for tragedy rest not with
fate and heredity but with a man and his fatal act of will?
Perhaps, in the end, it does not matter. A choice is made, a
step taken, a stone loosed, the landslide begun.

The particular avalanche that buried our three Fontanas started precisely at noon on September 7th of this year, ten months after Billy Wayne drove up the Winnsboro Road into town, Duane asleep in the capped bed of the pickup, pulled into his driveway, and walked up to the house holding Duane draped across his shoulders like a shawl. Billy Wayne saw Tami Lynne at the kitchen table, heard the squeak of a radio, and opened the screen door. Tami Lynne looked up from her crossword puzzle and was struck dumb. She thought she might be having a Russell Sikes–like mystical experience. Here was this familiar-looking ventriloquist and his limp dummy, both dressed in seersucker suits and white bucks, their brown hair short, parted, and slicked down with pomade like they were about to perform on the "Good Morning, Ark-La-Miss" television program. Now they might be Venusians, or angels even, but why were they coming down the hall toward her kitchen? Indeed, Daddy and son looked more like they'd just attended a weekend sales conference at the Holidome and not survived a year and a half on the road and in the swamp.

"Tami Lynne, let me explain."

"Billy Wayne?"

"I'm sorry."

Tami Lynne stood. "Oh my God," she said. "My baby Duane." She put her hands to her mouth.

"He's just asleep, Tami Lynne, that's all."

Tami Lynne cried. She kissed Duane and squeezed his hand. Duane muttered something in his sleep.

"He tried to stay awake," Billy Wayne said. "He was so excited. Engine trouble in Alto. We planned to be home hours ago."

Tami Lynne whispered, "I don't want to hear your trash now, Billy Wayne. Give one good reason why I shouldn't call Buddy Tidwell right now and have him haul your sorry ass off to jail." She took Duane from Billy Wayne's arms and carried him to the couch in the living room. She undressed him. She asked Billy Wayne where he got these outfits.

"The Wal-Mart in Winnsboro. We were looking pretty ragged."

She covered Duane with a sheet and an afghan, drew the shades. She and Billy Wayne went back to the kitchen. She sat at the table. Billy Wayne stood by the sink. Nothing had changed in the kitchen so far as he could tell. Well, the calendar from Spat's Pharmacy was new. He drank a glass of water. A commercial for Danny-Edwards's Dodge-Chrysler played on the radio. The salesman said, "When it comes to service, I mean business." Tami Lynne turned the radio off.

"I just came by to drop off Duane," Billy Wayne said. "I'm going to turn myself in." He put the glass on the counter. "I'm sorry," he said. "You and Russell, you take good care of the boy."

"Never mind about Russell Sikes," she said. "Russell Sikes is gone. What do you have to say for yourself?"

"I am truly sorry for what I've done, Tami Lynne. I had no right to take the boy. I know that. I was just . . ." Billy Wayne shook his head. "I don't know what I was."

"That's all you have to say? You stole my boy from me for a year and a half, and now you stroll into my house, hang your head like a bad dog, and think everything's going to be okay or something?"

"I don't think that at all. I did something wrong and I'll take responsibility."

"As if you had a choice."

They stared at each other. Billy Wayne blinked. Tami Lynne asked him why he'd done it in the first place.

"I don't know anymore. I can't remember."

"That's not good enough."

"I didn't want to lose everything I had."

"And now you have."

"Yes."

Tami Lynne watched Billy Wayne stare at the clock and then at his shoes. She slammed her fists on the table. "You stole my child, damn it. I can't never get that time back with him, Billy Wayne, not ever." Tami Lynne wept.

Billy Wayne wondered should he hold her. He pictured himself taking the two steps to her chair. Saw himself place his hands on Tami Lynne's shoulders. He didn't move.

Tami Lynne held her head in her hands. "You abandoned your little baby, tossed him away like leftovers." She looked at Billy Wayne. "What kind of human being are you?"

Billy Wayne shook his head. He was falling, it felt like. There was nothing, he knew, that he could offer his wife that could satisfy her grief and her rage, nothing that would even make sense. He held on to the sink, stared at the clock as if it had an answer. What time was it? Falling and falling. He tried to remember what it was had given him the resolve to do the right thing, to come home. The answer was in his mind he was sure, but was it retrievable? And if retrievable, could he decipher it? What kind of human being was he? Billy Wayne tried to grab hold of something to break this fall. Any particle of intuition might gain him purchase.

"I saw my life was a lie," he said. That was a start. "All of it." Billy Wayne told Tami Lynne about his dream of the fire on Moon Pie's forehead and the frogs that sprung from his own mouth. "Each frog was a different lie," he said.

He said he didn't know how this was possible, but he was somehow, out there in the wild, able in his mind's eye to scatter his insight and observe before him his entire past at once, like a landscape, and he could be still and behold every false move he'd ever made, from the fib he'd told Monsignor Pargoud about the poor-box money to the pleasure he'd felt at Angelo Candela's misfortune to the night he sat by the Dallimore place and convinced himself to be spontaneous, to wield a power he had not earned. Billy Wayne tried to let himself cry, but could not. Was this light the matter or Tami Lynne sitting there or his shame?

"I don't know that I can redeem myself," he said. "I don't know how to act." He looked at Tami Lynne. "I didn't leave Moon Pie behind for any good reason except that I was afraid of him." Billy Wayne punched his thigh. "I hurt the boy. I know that. And I can never do anything to make that up."

"You're right about that," Tami Lynne said. "I hope you understand it. There are no second chances. There's no start-ing over, no new life to run away to. You're stuck with your same old self."

"I know." That malevolent and disgraceful self that had been so horrified and intimidated by its unfinished son.

"You think Moon Pie's going to hurt you?"

"Of course not."

"So how are you going to get over this fear, Billy Wayne? How you going to make it up to your son?"

"I hope he lets me try."

"How you going to try if you're in jail somewhere?" Tami Lynne was not at all sure that this was a sensible door to open, but there, she'd done it. "Seems to me like you'd still be avoiding him, hurting him all over again."

Billy Wayne loosened his tie, undid the top button of his shirt. Was she right? Was he retreating to jail? Was coming home also running away? Would he ever understand his moti-vation for anything he did? "I don't think I have a choice in this, Tami Lynne."

"Or maybe you don't want a choice." She knew that nothing good would come of Billy Wayne's incarceration. He needed people, not solitude. He was in every way his own worst en-emy. He wasn't a bad person, just an unbalanced one, all weighted down with sin and guilt and doubt. Made it hard for him to move.

"You think I want to go to jail?"

"What do you want, Billy Wayne?"

He knew he wanted to stop. He wanted to feel as undistracted as he had in the swamp, but he wanted that here where he belonged. And what exactly was "here"? He said, "I want to be around my children, my friends. I want to stop hurting you." Billy Wayne closed his eyes, rubbed them. He saw him and his sons at the breakfast table and they're laughing their heads off at something Moon Pie said. "I want to stop feeling pity for myself."

"It's about time," Tami Lynne said. "I think we should try to keep you out of jail."

"How do we manage that?"

"For Moon Pie's sake," she said. "He needs a daddy."

"Well, I sure don't want to go."

"Don't make me regret this."

"I won't."

"No one thinks you're a criminal, Billy Wayne. Just another decent man who went psycho for a little while."

"I could get an apartment by the park, and I could be here whenever . . . or, you know, the boys could visit me."

"Let's take it one step at a time. You ain't out of jail yet."

"Maybe I'd better call the sheriff," he said. He looked at the clock. Was it really 9:30 already? "Tell him I'm on my way."

"You don't deserve it, but maybe you'll get one last opportunity to love your child." Tami Lynne stood, pushed her chair in toward the table. "Think about it, Billy Wayne. Is that what you want?"

"More than anything."

"Think hard. Because the next time you hurt that boy, you'll kill him."

"I know that."

"Well, before you leave, you'll want to see Moon Pie." She picked up the telephone.

AFTER SHE DROPPED Billy Wayne at the sheriff's and before she took the boys to Morrison's for Thanksgiving dinner, Tami Lynne called Dencil with the news. Dencil said, See I told you he'd come back. Took his damn time though, didn't he? Wait'll Hotson hears about this. Dencil phoned Hazel in Baton Rouge and Hazel called Tami Lynne with the name and number of a well-connected Italian lawyer from Natchitoches who happened to be the governor's chief fund-raiser.

"Thanks, Hazel."

"I'm not so sure you ought to be thanking me. Maybe you should let the asshole rot in jail for a while."

"I couldn't do that."

On Friday morning Tami Lynne called the lawyer who arranged for Billy Wayne's bail and set up a meeting for the three of them with Buddy Tidwell. Then Buddy spoke with Judge Noble Osborne, who in turn received a phone call from the governor's office and then met with the D.A. to set a date for the hearing.

It was this lawyer's suggestion that Billy Wayne move back home, which was fine with Billy Wayne but unnerved Tami Lynne. This was taking several steps at once, to her way of thinking. The idea is, the lawyer said, to present a picture of domestic harmony to Judge Osborne. Is it necessary? Tami Lynne said. I think so, the lawyer said. Then it's okay if he sleeps on the couch? she said. You can stick him in a closet if you want, the lawyer said. I don't care what's really going on. I care about what looks to be going on. That's what's important. Tami Lynne knew she couldn't back out now that Moon Pie was so excited and everything. Okay, she said. She knew if Billy Wayne did anything to hurt Moon Pie, it would be easy this time to toss him out. Her patience was all used up. Or was she kidding herself?

At the hearing Billy Wayne told Judge Osborne that he'd done a lot of thinking in a year and a half and realized now that even though his motive might have been honorable—he had only wanted to be with his boy—his method was sinful. Criminal, Judge Osborne corrected. In short, Billy Wayne explained, his conscience wanted him to return to Monroe from the first night, but he was afraid he'd lose his children, afraid he'd already screwed the family up beyond repair, and he had thought, maybe, this could be a new beginning. I was a fool. At any rate, a deal was fixed. Billy Wayne was sentenced to perform forty hours of community service work a week for two years. And he had to pay off the pickup and sleeping bags plus interest. Given Billy Wayne's background and experience, and perhaps mindful of past debts, Judge Osborne determined that the work should be done at St. Francis of all places. Billy Wayne thought that this really would be like starting over, like stepping back into his childhood before everything started falling apart.

While their parents spent the week in court, Moon Pie and Duane spent their school break getting reacquainted. The first thing that Duane said to Moon Pie was, "I thought you'd be walking by now." Moon Pie introduced his brother to Duane Junior, and the latter was charmed with his namesake, the way it changed colors like a river at dawn, the way it puffed up that deal under its chin while sitting on his shoulder. Duane explained to Moon Pie how he and his daddy caught a rattler one time in Billy Wayne's sleeping bag, how they killed it with the edge of a camp shovel, how they skinned it and gutted it (the heart is like a red bubble stuck to the ribs, you wouldn't believe it), how they grilled chunks of it on sticks, how it tasted like chicken. Moon Pie told Duane about Russell Sikes and his knives and his leaflets, but not about the dream he'd overheard Russell tell the sheriff. About the bobbed tail on the lizard, Moon Pie explained how his friend in gifted, Bobby Joe Wilcoxen, told him lizards would grow a new tail if you cut theirs off. I don't know why I listened to a boy who blew out all his teeth biting down on a blasting cap.

Billy Wayne knew that he and Moon Pie had a lot of catching up to do and that he had a lot to explain to his son. Billy Wayne pushed Moon Pie down Riverside to the Forsythe Avenue Boat Dock. Moon Pie engaged his motor for the climb up the levee. The *Twin City Queen* was at her mooring. It seemed to Billy Wayne like it must have been some other lifetime when he sailed on that thing. Earlene, he thought. She could be watching him right now. All the rain in recent weeks had turned the river maroon with soil. Fog settled on the crowns of cottonwoods across in West Monroe. An old boy in a Ford pickup backed his bass boat and trailer down the ramp and into the river. A kingfisher hovered over the shallows near shore, rattled, and plunged.

"What is it, Daddy?"

"We've never gone fishing, have we?"

"No."

Why did I do that? Billy Wayne thought. Why did I bring up something Duane and I had done? Too late. "We should," he said.

"Today?"

"Soon."

Billy Wayne knelt beside Moon Pie's chair, held his hands, apologized for the last year and a half. "It wasn't nothing against you, Moon Pie, you know that."

Billy Wayne stood, took the handgrips of Moon Pie's chair and walked down the oyster-shell path atop the levee, heading south toward the Louisville Avenue Bridge. My past starts right now, he thought. He didn't examine the thought to see that it was so obviously fraudulent. He bent and kissed the top of Moon Pie's head. With his eyes closed he could see it, the future, like a—what was it Vaughan had written?—like a great ring of pure and endless light. Or was it night?

BILLY WAYNE RECKONED it was more like browsing through a museum of his childhood than properly being at home again. After all, so much had changed at St. Francis. Where the grape arbor had been sat the attendant's shed for the new parking lot. The ornate chapel with its marble altar and stained-glass windows was now the oncology lab; another chapel, in the unadorned contemporary style, occupied a corner of the new pediatric wing just about where the tamale shack and Soul City Records had once stood.

Before punching in that first Monday morning back to work, Billy Wayne sat at a Formica table in the cafeteria and smelled the reassuring and evocative cigarette smoke and frying meat, aromas that drew him back to childhood meals in this very room. He peppered his poached eggs, sugared his coffee, opened the morning paper, and read the headlines. He once would just sit here, in the window light facing the cafeteria line, with Sister Helen. She would tell him stories about her da's potato farm, how he lost it to the bank and they moved to the city, and she would answer his questions about the world beyond the hospital walls. Billy Wayne closed his eyes and thought he could hear her voice in the room now. "People like us with the vocation," she was saying, "do not marry, that's all. There's prayer and there's work. The indisposed are more important than the self. Remember that, Billy Wayne." There were very few nuns left at the hospital, none of whom he had known. In their places was an army of efficient, vigorous, self-assured technicians. Medicine had become a business, not a vocation. Still somebody here would know where Sister Helen's at these days.

He took out his notebook and a pen from his shirt pocket and wrote this: "I have the sense of starting over, as if the fourteen years had not passed, as if I could save both the world and my soul." And then he scribbled over some lines and began a second page: "I fear that nothing will work out." And then this was circled in the middle of the page: "What God has joined together." And below that, underlined: "Like it's still summer, 1972." The notebook was found much later and tagged as evidence by Sheriff Tidwell. Found on the front seat of Billy Wayne's pickup. Billy Wayne looked at the clock and saw he had five minutes to report to maintenance. He folded his newspaper, took a last bite of his raisin toast. He got up, stretched. He didn't feel fourteen years younger.

That afternoon he went downstairs to Personnel and introduced himself to Ginny Thaxton in records.

"What can I do for you, Mr. Fontana?"

Billy Wayne explained who he was, how he had grown up at the hospital, who Sister Helen was and when, as near as he could recall, she might have resigned, and how he had been trying to reach her for so long, and he just wondered if they might not have some kind of recent address of hers that he might copy down.

"That was all before my time," Ginny Thaxton said. She smiled.

"Yes."

She wrote something on a slip of paper, tore the paper from the pad. "Let me just check through the records," she said. "Have a seat, Mr. Fontana."

Ginny Thaxton had a glass bowl of Mardi Gras beads on her desk and a photograph of herself and a young bald man, both of them in sunglasses, both holding cans of beer, both smiling into the camera. When did that start? Billy Wayne thought. All that smiling? He remembered old photos of homesteaders, Civil War soldiers, politicians. Not smiling, just posing naturally. When did everyone decide it was necessary to leave a smile for posterity?

"I've got a call through to Sister Mary Warren over to the convent," Ginny Thaxton said. "Sister Helen was never on the hospital payroll. None of them were. The Order took responsibility. A new one on me."

The phone rang. Ginny answered it, said, "Yes, he is, Sister. One moment," and gave the handset to Billy Wayne.

Sister Mary Warren said she was sorry to have to tell Billy Wayne this, but Sister Helen Lomasney had died more than a year ago.

"What do you mean?" Billy Wayne said. "Are you sure?"

"At St. Vincent's Hospital in Cork. Let's see. Alveoli carcinoma. Lung cancer."

"She didn't smoke."

"I wouldn't know about that, Mr. Fontana."

Billy Wayne pictured Helen in a hospital bed, oxygen tubes in her nose, leashed to an infusion bottle, an EKG monitor. He imagined her shrunk with disease and saw that she was generic, any dying man or woman, pasty, puckered, skeletal, inert. Hair thin as spun cotton, the mouth a toothless beak.

"I'm sorry, Mr. Fontana," Sister Mary Warren said. "She's in our prayers."

Billy Wayne got on Highway 80 and drove east out of town. In front of where the Palms had been was a sign advertising "Space Available" with a phone number. Every time he thought of Sister Helen he shook his head. Or Fox or George. No purpose, he thought, and slapped the steering wheel with the heel of his hand. His future with Sister Helen had been taken from him. No meaning, no answers, no God, no method, no reason, no solace. When Billy Wayne saw the

water towers and smokestack of the Chicago Mill and Lumber
Company he knew he had gone too far. He was in Tallulah,
had driven nearly sixty miles without remembering any of it.
He pulled to the side of the road. Across the street in what
looked to be an abandoned feed store, someone had painted
"Jesus" in red on both sides of the door. The road sign at the
corner ahead said "Vicksburg 25." Had he caught himself
running away again? He made a U-turn and stopped in the
breakdown lane in front of the storefront. Beneath a dripping
air conditioner in what had been a window, the someone
who had written "Jesus" had installed a plywood sign. The
message, printed in red capital letters, got smaller with each
line: "GOD IS USING THIS WOMAN. SISTER BOONE PRAY FOR YOU
AND GOD ANSWER HER PRAYER. IF YOU ARE WITCHCRAFT, SHE
CAN MOVE IT OFF YOU. IF YOU ARE SICK, SHE CAN HEAL YOU.
WHATEVER THE PROBLEM THROUGH THE POWER OF GOD. SHE
CAN DO ALL THINGS. SHE CAN GET YOU A JOB. WHATEVER YOUR
PROBLEM IS, PLEASE COME. SIS. B. BOONE."

In a window at the other side of the door, a window latticed
with wrought iron, a small boy held back a chintz curtain and
looked at Billy Wayne. Billy Wayne waved at the boy. The child
turned his head. A mile up the road, Billy Wayne stopped at the
Ebony Rest'rant and called Tami Lynne from the parking lot
phone. "I'm taking the Interstate back. No, I'm fine."

But Billy Wayne did not drive directly home. He went back
to St. Francis. He stopped in the janitors' room for bucket and
mop and walked to the north wing of the hospital. He rode
the elevator to 4. The moment Billy Wayne both feared and
desired had arrived. The room was as dark as a confessional,
as quiet as a sanctuary, and fragrant of the lilac blossoms in
the glass vase on the nightstand. He felt a shiver at the back
of his neck and switched on the light. He opened the windows,
cleared the flowers and the get-well cards from the bedside
table, and began to swab the floor. But it was too late to

scrub away the memory of Earlene deBastrop, the woman for whom, he now believed, he had sacrificed so much—his youth, his future, maybe even his God. And what was it, he wondered, that had driven him into her arms, that had persuaded him to put his world at risk? Billy Wayne closed the door to 412N and sat perhaps in the very chair in which he had heard Earlene's sins so long ago. It was love, he realized, pure and simple, that had done it. He realized now how much his heart ached for her.

When Earlene left Billy Wayne, she moved away, but not far away, just across the river in West Monroe. She bought herself a double-wide in a little trailer village near Kiroli Park and set up, as you know, an insurance business right out of her paneled parlor. Earlene had this boyfriend for a while, Royal Landry, a car salesman, you might recall, at Danny Edwards's Dodge-Chrysler. Earlene called off the affair. Seemed to take Royal by surprise. When she wasn't writing home and auto policies, Earlene wrote her songs and sent them off to Cousins Music.

Meanwhile Tami Lynne knew nothing about 412N but could see that once again Billy Wayne was driving her away and hurting his children terribly, and she told him why don't you stop. He'd taken up his old habit of reading his books out on the porch, shutting the family out of his mind. He'd work extra hours when he could, stay up late by himself. Said he couldn't sleep hardly at all. He even frightened himself the way he was because he knew what all this might lead to. But even as he held Tami Lynne and promised to display more affection, and even though that is precisely what he wanted to do, to be good, kind to her, he knew he could not. Instead he fantasized about returning to Earlene, a return he believed was divinely ordained even though he had not spoken to Earlene since that day she finally walked out on him—on the boat, on the river.

12

What It Is You Cannot Remember That Is So True

Billy Wayne watched Tommy Candela open a front burner on the gas range, bend over the flame, and light the cigarette in his mouth. "You're going to start yourself on fire one of these days, Tommy."

Tommy took two longnecks from the fridge, nodded to the pair at the kitchen table, and went back to join the party in the living room.

Billy Wayne looked at the Dutch boy on his glass. When he was little he thought that wooden shoes could make you fly. He poured himself an inch of bourbon, poured an inch into Hotson's glass, right up to the Dutch girl's knees. Ronnie had put on a Bobby Blue Bland tape, and Billy Wayne could hear him singing "Turn On Your Love Lights" at the pauses in the several conversations. He raised his glass to Hotson. "Here's to the Blues!"

"We did that one."

"To friends!"

"Hotson," Duane yelled. "How about this?" Duane walked into the kitchen and held out a cedar plaque in the shape of an outhouse with a dial on it that said, "I'm Reading"; "All Clear"; "Come In"; "Keep Out."

"Sure. Anything you want," Hotson told him. "Look through the plunder room."

"What are you going to do with that?" Billy Wayne asked Duane.

"Moon Pie wants this," Duane said. He held up a plastic sno-globe with three sombreroed Mexicans asleep against an adobe wall.

"He's got it," Hotson said.

"That's enough," Billy Wayne said. "Now go on back to Anna's room and play nice with the kids."

Hotson raised his glass.

Billy Wayne raised his and they sipped. "I'll miss you, Hotson."

"We should get drunk," Hotson said.

IN THE LIVING room, Ronnie told Tommy, No, we don't have any Johnny Mathis tapes. She put on Duke Ellington. Turned it low. Dencil sat in the overstuffed club chair and watched Tommy pick the cashews out of a bowl of mixed nuts. He could see from just the way Tommy leaned forward on the davenport, the way his foot was not quite keeping time to "Satin Doll," the new way he combed and lacquered his salt-and-pepper hair, that Tommy was in love. Tami Lynne told Dencil Duane's doing fine. Back in school and everything.

He's no brainwave like his brother, but Mr. Swan says Duane's got a nifty future for himself in the trades if he wants it.

On his way to the bathroom, Billy Wayne passed the living room and heard the name "Swan." Swan, he thought. Swan. He saw a pond, a white swan way off in the distance, and frogs splashing everywhere. Strange. Where had he heard the name? And then he remembered Earlene's confession that first night, he had met her in the hospital room. What was it? Mar . . . Marzell Swan. Yes. Earlene's old boyfriend was Duane's teacher. That's the kind of town Monroe is, he thought.

On his return to the kitchen, Billy Wayne stopped at the living-room door, leaned in, asked if anyone needed a fresh drink. They didn't. He sat at the kitchen table. "Is Earlene coming?" he said to Hotson.

"Coming here? No, she's not coming here."

"Don't look at me like I'm crazy. You all are friends. I just thought she might want to say good-bye, too."

"She did."

Billy Wayne sipped his bourbon, traced the outline of a blue pineapple on the tablecloth. When he thinks of Earlene, Billy Wayne remembers the gap in her front teeth, the way she kind of hopped when she walked, the yellow slicker and yellow boots she wore in the rain, how she could peel an orange in one long strip, how she would squeak an eraser on her front teeth when she wrote her songs. This was crazy, thinking she had any reason to ever want to see him again.

"You okay?" Hotson said.

"The boys don't even know I was ever married before."

"ANGELO'S DONE ALL he really can for the boys," Hazel told Tami Lynne. "It's become obvious to Tommy and me . . ."

(and here she smiled at Tommy) "that Angelo needs more care than we can give him."

This was the first Dencil had heard anything about Hazel's plan to divorce Angelo. Angelo sat there in the hallway with his ball cap over his eyes and his hands on his lap. Angelo still hadn't heard. At least Dencil hoped he hadn't.

"But hasn't Dencil been doing a crackerjack job?" Tami Lynne said.

"That's right, he has," Tommy said. "But Dencil . . ." he looked across the room. "No offense, Dencil. Dencil is not a therapist. We think that Angelo needs therapy."

"But why do you need a divorce to do that, Haze?" Dencil said.

Hazel put her hands on the hem of her skirt and tugged the skirt toward her knees. "It's very complicated, Dencil. Has to do with how much money the nursing home can get its hands on, and all that."

Dencil thought he might need a drink.

WHEN DENCIL SAT down at the table with his beer, Hotson asked him if he ever drank Hershey's chocolate syrup right from the can. It used to be fabulous when it was real chocolate.

"What are you talking about?" Dencil said.

"Kinds of things you ate as a kid," Billy Wayne said. "I did like a nice Vienna sausage sandwich, the sausages right out of the can. On white bread with Miracle Whip and sweet pickle relish."

Dencil said, "Earlene told me she used to make herself ketchup and margarine white-bread sandwiches."

"When she tell you that?" Billy Wayne said.

"Few months ago."

Billy Wayne drank his bourbon and stared at the bottom

of his glass until Hotson said, "We all see her, Billy Wayne. She's our friend."

"I didn't say anything."

"It's not a conspiracy, if that's what you're thinking," Hotson said.

"You can understand why you might not be her favorite person, can't you?" Dencil said.

"Let's drop it," Billy Wayne said.

"So, Hotson," Dencil said, "what are you going to do in New Orleans?"

"I figure I'll get my taxi medallion once I get to know the streets. Tend bar or something in the meantime."

Dencil said, "What about you, Billy Wayne? What are you going to do when this hospital gig is up?"

"I haven't thought about it." He thought. "I don't know."

"I'll be ready to drop this Reddy Kilowatt deal about then. Maybe we could go into business together or something."

They toasted youth, health, telephones, Harry Dean Stanton. And then they toasted chess pie and Elmer's Goldbrick candy bars. Dencil said that he'd miss Angelo, miss taking him to the movies. And then there was a knock at the back door. Webb and Ferlin had come to say good-bye before they headed on back to Baton Rouge. Choir practice early tomorrow.

Billy Wayne couldn't believe it. Hazel's little cowboys were in college now. He wanted to ask them why they still dressed alike. Then he thought that might be rude. Or they might think I'm just talking out of my alcohol. They both wore purple polo shirts, green chinos, and deck shoes. After many hugs and handshakes, Hotson told the boys to be sure to come see the new house in New Orleans. Your momma's got the address.

. . .

IN THE BEDROOM, Tami Lynne watched Ronnie take down the drapes. Tami Lynne sat on the bed and played with the tufts of fabric on the chenille spread. The drapes were a magenta and Nile green palm tree print. Tami Lynne knew they'd clash with everything in her house, but she loved them. Someday she'd have a house with white walls.

While they folded the drapes, Ronnie told Tami Lynne she was sad about leaving Monroe, leaving friends, but she knew it was the right thing. I had another life here, you know. Another marriage. And as long as I stay, the ex stays. She smiled. You know what I mean, hon?

WHEN THE POWER failed, Billy Wayne and Hotson were alone in the kitchen and Billy Wayne was saying that pretty soon no one would know who he was, know that he once had potential, spoke Latin, had a calling. That's when the lights cut out. Hotson yelled to the living room for everyone to sit still. Won't last but a minute. Ronnie yelled back that the streetlights were on, and the lights over to the Festervans' and the Autreys'. Hotson knew what it was then. LP&L shut the power off a day early. Tommy said he thought it was romantic. Ronnie checked on the kids.

"We'll have to finish all the beer, I guess," Hotson said.

Billy Wayne could just make out Hotson's face. The table-cloth pineapples were gray.

Everyone gathered in the living room. Ronnie set two red candles in pewter sconces on the coffee table. Billy Wayne sat on the floor, his back to the sofa, below Tami Lynne. He thought it was interesting how they'd all gone quiet in the dark, how they were all now staring at these fragile lights as if each person was afraid or powerless to look elsewhere, as if it were eyes that kindled the flames, as if the lights would vanish without their gaze. Tami Lynne touched Billy Wayne's shoulder. Billy Wayne shifted, smiled up at Tami Lynne, rested his elbow on Moon Pie's wheelchair.

He should tell Tami Lynne how he knew this misery was his doing, was his punishment, sort of, for having repudiated his priestly vocation. For that and for this unsanctified second marriage. Tami Lynne might be the natural mother of his children, he granted that, but Earlene remained his sanctified wife, no getting around it.

Moon Pie saw his daddy shake his head and wondered what was this hellhound on his daddy's trail. Here was Billy Wayne home at last, reconciled with wife and sheriff, sheltered in the bosom of his family, but for all it was worth, he might as well be gone. If ever Moon Pie mentioned going fishing, Billy Wayne would tell him, Soon, we'll go soon.

It was truly worse for Moon Pie having his daddy at home and still not feeling what it was he could hardly remember ever feeling anymore. He blamed himself. According to Duane, the feral life on Davis Island had been like heaven for him and his daddy. Moon Pie figured that had he been normal like Duane, they, the three of them, would be on that island now, pioneering like the Fontanas of old, the ones he'd heard about from his daddy.

Hotson placed a large portable cassette player on the coffee table and put on a tape of Bach organ fugues. No one spoke. Billy Wayne shut his eyes and felt the music hum through his bones. This could be church. We have eyes because there's light, he thought. When he opened his eyes, Billy Wayne noticed that the flame of the candle in front of the speaker was dancing, pulsing, beating in precise harmony to the music. Even sound was made visible by light.

Hazel giggled and told Tommy not to be fresh. Dencil

snored. Billy Wayne remembered Monsignor Pargoud's votive candle, the one he lit for Billy Wayne one evening in the grape arbor and used to explain the Blessed Trinity. Told Billy Wayne how the flame was like God—the heat was the Father, the form was the Holy Ghost, and the light was Jesus, and they cannot be separated. Billy Wayne didn't say it then, but even at age ten or whatever he was, he knew there was still only the single flame with three attributes, not three flames.

"What are you thinking about, Daddy?" Moon Pie whispered.

Billy Wayne shrugged. "Just listening to the music, honeyboy."

"Me, too," Moon Pie said.

13

Put Out the Light, and Then Put Out the Light

*T*his is what happened on September 7th near as we can tell from what Tami Lynne recalled and what Sheriff Buddy Tidwell and others surmised. Billy Wayne, who hadn't slept well again that night, who had, in fact, already fed the cat, gone down to the 7-Eleven for the paper, done the crossword except for 65 across and 71 down, and shined his shoes, kissed Tami Lynne on the forehead, and left for work at six-twenty. Tami Lynne, for her part, was so touched by her husband's unexpected gesture that she lay in bed imagining kiss after luxurious kiss and determined to do something sweet for Billy Wayne today as he had done for her.

Duane's project for the day was to build a possum trap

out of parts he could salvage from neighborhood dumpsters. Moon Pie could watch, he said, but that's all. So at about nine-thirty, Duane sat reinforcing an orange crate by weaving net fencing through the wooden slats, while at the hospital his daddy sat in the cafeteria on his break. Billy Wayne drank iced tea and stared at the phone number he had jotted down on the notebook paper. He walked as far as the pay phone in the lobby before he hesitated, wadded the paper in his palm, and dropped it onto the gray sand of the ashtray.

Tami Lynne heard the boys bickering out back, went to the window, and yelled for them to hush up and be sweet to each other. Moon Pie was crying and said that Duane had tried to haul the battery off his wheelchair. Seems Duane wanted to somehow electrify his possum trap.

"What, you ignorant, Duane?"

"No, ma'am."

"How you think Moon Pie's going to get around without the battery?"

"I'd just be needing it at night when Moonie's sleeping."

"Stop this foolishment, Duane."

As soon as Tami Lynne drove off to the fish market in West Monroe, Moon Pie turned on the sprinkler and drove his wheelchair back and forth through the spray. While Moon Pie played car wash, Duane pondered his possum trap. All right then, he figured, he'd use gravity, not electricity. One little whatchamacallit fixed into the frame, he reckoned, would hold the door up, but just barely, so's any vibration would drop the door shut like a guillotine. He fetched his daddy's old electric hand drill out of the shed and ran the extension cord across the lawn and in through the kitchen window. Damp feet, metal motor housing. You can see it coming, can't you? As soon as he squeezed the trigger, Duane got himself straightened up with 120 volts of electricity, and when an upper filling touched a lower filling in his mouth, he screamed, collapsed on his back. His eyes started jiggling in their sockets. Had Tami Lynne returned then as she had intended, she might have found Duane groaning in the dirt, seen how mightily he perspired, and heard how he told Moon Pie how his heart had skipped some beats. She might have brought him to the hospital. But Tami Lynne, because of what she heard, did not come directly home.

Billy Wayne had been unable to concentrate on his work all morning. Sure, he'd discarded the phone number; he'd memorized it anyway, and why did he need the number when he knew the address, had even driven by the home twice in the past week and parked a block away and watched until the parlor light came on at dawn and a face peeked out the window? He knew that he belonged to Earlene and she to him, else why ever would they have met, married, and pledged undying love? Surely there had to have been a purpose, reasoned Billy Wayne, elsewise this world and everything in it were all merely accidental and random—not the kind of world a God would create. Moon Pie was on the right track that way—there must be some idea of order even if we can never figure it out. Not even the kind of world that the laws of physics would tolerate. Be they God's or nature's, no one escapes the laws. So when the lunch buzzer sounded in the janitors' room, Billy Wayne decided to forgo the corn dog special in the cafeteria. He took his fate in his hands and drove to Earlene's.

Tami Lynne wanted this to be a special night for her and Billy Wayne. Perhaps his kiss had been the signal that their life was going to change. Tami Lynne felt buoyant, happy, as if the sun had shone after days of gloom, cold, and rain. She planned to make Billy Wayne's favorite that night—crawfish etouffe. Maybe she was right to have been so patient with him. After all, she had turned away from him once, and that had ended disastrously. So on leaving Bayles Landing Fish Market, Tami Lynne drove to Green Acres, the florist shop on Cypress run by the Oglesbees. Azzie Lee was working the store for her momma, it being a Saturday morning and all. Tami Lynne ordered a half dozen blood red roses, and Miss Azzie Lee remarked how it must be Tami Lynne's anniversary.

"Why do you say that, Miss Oglesbee?"

"Promise you won't tell."

"Tell what?"

"Your Billy Wayne. He was in here not three minutes ago buying you a dozen of those long-stemmed Mr. Lincolns."

"You must be mistaken."

"No, ma'am, it was Billy Wayne for sure. First time we'd seen each other since . . . well, you know."

"But he's at work."

"And now both of you got roses. Won't he be surprised?"

"Just three minutes ago?"

"Yes, ma'am, that's right. Drove off down Cypress toward Kiroli Park."

Tami Lynne borrowed Azzie Lee's phone book a minute and looked up under "Insurance" in the Yellow Pages.

"Thank you, Miss Oglesbee."

Moon Pie persuaded Duane he should take a bath on account of he was covered with dirt, and he promised not to tell anyone what happened. Billy Wayne convinced Earlene to let him speak to her just a moment in the privacy of her office. Duane locked the bathroom door to secure his privacy against his mother's imminent return. Earlene backed away from Billy Wayne, and without saying a word, drew the blinds shut and locked the front door. In God's eyes, Earlene, we're still married, Billy Wayne said. Always will be. Billy Wayne handed her the roses that he held out to her like a torch or like, he thought, Jesus offering you his burning, bleeding heart on

Moon Pie's holy card. Not in my eyes, Billy Wayne, Earlene said. It's this other marriage, he went on, that's the sin, that's driving him to hell on earth.

"I need your forgiveness, Earlene."

"I can't give you that, Billy Wayne."

"I've sinned."

"It would have been better if you had killed me," Earlene said. She sat on a folding chair.

Billy Wayne sat on the ottoman facing her. "Just listen to me, Earlene," he whispered. "I need to tell you."

Earlene held the roses on her lap. "Why?"

"You deserve to know."

"I don't care to know. It won't change what happened, will it?"

"I couldn't stop myself, Earlene. I knew the affair was wrong, but I couldn't stop. I ached."

"I know what you did, Billy Wayne. I don't need to hear about it."

"But you don't know why."

"And you do?"

"I think I do." Billy Wayne shut his eyes, dropped his forehead onto his folded hands. He heard the squeak of old wood as Earlene stood, heard her say, To want to know why I'd have to want to understand you, Billy Wayne. And I don't.

"I would have done anything for you, Billy Wayne."

Billy Wayne opened his eyes and saw Earlene standing by the sofa with her back to him. Earlene's telephone chirped. He heard the click of her answering machine and her voice say that she could not come to the phone right now but the call was important to her. Whoever it was hung up. Earlene walked to the desk, set the flowers down, put the phone line on hold. She began to cry. Billy Wayne wanted to say something. He couldn't believe that after all these years, he was with Earlene again, that, though he did not deserve this, he was being given a chance to witness his love for her, and that, he knew, would be enough. He would tell her how he believed that they would one day be together again and how that faith alone endowed him with patience and fortitude. He could almost touch her. "I love you, Earlene."

"Stop this."

"Earlene, have you been waiting for me?"

Earlene sat in her desk chair, wiped her eyes with tissues. She bit her lip, tried not to look at Billy Wayne.

"Earlene, we need a person to tell us we're still good after all we've done."

Earlene took a deep breath, sniffled. "Billy Wayne?" she said.

"It's all right," he said. He walked to the chair and touched her shoulder. "It's all right."

And whatever else Billy Wayne confessed to her in the dim light of the mobile home beneath the sofa-sized painting of waves crashing on a stormy beach so stirred Earlene that, well, they didn't hear the doorbell ring.

Over the hum of his wheelchair, Moon Pie thought he heard a thrashing from the bathroom. He called to Duane, heard the thrashing again and then the racket of metal and something else hitting against the porcelain. Moon Pie repeatedly rammed the bathroom door with his chair, then went for Russell Sikes's cleaver. Crying and yelling for Duane to hang on, Moon Pie hacked a hole through the door panel large enough for him to see Duane faceup in the water, his eyes staring back at the door. When he had fallen, Duane ripped down the vinyl shower curtain and now lay covered in pastel flowers. His lips were blue. A trace of blood leaked from his ear. His heart had shorted out and fluttered to a stop.

What happened after that happened rather quickly. Tami Lynne found the side door of the double-wide unlocked and walked in. She discovered the couplers on their backs in the middle of the living-room floor, their shirts and shoes on, their eyes closed. She picked up the pen-and-letter holder shaped like a cat from Earlene's Parsons table. She dropped it and drew their attention. Earlene reached for her skirt and draped it over her middle. Billy Wayne sat up.

"How tender," Tami Lynne said. "Father Fontana and his child bride reunited at last."

"Tami Lynne," Billy Wayne said. "What the hell!"

Earlene shook her head. "Jesus Christ, Billy Wayne, you're still trouble."

"More than you think, sweetie," Tami Lynne told her. "Billy Wayne, don't you even think about coming home. The boys and I are through with you."

"Look, I'm sorry," Earlene said.

"Not so sorry as you will be."

"I had no choice, Tami Lynne," Billy Wayne started to explain.

"Yes, I know. This is your salvation."

While Tami Lynne confronted Earlene and Billy Wayne with their tawdry behavior and told her husband that she was leaving him for the second and final time, Moon Pie was driving his machine up Forsythe to 18th and from 18th to DeSiard and down DeSiard past Hub Cap City, past the city cemetery, past Cloyd's Beauty School, past Haddad's Pest Control, all the way to the river. He wasn't looking for his daddy this drive. He was looking to get free of what his daddy had called this genetic knowledge, free of the disaster, the heartbreak, that shadowed his family, every maniacal, suicidal, criminal, diseased one of them.

When Tami Lynne found Duane the way he was, naturally she snapped some. Neighbors found her dragging Duane's naked body across the front lawn and called the police. Tami Lynne was sedated and hospitalized. When the social worker arrived to collect Moon Pie, he was, as we have said, long gone.

He had by then reached the Forsythe Avenue Boat Dock back near his house and sat staring past the *Twin City Queen* into the silty Ouachita. He wished his daddy had never come home. He wished it were like it used to be before the dreamer Russell Sikes, before the lizard, before the milk cartons. He wished he could disappear like Duane. And then he started the long slide down the hundred-foot boat ramp. According to the jogger on the levee who witnessed the whole spectacle, when the chair hit the black water, Moon Pie was thrown ahead ten feet, went under, surfaced, just his head above the water. He looked around, smiled, and then dove. Damndest thing I ever saw, the jogger said.

Later that night, Sheriff Tidwell came for Billy Wayne at Earlene's, asked her to stay in the house, told him to step outside for a minute, and confronted him with the news of his two dead boys and a wife shattered with grief. "And here you are having yourself a tomcat time of it."

"Oh my God." Billy Wayne slumped to the ground and kept on moaning and saying, "What have I done? What have I done?" over and over again. The sheriff let him go on for a bit and then hauled him up by the armpits, sat him in the back of the cruiser, slapped his face, and shook him silent.

"Look here, Billy Wayne. I don't know what the hell you done. I just know you done something. You're the goddamndest Fontana of all, you are. No matter how bad things ever got out there in the Bottom, the Fontanas always took care of their children. Boy, you ain't fit to roll with a pig."

Billy Wayne cried into his hands.

"This whole parish is finished with you. You best go somewhere, son."

Billy Wayne drove home, drew the shades, put out the lights, sat in the dark in the boys' room, holding their bedsheets against his face. Smelling his sons. Half the time he thought he must be making this up, that the horror couldn't be real. He closed his eyes and waited for the nightmare to end. He curled up on the floor and drifted toward sleep. In his drowsiness he imagined Duane with an exterior heart that pulsed fire and Moon Pie as a helium balloon tethered by the string in Billy Wayne's fingers. Any gust of wind could extinguish the flame, carry his boy away. He shook himself conscious.

Now that his boys were gone, they were impossible to ignore. He'd killed his sons, and now they would not die. In this unlit room, Billy Wayne could see his sons plainly and could see his own depravity, and he understood that he was an abomination, the murderer of children, destroyer of lives. He lay there now alone, afflicted by darkness, cursed by light, and prisoner to the magnifying power of memory.

And so Billy Wayne decided to punish himself since we could not and went to the backwash of Chauvin Bottom, where he fashioned himself a crown of nettle as some kind of penance. The nettle, of course, itched, stung, blotted his skin no doubt, and within hours swelled his eyes shut. So there he was, the final Fontana, stumbling through his ancestral home, blind as his daddy, eyes without light, trying to exorcise his tenacious demons or atone for this original sin he carried in his genes, when he fell into a nest of cottonmouths. We found him in the morning, bloated with swamp water and venom, and covered with snakes.

14

What Peace We Often Forfeit, What Needless Pain We Bear

The staff at St. Francis was keeping Tami Lynne under observation. She was refusing to eat or to speak with the psychiatrist. Medication kept her calm but could not relieve her wretchedness and sorrow. When Dencil came to sit with her that next morning and brought along her robe, slippers, and nightgown, all Tami Lynne would say was "Where are my babies, Dencil?" Dencil squeezed her hand, told her he would see to things, and went home to make the funeral arrangements.

He called Poteet's Funeral Home because it had the biggest display ad in the Yellow Pages and the motto "Large enough to fit your every need, and small enough to know you personally." He spoke with Homer Poteet himself. He said, "What is it you're getting at with that slogan of yours?"

"Who is this, please?"

"Dencil Currence. Your ad here sounds a little peculiar to me."

"I'm sorry, but I don't think I understand."

"This 'fit your every need' part. That's not some kind of mortuary humor, is it?"

"I can assure you, Mr. Currency, it is not. We have been in business since 1948, and we do not take death lightly."

Now Dencil wondered if he'd heard his name right and if that last remark was meant to be funny in an uppity way. It was as if language itself had decided to be illuminating no longer, but rather opaque and disheartening. Like the world.

"Are you still there?" Homer Poteet said.

"I've got three dead bodies for you, Mr. Poteet," Dencil said. "Is that redundant?"

Before the burial, a small memorial service was held in the Eternal Light Prayer Chapel at Poteet's at which the Reverend Guice said a few words, mostly about Moon Pie, whom he said he was blessed—we all were—to have known, if even for so brief a time. He said who could know God's plan, and he quoted the Wisdom of Sirach: "When you are born, you are born to a curse," he said. "And when you die, a curse will be your lot."

Azzie Lee Oglesbee stood in the vestibule of the chapel, waiting to collect the funeral baskets, the spears of gladioli, the wreaths, and bring them to the grave sites at the city cemetery. She wondered why it had been her fate to have gotten all mixed up in this Fontana business, wondered what it was God was trying to tell her. She remembered Duane as a cute little boy with respectful manners who didn't know the first thing about geography. Couldn't point to Louisiana on the U.S. map. Good with his figures, though. She hardly knew the little one.

Webb and Ferlin sang "What a Friend We Have in Jesus." When they had finished, Earlene asked them if they knew "There's a Fountain." The boys looked at each other. Webb or Ferlin said, "About the sinners plunged beneath the flood? That one?"

"Yes," she said. " 'Lose their guilty stains.' "

"We know it," he said, looked at his brother, nodded, and they began.

"Redeeming love has been my theme," the boys sang. "And shall be till I die."

Father Guice blessed the caskets. Homer Poteet escorted the mourners out the side door to the parking lot. Earlene shook hands with Webb and Ferlin, thanked them very much.

Earlene sat in back with Ronnie and Anna. Anna asked why was Moon Pie dead. Nothing lasts forever, she said, not even school. Nothing except this one thing, Ronnie told her. Earlene looked out the window at the wild mustard and sparkleberry growing alongside the lot. She wondered where Tami Lynne would find the strength or the will to survive all this. Sheriff Tidwell lit the rotating beacon on his cruiser and pulled out onto Oliver Street. Hotson followed the hearse.

The funeral drew lots of attention, naturally. It was not only the sensational nature of the deaths, not just that folks were jolted into an uncomfortable awareness of their own vulnerability, but that these, we realized, were the last Fontanas. This was the end of a presence that we had all taken for granted, and we weren't at all sure what we would do from that day forward. It was as if something in the soul of the town had died, or worse, we feared, that we had let something precious slip away. What would happen to Monroe now? The city cemetery was crowded with spectators who lined the walkways and stood along the iron fence. Claudia Simmons and her cameraman stood by the gate as the hearse pulled in. One photographer climbed the Saunders monument for a picture, but Buddy Tidwell suggested he climb down on the double.

We have a truckload of folklore and superstitions about death in our part of Louisiana. If your name, for example, is carved on a tree, and that tree falls, you'll die. A bird in the house means someone there will die. If a dog howls on a moonless night, a neighbor will die. If a buzzard sits on your chimney, someone inside the house will die before the year is out. If you were to stand and watch a person walk out of sight, that person would die. Now you might not believe that, but you would never want to test it out. Another thing that you might not believe is that it is bad luck to keep a crippled person's crutches when he dies, and maybe we don't believe it either, but we do abide by the tradition of burying them with the departed, and that is why Moon Pie's wheelchair, the brightwork polished, the leather cleaned and oiled, the battery removed, was folded and placed atop his lowered casket. Mr. Glass and the students from Moon Pie's gifted program filed by his grave. Each child dropped something onto the casket— a pencil case, a flower, baseball cards, a drawing of Moon Pie flying over Monroe, a picture of Einstein, a calculator, a radio, a box of Sugar Pops.

Father Guice talked about the joy of the desolate, the light of the straying. "Earth has no sorrows that heaven cannot heal," he said. He played a tape of Moon Pie talking on the radio about the need to suffer. "The Fontanas," Father Guice said, "have suffered. There is surely a place for them in heaven." Earlene saw Royal Landry standing by the graves of the Chinese laborers and saw that he was watching her. She closed her eyes. Hotson put his hands on Anna's shoulders. Ronnie held his arm and leaned against him. Father Guice asked if anyone would like to speak. How silent it was—a rustle of wind through magnolia leaves, the hiss of passing traffic, a cough, sniffles. And then from the front of the semi-circle of mourners by the graves, Cecil Pilcher, in his sanfor-ized, green Zodiac Car Wash uniform, looked to the sky, called out, "You son of a bitch, give me back my friend!"

The friends of Billy Wayne met back at Hazel and Tommy's for food, drink, and solace. This was the bayou house that had been Angelo's. On the drive over, Dencil had stopped at the Bethel Manor Convalescent Home and picked up Angelo. Right away, though, Dencil had to carry him upstairs and put him to bed. When he came back down to the kitchen, Dencil told Ronnie, "They keep him so medicated, he can't stay awake."

As it grew dark, they all ended up crowded together in the kitchen. Hazel and Tommy standing shoulder to shoulder, leaning against the counter, Anna on Hotson's lap, Ronnie scrooched over to make room for Earlene on the chair. Dencil realized who wasn't there, besides Billy Wayne and his sons, Fox, and George. Just then they heard Webb and Ferlin out in the yard, singing "Higher Ground." They listened. Dencil excused himself, walked upstairs to check on Angelo. He opened the door, listened, heard Angelo's stomach churn. Dencil took out his Reddy Kilowatt pen light and tiptoed to the bed. Angelo's eyes were wide open. Dencil wiped the drool from Angelo's cheek, wiped his eyes. "It's okay, buddy, we'll get out of here. You won't have to go back. We'll just drive." He heard Webb and Ferlin's harmony: "A higher plane I have found; Lord, plant my feet on higher ground." What am I talking about? Sentimental crap, Angelo. The kind of talk that leads to trouble. Where would we go anyway? Dencil saw that Angelo's eyes were turned toward his little light.

Epilogue

T hree months have passed since the deaths of our Fontanas, and we have had plenty else to think about. At the college, a coed was strangled and stuffed into a dumpster outside the Education Building; the parish suffered its worst cotton harvest in twenty-three years; the paper mill's on strike; a Ouachita Parish High School chemistry teacher was arrested for manufacturing and distributing angel dust out of his home; two pistoleros shot and killed a 7-Eleven clerk and got away with seventeen dollars; and they're finding tumorous bass in the bayou.

Through it all, the name Fontana has remained on our lips, primarily because of some news—distressing news some have said, though most folks, whether they admit it or not, are, if not joyous, then let's say, cheered, at least, by what they heard. Earlene deBastrop Fontana is pregnant with Billy Wayne's love child, and, yes, that does bother some people worse than all our mayhem and decay. Others, however, are inspired by this indomitable and resolute Fontana bloodline. Indeed, it had seemed certain to us that the Fontanas had at last closed their eyes, doused their ashy lights, but now they had risen from the embers.

It'll be a boy. It'll be named either George Jones deBastrop Fontana or Willie Fox deBastrop Fontana, Earlene hasn't decided. He'll have Dencil Currence and Ronnie Flacy as godparents. That's what we know. What we wonder about is will it be entire. Will he have those hooded Fontana eyes, those smallish ears, or will he favor Earlene? All of that speculation should keep us busy until the birth. Yesterday, the *Citizen* published an ultrasound photo of the child that had been released by the St. Francis PR staff. The caption noted how at that age all fetuses look alike—gills, tails, and all of that— how you couldn't tell a frog from a child at this point. What you see in the picture is this cranium and spinal cord. Looks like a number 9 or a banjo.

Last week at the Great Books meeting, in a departure from the usual regimen, a departure, by the way, which rankled Margaret Grimes though she tolerated it, Professor Johnny Ash from NLU read his story about the Fontanas called "The Fontana Gene." Johnny didn't have all his facts exactly straight, but he meant well, and he was entertaining. You know, like some of his dates were wrong. And Moon Pie never did have a harelip; don't know where Johnny got that idea from. One funny error was where he explained that a chapel at the hospital had been converted into an ontology lab. What he meant to say, of course, was "oncology." (It is, in fact, the Hershel and Mildred Stubbs Cancer Center.) But if you think about it, wouldn't it be rich to have these researchers discussing the formal and universal essences of what's there in the petri dish? Dr. A. sits at his microscope, says to his colleague: Dr. B., take a look at the specimen on my slide. Dr. B. looks, says, I don't see anything.

And it's true what Johnny said, how when the Fontanas are gone, we'll have lost a way of life, a mythology unique to our community, something valuable to preserve. When we all hear stories about the Fontanas, he said, we're learning about ourselves, about what it's like to be a human being and how that feels. The Fontanas, he said, are just like us, only more so.

Shug Johnson asked Johnny did he know the Fontanas who tried to break into show business, in a manner of speaking. Johnny said he didn't. You might could use it in your revision, Shug said. In 1917, a movie company had come to south Louisiana to film *Tarzan of the Apes* down to Wax Bayou. When Romeo Fontana heard about it, he got down there and got himself a part in the movie. He's a deckhand on the Greystokes' ship, the one that wrecks. Got paid two dollars and got to shake Elmo Lincoln's hand. Then in 1929, Roebuck Fontana took a train to St. Martinville to meet Dolores del Rio, with whom he fancied himself in love. Dolores had posed for the statue of Evangeline, who was really Emmeline Labiche. Anyway she was there for the unveiling. When Roebuck, who was rabid with infatuation, refused to cease and desist in his salacious harassment of Miss del Rio, her inamorato retained the services of a robust Cajun gentleman who shattered Roebuck's nose and then crushed his thumbs.

Ted Muto had it on good authority that there were discussions under way at city hall, as we speak, pertaining to the development of public lands in Chauvin Bottom. Then again, Ted Muto might not know what he's talking about. Said he had it from a reliable source that a New Orleans developer, representing Pakistani interests, has spoken with Mayor Tommy Candela, with Hazel Candela, and with the directors of the Pelican Bank, about proceeding with one of the following plans, either of which would both preserve and capitalize on the Fontana way of life. Sort of. The first is Fontanaland, a modest Disneylike theme park. The alternative would be called Fontana Village and would be a historical reconstruction of the homestead, dedicated to the preservation of Fontana cultural folkways, mussel gathering, cypress knee art, soap making, and so forth. But first, Ted said, the city's got to attract some federal dollars to jump-start the project.

"Fat chance," Margaret Grimes told him.

Before Maryalice Wiggins flicked the Boscobel Room lights and the meeting ended, the Great Books folks each tried to summarize what he or she had understood the significance of Johnny Ash's story to be. Perhaps they have been too analytical for too long, too reasonable, too self-improving, because though Johnny assured them that would not be necessary, they could not help themselves. Bobby Sistrunk insisted not to do so would be like going home empty-handed from the Ark-La-Miss Fair.

"What I was thinking," Chiquita Deal said, "was how, you know, we aren't always free to be ourselves. We're more like forced to be ourselves. That's what I think Johnny means about the gene."

Ted Muto nodded and smiled.

Margaret Grimes said, "Self-knowledge can be a dangerous thing," she said. "Ain't that right, Shug? Turns out to be dismal news."

Tommie Nash said, "You all realize we're talking about real people here. This ain't no let's pretend story. Earlene is over across the river right now, probably nauseated and all. I don't know that we have the right to put thoughts into their heads. I'm sorry, Professor, but that's what I feel."

"The meaning of life?" Royal Landry said. "That it ends. Just that."

Cicero Wittlief said, "You know, we never did find out why the Fontanas were cursed or whatever they were. We didn't get answer one."

"You uncomfortable with that, are you, Cicero?" Shug Johnson said. "There went the lights. What's on for next week?"

Buddy Tidwell has his own notion about the Fontanas, and he sat one night alone in the Rise 'n' Dine and told Tenille Suzenau all about it. "I wasn't born on crazy creek, Tenille, you know that," he said. "But I wonder sometimes if Russell Sikes hadn't hit the nail right on the head."

Tenille freshened his coffee. "How's that, Buddy?"

"About them being from Venus."

"Venus?" Tenille said. "That's over the parish line, isn't it?"

"Eros, you're thinking of."

"That's right."

"I mean Venus the planet." Buddy pointed to the ceiling with his thumb.

Tenille didn't know whether to smile or not. Buddy had never been the teasing kind.

He told her he'd been doing some research. He took a notepad out of his shirt pocket, opened it, flipped a couple of pages, laid the notepad on the counter. He put on his reading glasses. "Since 1954 there have been 1,723 UFO sightings in Louisiana, more than any other state."

"Buddy Tidwell," Tenille said. "I'm surprised at you."

Buddy looked over his glasses at Tenille and held up his finger to indicate he was not finished. "A full 347 of our citizens, two of whom you know personally," he said, "have been abducted by space aliens." He closed his notepad. "Is there something about Louisiana, do you suppose, that appeals to spacemen?"

"Maybe you'd best switch back to decaf, Buddy."

He smiled.

Tenille answered the pay phone by the door. "Haven't seen him," she said. "If he comes in, I sure will. You have a good one." She told Buddy, "If you see Eddie Pettis later, tell him to get his butt on home."

"So where do you think Peregrine came from?"

"I think it's more likely he came from, say, Cooter Point than from Venus, don't you? I sure don't know where my long-ago kin came from neither."

"What about all the male children?"

"Well, if there is a curse on the Fontanas, that's got to be it." Tenille opened the refrigerator. "Some kind of hitch in the Y chromosome." She moved a plastic tub of Crisco aside. "Let me fix you up some boudin, Buddy."

"Maybe I need a vacation, Tenille."

"You and Boogie ought to go on up to Stuttgart for duck season."

"Duck season's finished with." Buddy took off his Stetson, put it on the stool next to him. "I'll have some dirty rice with that, Tenille."

Tami Lynne, by the way, has moved into Tommy and Hazel's. She's under a doctor's care for her melancholy. She's trying to sell the McKinley Street shotgun. Whoever's interested should call Darcy Filhiol at Bilbo Brewer Realty. And Russell Sikes is back. He spent some time in a Trappist monastery up in Massachusetts after Sedona. He called on Tami Lynne, brought her some jars of jam. She told him she needed time. He said he'd be at Dencil's.

Some of us are getting together tonight at Herb and Marilea Bryant's, drink some beers, pitch some horseshoes. We'll end up, those of us who stay late, sitting on the front porch. Herb will bring out a pitcher of gin-and-tonics. He'll shoo Vera over to her rug in the corner. Someone, Grayson Berard maybe, or Danny Whatley, will start in on a story. Maybe it's about a man in Holly Ridge who had Jesus appear on his freezer, or it's about a log hauler with a sick little baby at home. Whatever it is, we'll feel different when it's over. We'll feel wiser, even if we aren't. Wise and fortunate. And we won't want to leave or say good night. We'll count the seconds between the lightning and the thunder, listen to the squeak of the glider, wonder what's that smell in the air, is it lemon or vinegar? Is it rising from the soil?